Cover image, "Aphrodite," used with permission of the artist, Alexander Scaramanga, of Greece.

DEDICATION

To Vicki
For your patience, well-considered advice, wisdom, and for always having my back.

To Bryan
For sharing your experience as an author, for straight talk about my work, and for being a pal going all the way back.

FLIRT

A Novel of Lust, Love, and Murder

By Ric Bohy

Prologue

She leaned into the mirror on her grandmother's dressing table, keeping her back arched as she had been taught, and touched the tart-cherry color to her lips. It was on a No. 2 flat red sable art brush, costly, useful for painting sharp edges with oils. It worked as well with lip rouge.

Using just enough pressure to flatten the silken animal hairs into a crisp line, she guided it beyond the outer edge of her lips, but not so far as to be noticeable without getting very close. She traced her upper lip, then the lower, and then returned to the gentle cleft at the top to limn a bit more shape.

"Marvelous, darlin'," Ruby Bliss said. "You are a natural beauty, a supernatural beauty, no doubt of it. But even a beauty such as yours, as ours, can use accentuatin', a little boost. It is not gildin' the lily. It is makin' the most of what we have."

The girl adored Ruby Bliss, a genteel Southern belle long known to her admirers as Miss Ruby. The child was abandoned by her mother – Miss Ruby called her "that whoo-er" – and the father, an effeminate ponce, when she was a tot. One morning, they brought their child to Miss Ruby's for a visit. At the first chance, they skulked out the door and vanished.

She committed to raising her granddaughter as a healthy, well-loved child, and to teaching her how to face the world alone, strong and smart and unafraid, comporting herself in Miss Ruby's own image. The only difference – Miss Ruby had to persuade the child never to be ashamed of, never to be angry about, and never to think she was diminished in any way by her anomaly.

When the monthlies first visited the girl, Miss Ruby told her she was blossoming as a woman, and began to school her in the ways to use her looks to support herself. Men were quite simple creatures when it came to their libido. Generally, she taught, when it became clear that they could look but would not be allowed to go any further, most would be grateful just to look. Many of them are voyeurs, Miss Ruby said, explaining the meaning of the word. If they have something material to offer that you need for your support, show them a little more. Be proud of your body and its power. Use it.

"When I was young and surpassin' lovely from my hair to my pretty painted toes, I was able to use my looks and my body to provide near ever'thin' I now have," Miss Ruby told her granddaughter. "The more money they have and the more you grant them glimpses of your physical attraction, the more they give 'cause they hope to get more. That is a lot of 'mores,' is it not darlin'?

"But here it is: You must never give yourself to them, as that whoo-er does for money. You must learn to dress provocative, not trashy as that whoo-er does. In today times, I keep hearin' angry women usin' the word objectifyin', us all bein' sex objects and such. You should know that this is not all that women are, but all women are sex objects at one time or other. That is because of the very nature of men, who carry the instinct to breed to keep the herd goin'. In that way, they are always a bit of the beast that they come from in early times. That is no excuse for their animal behavior, when it gets to that. But it is what they are, child.

"There is much more I have to teach before you are a grown woman, and much you have to teach yourself. Never stop feedin' your mind, child. Study art and science and history and literature and politics and music and whatever you discover on the way. I know I talk like the hillbilly I used to be, but I've found that usin' it as a Southern belle holds its own charm for the simpler sex. You must find your personal way of speakin' and movin' that attracts them. Just be sure to speak proper. No contractions, you, like can't 'stead of cannot, and won't 'stead of will not."

The granddaughter thought of all this a dangerous game and one that would not accommodate her disability, which is how she thought of it. She wanted to fit in, not stand out. Some nights she wept as she tried to sleep because she could never be perfect. She could only try.

It didn't occur to her, ever, that Miss Ruby never spoke of love, God, or religion.

It didn't occur to the girl to ask.

CHAPTER 1

Jimmy Noze faithfully iced his eye before each outing until the swelling died and the blue-black color faded to yellow-green and only a black scab remained, splitting his right eyebrow. Now he regretted having earned it, which he knew was true even if he couldn't remember why. She might think he was disreputable or, worse, physically repellent. She probably wouldn't remember him, and if she did, might not approach a second time. In that case, he had no plan. But he had to look at her again.

He returned to the trendy Train and Tunnel club eight nights running, nursing Jack Daniels sours and eating the orange slices and cherries for hours and fighting the urge to go outside for a smoke until he saw her again.

Each night he showered and shaved and pressed a clean Hawaiian shirt, leaving it untucked over his least faded black jeans for comfort, and as cover for the piece he carried in his waistband at the small of his back. Using an old cop trick, he'd wrapped the grip entirely with rubber bands to prevent the gun from slipping down his pants. He dropped a fresh box of Kools into the shirt pocket. Pulling on his treasured Ariat boots, he tucked a Spyderco fixed blade knife into the boot sheath clipped inside the right. He shoved a fat Michigan bankroll, with a twenty on the outside covering a few tens and a pile of singles, fold-down into his right pocket.

The first and only time he saw her, he was sitting on the same stool at the same bar in the Train and Tunnel in Birmingham, a suburb north of Detroit that was rife with the same preening, self-involved, new-money people who made this joint one of his favorites for people-watching.

Mixtapes broadcast from Bose speakers played Leonard Cohen and Renee Fleming, TLC and Boyz II Men, showstoppers from *Les Misérables* and *Cats*, Judy Collins and Judy Garland, Warren Zevon and Anita Baker, theme songs from '80s sitcoms, Sinatra and Nirvana, but never country – though Lyle Lovett made an occasional appearance.

The tables in the room were made of burnished teak and in a utilitarian assortment of two-, four-, and six-tops, which could seat eight. They were nearly chest high and matched with straight-back stools that allowed the women to stretch and display their legs and shoes. The men did what they could to avoid dangling their feet.

Incautious after an hour of slow drinking, Noze had watched while a lady with lustrous hair the color of fresh-stripped copper wire and wearing a low-cut dress in vermillion stood from the table she occupied alone, threw a glance his way, and walked toward him, casually cooling herself with a matching carved-wood fan. She had a hitch in her step that exaggerated the sway of her hips. The clingy dress ended just below the knees and parted in a slit that exposed her right leg to the hip as she moved. She brushed against him lightly and took the stool next to his, facing the bar as he faced away.

"I am thirsty," she said, looking straight ahead in the mirror on the back bar.

"I'm good for it," Noze said. "Anything you want."

She also caught the attention of the bartender, a girl in a tight white blouse and black dress slacks who wore a fine gold chain between pierced eyebrow and ear, a small blue star tattoo on her right wrist, and a simple silver ring on one thumb. Noze reckoned that she could kick-start a 747 on an icy morning. When she tended him, her lips were frozen in a grim line. When she spoke to the lady in red, they parted in a smile that showed sharp bleached teeth.

"Well, hello there, peaches. What'll it be?"

"Campari rocks lemon twist. He says he is good for it."

Jimmy Noze was hooked on her style, from dress to drink. Who drank Campari? He turned his stool to study her profile while the liqueur was poured, and paid from what was left of his cash on the bar. He noticed that the red of the drink nearly matched her lips, and wondered if it had been calculated. She smelled like flowers. He had no idea what they might be.

"So," he said, feeling stupefied, "come here often?"

She reacted as though his seat was empty, pursed her lips in a way that put a little knot in his colon, and sipped the aperitif.

"That was kind of a joke," he tried.

Nothing.

"Am I intruding on your private time with the drink I just bought you?"

A trace of a smile, and a sweet, smoky voice. "I do not know you, and I am not sure I want to." It was barely above a whisper and required Noze to lean closer. As he did, he let one palm rest on her exposed thigh. It was cool and smooth as – Noze couldn't think of an adequate simile – soft but well muscled. She looked him in the eyes, without offense.

"No, no," she said like a schoolmarm, and he removed his hand. "People do not value what they get for nothing. Give me everything in your pocket."

He reached in and pulled out the rest of his money and handed it over. Even when she took it, silently stood, finished the rest of her drink, and walked off as he watched that sway, Noze thought it was the best eight bucks and change he'd ever spent.

The nights when she had not reappeared were at least interesting. Noze collected characters like the swells collected fine possessions because there was that novel he was still going to write and he didn't trust his imagination as much as his power to see and note details and remember.

To say that the crowd at this club was of a type wasn't entirely accurate, and he knew his own prejudices, tending to generalize when it came to those with money. They were a little loud, even in a quiet room. They had no manners when dealing with those who served them, issuing orders instead of making requests. Some reeked of entitlement and exaggerated self-worth. They were keenly competitive, which could be admired, but not averse to lying and cheating and stealing to overtake the front of the line. Some had taste gleaned from lifelong exposure to costly things. Some would always assume that money alone meant their tastes were refined. Many were bullies, but believed they were compassionate. Few promoted charitable causes that did not directly benefit their class, tax status, or self-promotion.

Jimmy Noze stood out from the crowd in the club. His teeth didn't gleam with an unnatural whiteness, and the bottoms were skewed and overlapped. His fingernails were ridged and the cuticles torn. His hands weren't soft, but neither were they horned and heavily calloused. His skin was not tanned during cold months. His eyes were alive, but without malevolence. His hair was untouched by anything but shampoo, and trimmed at home once a month with electric barber clippers fitted with a No. 4 comb.

Others in the club dressed casually, but the clothes were new and the look affected. The place prided itself on eclecticism, which its clientele thought was grand, so tennis skirts mixed with business suits, slutty clubwear mixed with boating togs, and a Hawaiian shirt and black jeans were not entirely out of place. It was a noisy room, indirectly lighted with strategically placed pink reflectors to give everyone a healthy glow, though few needed the help. The room gave anyone who entered the club a quick once-over.

When she walked in, pausing to survey both competition and prospects, conversation stopped, and a few women snickered maliciously. Noze didn't know her at first sight. She was an entirely new character. But there was that hair, and as she walked with a subtle pony's gait to an empty two-top near the front of the room, he remembered the slight hitch in her step and the pronounced movement it gave those hips. Many of the men stared. Noze heard some of the comments by women.

"Please," said one, drawing out the word. "What does she

thinks she's doing?"

"What's with the limp?" said another. "She thinks she walks like a model or something."

"Look at daddy's little girl. I don't know what she's peddling, but it's disgusting."

"The bitch isn't as hot as she thinks. I've got way bigger tits."

"Maybe so, Lindy. But you also have a way bigger ass." Boozy laughter.

Noze thought them all typically rude. He couldn't take his eyes off of her.

Her hair was parted in a T, with some teased forward to play across her brow. A glossy hank was gathered on each side and tied with a lace ribbon that closely matched the tart cherry red of her lips. Another length of the same ribbon was tied as a choker around her neck.

Tonight's costume included a white blouse, cut to pinch at the waist and flare over the hips. It buttoned the full length of the front and the neckline was low yet nearly modest. The cloth was scandalously sheer, but doubled at the breast pockets, providing a pretense of decency. The skirt was inky black. It rode her hips and fell in wide pleats almost to her knees. She completed the look with ruffled white ankle socks and black patent Mary Janes with just enough of a heel to heighten interest by shaping her butt. It was a cliché, but clichés became so from effectiveness. A subtle scent of freesia and violets arose from her hair, neck, and thighs, a custom blend prepared exclusively for her by a perfumer she'd enchanted. She called it Vestal. She slid effortlessly onto a stool from the left side, set her purse on the table – it was kicky, chic for its reuse of a piano-black Cohiba Comador cigar box with a glass bead handle – and crossed her legs, right over left, the left heel hooked over the stool's foot rung. She raised a hand to signal for a server, but one was already on his way, wending between the tables, moving urgently, leaning so far forward that he seemed in danger of falling on his face. Noze watched her look up with shimmering gray eyes, showing perfect teeth in a delectable smile, flirting. The young man leaned closer as though he could not hear, she said something, and he scurried off. She began to scan the room.

Her eyes met his for a two-count, then moved on. He felt he had been judged and discarded. He turned to pick up his sour and drained it.

"Oh, barkeep," Noze said to the same black-and-white and pierced girl who seemed always to be here, "Jack on the rocks, *el doble*." She was in mid-show, adeptly keeping two of three bottles aloft while combining tequila, triple sec, and lime juice over crushed ice in a salt-rimmed shooper. When she finished, slamming each bottle in turn into the well, she stirred the cocktail with a gold-plated barbed wire swizzle, shrieked "*Arriba*! *Arriba*! *Andale*! *Andale*!" in a mocking Speedy Gonzalez impression, looking sideways at Noze, handed off the drink, and gave him a straight pour.

He took it and swallowed about half, the enervating brown creeping forward from the back of his brain.

He continued to watch the copper-haired girl as she sipped at her drink and smiled and dismissed approaching suitors while he assigned them each a type. The Viking was not accepting his fate.

He wore a slate-gray bespoke suit that fitted tightly on his trim bulk and set off his golden mane, which in turn set off his store-bought tan. He grinned and said something Noze couldn't make out. She showed him a palm and looked down at her drink. He leaned heavily on the table and spoke again, the grin gone. She refused to meet his glare, showed him the hand again.

The Viking gripped the tabletop with both big hands, shook it hard, and pushed off, turning to walk the walk of shame back to his seat. His jaw was set hard. He sat alone with a fixed stare in her direction. His lips moved between swigs of light beer, until he slammed the glass down on the table and stood. He began to pick his way between tables, heading again for Noze's dream gir

She saw him coming, set down her drink, stood, picked up

her purse, and began making her way toward Jimmy Noze. As she tried to sidestep the Viking, he lunged and grabbed her left arm. Noze saw alarm and anger distort her face as she wrenched her arm away and toppled to the floor, legs splayed. Two men at an adjacent table looked down at her and grinned when they saw her exposed panty. Noze's eyes were instead drawn to her left leg. The hum in the room was dropping. The Viking bent down, hooked a paw under her closest arm and stood her on her feet, lifting without effort.

"You don't get to just blow me off," he rasped, a catch in his throat. "We're leaving," he ordered. She hissed. She tried to push by again and he seized her shoulders until she mewled in pain. He shook her and snarled, "Look at me," and, turning her around to face him, saw past the top of her head as Noze hurried from the bar, reached behind his back and stopped out of reach pointing his pistol – a Glock 31, its magazine filled with fifteen .357 hollow point rounds – at the center of the Viking's face. He had everyone's attention.

The hum stopped dead and Mellencamp sang about a lonely ol' night and the bartender said, "Sir, sir, we don't allow firearms in here." Jimmy Noze thought that was about the funniest thing he'd heard since whenever.

The Viking froze, still gripping his prey by the shoulders. Noze told the bartender and the room, "It's OK, I'm a cop," and for all they knew he was. The Viking kept his eyes locked on the piece and didn't move. Noze looked him hard in the eyes and said, "Looks small, but punches like Tyson. Turn her loose."

The Viking opened his hands, but she stood still, looking up into the big man's face. "Got a good job?" Noze asked. The Viking subtly nodded, keeping his eyes on the gun. "Enjoy a good rep in your community?" The Viking nodded. "Ever been arrested?" A silent no. "Want to change any of those?" Another two-step shake of the head.

"Miss, is there anything you want to say to this guy?" Noze asked. She took a half step back toward Noze, cocked one shoulder, balled up a little fist, and landed it dead center on the

Viking's gullet. He made a gurgling sound, eyes popping, but stopped himself from grabbing at his injured throat. "Go away," Noze said, and the Viking did as he was told.

Jimmy Noze tucked the gun back under his shirt and returned to his barstool, still facing the room. He heard bits of can-you-believe conversations starting as the bartender said she had no idea he was a cop and she was usually pretty good at spotting them and she set him up with another double without him asking. "On me," she said.

The redhead slid onto the stool next to his, back in character.

"I want a drink, just like his."

The bartender scooped another glassful of rocks, rocketed the bottle of Jack into the air, turning once, turning twice, and caught it spout down, filling the glass. "This is on me too, cutie." Everybody was back in character.

Noze felt a quiver in his legs as the adrenaline subsided and he hoped the copper-haired girl didn't notice and he let his drink sit until his hands settled down and smelled the same faint scent of flowers he didn't know. She turned her stool to face him and pursed her red lips and sucked a little Jack through the cocktail straw. Noze filled his lungs and let it go slowly.

"Dangerous, huh?" she said.

"He wasn't all that dangerous. Mostly a coward."

"No, you," she said, and took a big swig of the fiery sour mash. Noze shrugged and felt like a stupe. He turned his stool to look into her face, but couldn't stop a glance down at her breast pockets, then looked back into her glinting gray eyes.

"What was that about?" He hazarded a good swig from his glass and appreciated the burn.

"Oh, we saw each other once when he bought me dinner and said we should get to know each other better. I was not so sure." She pursed her red lips and sipped, again through the little straw. "I let him take me to his house. Just for snacks." She sipped some more, and pouted.

"But he was mean. Some men are mean. He was really

mean. He did rude things and I said they were rude. He expected something other than what I was willing to give. So I left his gaudy house. I guess he was waiting for me to come back here." Red pucker. Sip. "I think you too were waiting for me to come back here." She looked him square in the eyes. "Are you mean?"

Noze didn't know how to answer.

"What is your name, dangerous man?"

"Jimmy. Jimmy Noze. With a Z."

"Are you really a police officer, Mr. Noze?"

"Far as you know."

"My name is Mary." Sip. "Bliss."

"Is that your real name?"

"Far as you know," she said, then, "Have you eaten yet?"

CHAPTER 2

He led her to his ancient, faded, unwashed Ford Ranger parked down the street from the Train and Tunnel. She didn't expect him to open the passenger door for her, but there he was, looking sheepish as he yanked on the handle and opened it fully on tired hinges that made a mournful groan. He was a surprising man.

As she turned to face him and settled onto the seat, he took her right hand to help as she lifted her legs over the threshold and faced forward. He asked, "Ready?" She smiled, amused. "Yes, thank you." He closed the door without slamming it, winced at its rusty complaint, trotted around the front of the truck and let himself in. Mary Bliss watched his face as he started the truck, let out the clutch, and pulled into traffic.

"Is something wrong?" she asked.

He glanced at her and looked back at traffic and said, "Not exactly. But I have to think this isn't something someone like you is used to."

"Oh? And who is someone like me?"

Trapped. He never felt trapped. Jimmy Noze was stubborn about speaking his mind, and hadn't made the connection between that trait and being mostly alone. Mary Bliss made him care about the effects of his words. In the considerable time she had spent in his head, he had not once thought they might share the same space. He hadn't prepared for conversation. Now he could only speak his mind.

"Someone who doesn't look like she's hopped in many trucks. Someone who looks like she takes care of herself in every detail. A really unique kind of beauty." He paused to swallow saliva that pooled under his tongue. "I've seen you, before tonight."

"I remember."

"You looked very different each time, different hair style, different clothes – both times the same woman, but reimagined. Always graceful against the odds. You're bathed in mystery. You offer and you withhold. You are so frankly sensual, but so easy and comfortable with it." Jimmy Noze felt the words spilling out and regretted giving voice to thought, to the phrases he had written in his head, trying to describe her. "You are that rarest thing, Miss Mary, a warm jewel, genuinely one of a kind." He was afraid to look at her.

"'Against the odds.' You must mean my leg." Jimmy Noze squirmed. "Why, Mr. Noze, can you possibly think I am not aware of the interest in my limb, that it is the first thing most people notice?"

"I think you're wrong about that."

"Many for their own reasons fixate on it and think their thoughts and want to know about it but do not have a way to decently broach the subject."

Jimmy Noze said, "Please call me Jimmy," and hoped the topic was closed.

"There was no grisly accident, Mr. Noze. I was not maimed. I was born with a leg and a stump, as simple as that, and have always accepted it just as I now accept that my adopted leg is as much a part of me as any of the rest of my body. Mr. Noze, you would disappoint me if you felt this is somehow heroic or sympathetic or admirable. The only thing admirable is the leg itself." She shifted her body to position it closer to him and hiked up her skirt a bit. "Do you not agree?"

"Miss Mary, there's nothing about you that isn't admirable." He allowed himself to look at the leg and slide his eyes up until they settled on her face. He felt his breath shorten and relaxed when she parted her lips and winked.

"'Miss Mary.' That's sweet. Are you from the South?"

"I have family there."

"Oh, that reassures me. It says good things about you, Mr.

Noze. My grandmother was from Dixie. That is what she always called it. Her name was Ruby Bliss. Everyone called her Miss Ruby. She was a true daughter of the Confederacy, which gave her certain primitive views on some people – views that I do not share, you should know – but it also bred in her the finest qualities of the classic Southern belle. She was made of iron, you see, but she was physically dazzling and her demeanor was soft and delicate. I do not want you to think badly about her, that she put on a façade, or was somehow deceitful. But in her time, it was necessary for a woman to make her way in the world as best she could. She knew about men and abided their frailties. She knew how to charm them, how to enchant them, how to please them and – I will be frank, Mr. Noze – how to manipulate them to get what she wanted." Mary Bliss leaned forward, soft and exquisite, and turned her face toward his. "She had a profound influence on me."

Jimmy Noze felt, unaccountably, that he was looking at an adversary, one who was offering him the key to winning the contest. He didn't know what to do with it, and doubled back.

"What I was trying to say was that I don't imagine you spending any time with characters like me. That bit with the gun back there wasn't very bright. There could have been all kinds of trouble after a stunt like that. I didn't think it through."

"But you did it. Why? No one else did a thing to help me. They just enjoyed the show."

"It looked like you needed help." He paused and turned to see her reaction. "I'm afflicted with that, with rescuing. I've been told I have to give it up."

"Why, Mr. Noze, I do believe you are an old school gentleman, coming to the aid of little ol' me." She gave it just a touch of Southern inflection. "You, dear man, are my hero in Hawaiian rayon."

He looked to see if she was taunting, but there was warmth around her vivid silver-gray eyes and a benignly teasing smile as she reached over to stroke the back of his hand once with her perfectly manicured fingertips.

"If I can be candid, sir, I found it very – you simply must forgive me – *stimulating*." She took her time saying the word. Jimmy Noze tried to pay attention to traffic.

She did not know whether her companion caught the import of her comment. For a woman whose métier was being able to accurately read a man and his intentions – most of the time – Mary Bliss was confounded by Jimmy Noze. Was he good? Was he brave? He seemed to be both. Not everyone would confront a predatory ape like the Viking in defense of a stranger. Still, it was possible that he had his own motives. There was no way to be certain given the limited time they had spent together. Was he a ne'er-do-well, a mooch, and not the mensch she was imagining? Perhaps she was letting wishful thinking overshadow her usually reliable instincts. She had a hunch that he might be unable to provide anything to support her needs for daily life. This was something else. She reluctantly accepted that, for the first time, she might want a very different gentleman friend, someone she was just happy to be with and who filled a need that had nothing to do with durable goods. Mary Bliss had never trusted listening to her heart.

They rode in silence for a while until she broke it. "You talk almost like a poet sometimes, Mr. Noze. 'Bathed in mystery.' Where did that come from? Who are you?"

Jimmy Noze had long defined himself by his work and told her who he used to be, going into more detail than might be prudent, because like many newspaper people he wrongly assumed civilians thought the work glamorous and were fascinated by it. He didn't tell her about the incident at the root of his resignation. He said he left the business to pursue other options that hadn't yet panned out, but he had feelers out, irons in the fire, attractive options, and so forth. Something would come up any time now.

"As it is now, though, to be honest with you Miss Mary, I hate to admit it but I have somewhat limited means. I've been running down a list in my head of places to eat and can't decide because I think your expectations might be more than I can deliver."

"Who do you think I am, Mr. Noze?"

"Do tell."

"I know some very well-to-do people, yes. I do not judge those who are not. I am not an aristocrat. It is true that I like nice things. But I am not a gold digger and would be terribly hurt if you suspected anything of the sort."

"Perish the thought."

"'Perish the thought.' That is quaint, is it not? Like 'gold digger.' You are an interesting man. I like interesting men. I also like interesting women, but some of them are quite mean. They can be judgmental of one another, jealous or superior, often a little insecure. When that type of woman looks at me, her eyes are hard. I attended school with some girls like that."

Mary Bliss calculated whether to add any more gender criticisms that might be welcomed by a man. These were enough. "I just want to know people who are nice. A girl cannot have too many nice friends, and it does not matter if they eat caviar or canned soup. Mr. Noze, do you know what I would really like? What I would really like is a big sloppy hamburger, with streams of warm juice, just a little bloody, that flow down your chin. And thick, hot, salty *pomme frites*, as the French call them. Fries. Ooh, and an ice-cold beer or two. How would that be?"

Noze grinned and turned hard at the next light and gave the truck a little more gas and drove another few miles south into downtown Detroit. He continued to the so-called warehouse district, where humming industry once stashed its goods for entry into the supply chain, but now was a ghostly reminder of what once was, an eyesore where tumbleweeds sometimes rolled down the mostly empty streets.

He pulled into the parking lot of a tatty bar and restaurant called the Red Oak Stables. It was where he usually went for nourishment after a championship bender. It served out-of-fashion dishes like Salisbury steak and a half-chicken platter and an iceberg lettuce wedge with bottled Roquefort dressing and thick chicken noodle soup and chewy smothered pork chops, and excelled at grilled hamburgers with fries and packaged slaw. He could swing two of the plates and still have enough for a Jack Daniels appetizer with beers back and some post-prandial refreshments. He parked next to the long-abandoned valet shack, hustled around the front of the truck and offered a hand to help Mary Bliss out of her seat, which she accepted with a gorgeous downward glance and an air of you-are-too-kind.

He saw some husbands do double takes as they walked in, and some wives scold them or busy themselves telling their children to eat up. The same men wondered how a worn out jamoke like that guy could be out with her. A pair of truckers at the pool table leered and grinned and one stroked his cue trying to catch her attention. Noze took his seat, back to the wall as his old man taught, so he could keep an eye on the room. Mary Bliss kept her eyes on him.

A smirking waitress who knew him by name showed up with water and paper napkins and cheap flatware and Noze placed their order, two double Jack rocks, two PBRs, two burger platters, and Mary Bliss agreed that grilled onions would be wonderful. She continued to study his face.

"Well?"

"What? Is there something else you'd like?"

"Conversation would be nice."

"What do you want to talk about?"

"Talk about you," she said, knowing what she knew about men. "If we are going to be friends, I want to learn all about you, not just about your work. We are going to be friends, Mr. Noze, do you agree? Move your chair a little closer so we do not have to raise our voices. You, the wordsmith, could probably say it better, but I feel, I do not know, soft and warm and safe with you. Still, you look sad. My other male friends do not ever seem sad when they are with me. Are you sad?"

"No. Not right now. Not with you. I can get gloomy sometimes. People disappoint me generally. I know my work had a lot to do with it. I'm aware of that. I'm supposed to remind myself that there's plenty of good to go around, good people, beauty, happy endings, and rosy sunsets. Well, do you know that when you stand by the river downtown and look west at a brilliantly colored sunset, the colors come from the light filtering through thick air pollution? Hard as I look I don't see much evidence of goodness, let's put it that way."

"Where do you look?" The waitress returned with their drinks. Noze picked his up a little too quickly, plucked out the cocktail straw, and tossed down half. Mary Bliss pursed her lips and sucked on her cocktail straw, again studying his face. His eyes were on the table, not on her. She would have to make some adjustments. She idly ran the tip of one finger along the neckline of her blouse, rhythmically, sucked a little more Jack, and set down her drink, giving him her full attention. Noze raised his eyes, caught himself staring at the tracings of her finger, and brought them up to her face.

"Everywhere. Look around here. This used to be a pretty nice place, a family place, where Mom and Dad could have a cocktail and relax over dinner with the kids. Now it's run down, saw better days go by, started relying on lowlifes like the mooks at the pool table to bring up the head count. Families still show up just because it's better than fast food and cheap." He corrected himself, remembering that he brought Mary Bliss to this place. "Inexpensive. What I see are regular people, maybe even good people, subjecting themselves to whatever the fringe might do because they can't afford much better. Grim. It's just how I'm wired."

She looked at him disapprovingly, and reshaped her face into her best little pout, then shifted into an expression to show him that she had reached some kind of conclusion. She dipped a finger into her drink and sucked it, then leaned closer.

"Well, here is how I am wired, Mr. Noze. I enjoy good company, and find that men are more capable of providing it. I want them to feel that I am good company as well. I want them to feel happier for spending time with me. I have educated myself, and continue to learn about art – especially art – music, literature, history, science, the contemporary world around me, food, drink, dance, the theater, film, fashion. I just cannot abide sports. They are silly. I am a serious person, Mr. Noze, when it comes to improving myself to be prepared for conversation, friendly debate, an appreciation of fine things, all to be good company, a treasured companion. This means that I also make myself as pretty as I can be in as many ways as I can. Men are very, very visual creatures. I try to gratify that. But you, you seem almost afraid to look at me, and that makes me sad. Do not make me sad, Mr. Noze."

He raised his eyes to look at her dazzling face and allowed himself to deserve it. "You sound like some sort of geisha," he said.

Mary Bliss contrived a look of mild shock and hurt. "What do you know about geishas? Merely the old soldier stories from the Second World War? The geishas they knew were sordid poseurs, street girls who imitated the makeup and hairstyle and kimonos, tawdry mimics who enticed army oafs with the promise of something exotic, with some 'strange,' as those men called it. If you think the true geishas were prostitutes, like most people you are mistaken. They were highly skilled artisans and their art was beauty and grace and skill in the flawless provision of gentle relaxation, entertainment, and excellent company. Do you know that their kimonos, which covered almost their entire bodies, hung low at the back of their necks for clever, modest, erotic attention? Just one glimpse of pale bare skin framed by rich silk. They were sexually appealing, brilliant at creating desire, but not sexual playthings. If you mean to compare me to the true geisha, you compliment me, and very highly. If you mean to suggest otherwise, I will be offended and wounded and believe that I was mistaken about you, Mr. Noze, and will ask only that you call for a cab to take me home."

Jimmy Noze listened, chastened and impressed. The recitation sounded memorized, her resentment contrived. But she did her homework and he wanted to know what else she had studied. And he was happy that, if the geisha was a role model,

Mary Bliss seemed to have left modesty out of the equation. When she finished, they sat silent, their eyes on the waitress as she unloaded her tray, dropped a condiment basket on the table, and said anything else, Jimmy? No, this is fine, Noze said.

Mary Bliss sat straight, hands in her lap, graceful arms framing her lightly veiled breasts, and looked for an explanation.

"I know the difference," Jimmy Noze said. "I didn't mean anything else. And believe me, I'm happy to be here with you. I'll do a better job of showing that." He smiled, and it felt foreign, but he saw her brighten and he felt a cloud pass. "Still hungry?"

"Ravenous."

Mary Bliss picked up her burger, opened her mouth wide and took a big bite. She leaned over her plate as wet warmth run down her chin, set down the sandwich and lifted two fingers to the bottom of her chin, wiping up to collect the juice and put the fingers in her mouth, which she sucked as she slowly withdrew them. She scrunched her nose and grinned a carefully calculated grin, gave her fingers a lick, and said, "Good," stretching out the word.

Watching her, Noze felt a jolt of desire and quickly took a bite of his own burger. He caught the juice with his napkin. He was happy and he laughed, trying not to spit food as he chewed.

"Miss Mary, you're a wonder."

"That is more like it. Much better."

They ate and talked and Mary Bliss sometimes interrupted him in mid-sentence to dip a chubby fry in ketchup and feed him. She continued to suck her fingers, a bit noisily, as she ate and listened with interest – unfeigned, uncalculated interest – as he answered her questions about himself and opened up to her gentle prodding and probing and, he thought, remarkable skill at interviewing. It was an interesting, unfamiliar turnaround, being the subject instead of the interviewer. He talked easily and drank freely and told her war stories from the streets and was encouraged by her reactions, and told her a little about his old man and a childhood without a mother, and confessed some regrets about certain lapses in judgment and some pride in certain achievements and told her, when she asked, why he had a potent handgun tucked under the back of his shirt.

"I've always been around guns, the old man being a cop. He taught me to shoot when I was a kid. After I got into newspapers and mostly worked the streets, he thought I should pack. But I never thought I needed to, even though it was Detroit, and never got into a situation that proved me wrong. Then I got this phone call, not long ago, and it was a guy who had seen too many movies and worked at sounding sinister and just said, 'Know who this is?'

"Strange thing, I did, even though I heard his voice only a couple of times before. I covered his trial for kidnapping a few years ago, and wrote a profile of this weird scrawny guy who looked like a low-rent Alice Cooper, and how he came to swipe his son from the baby's teenage mother. It was the dumb theatricality of what he said on the phone and how he said it. I knew as soon as he spoke that it was this guy. Then he said, 'You got a debt.' I told him to piss off – sorry – and lose my phone number. But he kept talking, pouring menace on thick, playing the part of scary guy. 'Lost my son 'cause of you,' he said. 'He's mine. You'll pay for that.' I told him he had really picked the wrong guy to try to shake. I told him I had nothing to lose. Then he said, 'Well, let's find you somethin',' and hung up."

Mary Bliss listened wide-eyed, and sipped her beer while he told the tale. "Has anything like that happened before?"

"Oh, there've been guys, bad guys, who didn't like things I wrote, and called me at work or even showed up to bitch – sorry – but they usually just wanted to get it off their chests. I listened, and they went away. This guy is different."

"Why?"

"Because he's dumb and he's a wack job, I mean really nuts. Maybe he means what he said."

"And that is why you carry the firearm?"

"Couldn't hurt," he said. "And maybe now I have something to lose."

Mary Bliss measured his meaning as he looked at her, a little blurry but really quite pleasing now that his brow was relaxed and his gloom had lifted and he had exposed himself as a man of some frailties and much strength. Now it was plain that there was not much he could do for her, materially, not like the others, she reckoned, and that was a matter of some concern. But he was much more real than any of them.

They ordered coffee, and before it arrived Mary Bliss swallowed the rest of her Pabst. Jimmy Noze, his tongue loosened, said with admiration that she seemed to be able to handle her drinks.

"Some people say I have a hollow leg." The look on Jimmy Noze led her to add, "Is that not cute?" He let his breath go. "You are sweet, Mr. Noze. Just the sweetest man. And for all your worldliness, whatever those experiences and people who have left their marks on you, you are better mannered, more sincere, and better company than most men I have known. I can tell you like me, and not just like others do. You treat me with respect. You honor me with your behavior. Do you know how unusual that is?"

Then Mary Bliss asked something that she had been asked many times, but had not once said herself.

"Do you think I can see you again?"

An explosion outside rattled the walls, broke two windows, rocketed a side-view mirror into the room, and left children and their mothers terrified and crying. Two men also wept. Jimmy Noze recognized the beat up mirror and knew at once that his truck was no more.

"Stay here."

Noze walked over to the wall and peeked around one side of an empty window jamb and saw his ratty but reliable old Ranger with black smoke and orange flames pouring out of the now-missing windshield and every window.

He felt a presence behind him, smelled flowers he did not know, and turned his head to see Mary Bliss. Her eyes were wide but she seemed unshaken.

"Why would someone do this?"
"It's him."

CHAPTER 3

Haynus Geasley thought himself clever when he added a lightning bolt to his online signature "SS" to complement his photo, stone-faced with what he thought of as a withering gaze, and a Nazi officer's peaked cap perched perfectly on his smallish head. They would see him immediately as the embodiment of terror and menace and, what was the word? Nonstoppability.

"Tremble in the black shadows of my nonstoppability," he said as loud as he could, as always frustrated by his thin voice. "Throw yourselfs down. Lick the floor. Lick my boots. Beg for mercy. Die. Die again some more."

Geasley spat, and felt a stirring between his legs.

When he finished the SS blog, he clicked over to check for comments on Samson Stiff. It was hard work maintaining – how many now? – nine blogs. He had so many sides. There were the costumes and the props and staging for the photographs, the creation of images for each persona, some of them costlier than others. Samson Stiff the porn producer, wearing only a lightly filled banana hammock, lolled in a grimy beanbag chair, legs spread wide, and grinned at the attentions of two meaty street whores who had cost him twenty dollars each for an afternoon of posing bare-ass in the light of a cheap floor lamp. He made them sex him up to get his money's worth. He replied with fury to every comment posted by those who would belittle him and scorn him and try to unmask him as just Haynus Geasley, pretender and goofball, as if they really knew him. "Die cock-a-roaches. Die shit gulpers. Die piss drinkers. Die," what was the word? Dooshbags. He two-finger typed it. Dooshbags will do. "Die dooshbags."

When nobody commented on one of his blogs, Geasley seeded it with remarks trashing himself under an assumed name. It often got others to join in. Then too, there was something about smearing himself that got Geasley a little excited.

The first of the blogs had been the easiest to create. It was the one that best reflected Haynus Geasley as he saw himself. He was Satan's Spawn, terrifying headbanger and black metal screecher and godlike slasher, an object of wicked desire and dread, adulation and loathing, envy and worship. He was Satan's Spawn, made in His image. He was a solo act.

Only Alice was better. He was the original godfather of gore. Alice was the Creator. Satan's Spawn demanded worship for himself, but he worshipped only Alice, and practiced his spiels ranting at one or another of the Alice Cooper posters covering his bedroom walls. Haynus Geasley spent a lot of time talking to walls.

"We'll see 'em all burn, on earth like it's in Hell. They'll beg, cry, plea for our mercy and die stranglin' on buckets-a their own foul blood while their skin melts and we party hard in their agonies and beggings," and so on.

He worshipped with coal black hair grown past his shoulders and blackened eye sockets dripping black tears and black lips and black fingernails. He worshipped with homemade blood spewed from between crooked brown teeth and black lips, covering his chin and his bared hairless chest and tasting sweet from corn syrup and cornstarch and mostly red food coloring with a few drops of green and yellow for that desirable depth of color. He worshipped with choker chains and spiked armlets and skull rings and chain mail vests. He worshipped with black leather codpieces, the pouches far bigger than needed.

Haynus Geasley was a pretender to violence. He was enraptured by the crimson theatricality of it. As a sour-smelling pimply kid, before his Birth, he'd gone to the public library for a dictionary when he read the words *Grand Guignol* – mouthing "gran gwig-null" – in a newspaper review of the Alice Cooper concert he crashed last night. The dictionary definition led to an encyclopedia and that led to source books and brittle periodicals and Geasley fed on what he found in them. He felt very smart because this Grand Guignol was from the 19th century and better still it was French.

His adolescent weenie twitched when he read the phrase *la douche ecossaise* and he couldn't pronounce it, but he learned it meant the usual mix for a night at the Théâtre du Grand-Guignol in Paris.

This garish, gory entertainment was a product of its place, a steaming dead-end street just off the lurid sex-trade center in Montmartre called the Place Pigalle, the end of the line for women who, however desirable they might once have been, now functioned mechanically as the only possible release for a class of men who were utterly incapable of charming their way into anyone's knickers. Deformed women, young and old, charged premiums for unique servicing in alleys and doorways and cellars. Urine scented the air and mixed with a funky, thick stink of ejaculate.

But the perfumed wealthy also braved the sensory and sometimes physical assaults of the streets and alleys outside the little theater to lap up what went on inside.

Murder most foul was enacted on its stage, lovingly portrayed with every spilled gut, quartered corpse, scalped skull, slit eyeball and garroted throat shown as realistically as the company could manage. One popular leading lady named Paula Maxa even appeared to decompose into a putrescent corpse after her demise, and she pulled it off every night for more than three months.

The nascent Satan's Spawn, alone in his library carrel, indulged his own urges as he pored over the yellowed magazine pages and musty tomes that told the story of this largely forgotten entertainment. The janitorial staff was not accustomed to scrubbing such stains.

Geasley went about his transformation with singular

purpose. Hair already long, he blackened it with Rit dye, and practiced drawing black and blood-red tattoos on his arms, knuckles, and birdcage chest with permanent markers that did, in time, wear away anyway. He used the black marker to color the nails on his fingers and toes. He shoplifted a T-shirt wardrobe from resale shops, concentrating on Alice above all but Ozzie and Lars and Kiss for their monochromatic color scheme and sometimes blood, and Slayer too. He tried to pierce one eyebrow with a darning needle from his ma's abandoned sewing things. His resolve withered because it hurt too much. But he succeeded with one ear lobe and, when the infection passed, wore lightning bolts and question marks fashioned from paper clips. Classmates, always mostly oblivious to young Haynus, were no crueler than they had been before his transformation. They just had new material.

When he was seventeen, Geasley accidentally bred. It was with a girl who stood alone facing the Geasley family garage when Satan's Spawn swept aside the bedsheet curtain to begin his show. He had promoted his performances a dozen times with gaudy notices hand-drawn on paper stolen from the high school library and posted with masking tape throughout the building. "Do you Dare?" and "Is It Real?" and "Buckets a Blood!" and "Guitar Slasher!" and "Snuff!" and "Will you Survive Satan's Spawn of Grand Guignol?" and "Admission FREE" and the street address of his ma and pa's home with "One Night Only" and "Theater in Back." With each show, he felt himself getting more powerful and soaring above the insects that infested his existence and emerging as the One True, like the blossoming of a thorny black rose. No one attended, until this girl.

Everything about her was thin. Long thin hair, thin acne-ravaged face, thin lips, long thin nose, thin arms, thin fingers, thin frame, thin legs, thin clothes. Her lips and eye sockets were painted black and she wore a black teardrop at the corner of one eye. An inverted cross dangled from a string of black plastic beads and lay on her wasted chest. Satan's Spawn swallowed his surprise at seeing her – anyone – standing there, and imagined he saw more than he saw through the yellowed sleeveless undershirt she wore as a dress that stopped well short of her potato knees and was cinched on an undefined waist with a black web belt. She had hand-lettered "SATAN SPAWNS" on the front of the wife-beater in dripping blood-red capitals. For a long moment, Satan's Spawn dissolved into Haynus Geasley, who nearly wept. Then he slashed the first chord on his Wal-Mart guitar, kicked over a plastic cup brimming with corn syrup blood, and made the family garage shudder with the thunder of the paean he wrote on the spot for this lone pilgrim. She held her hands high, pumping the sign of the devil's horns, and bounced on her heels and swayed and shuddered and closed her eyes and did her best to mimic ecstasy. Both idol and idolater poured sweat until makeup streaked their faces in black tracings and her dingy undershirt dress clung to her body.

When he raked the strings in one final misshapen chord, Satan's Spawn froze in a posture of imagined majesty and the girl squealed, clapping her little hands and pressing her knees together, jerking her angular torso forward as though succumbing to a terrible cramp. Satan's Spawn beckoned her to join him on stage. When she did, he closed the curtain behind them.

Their coupling was brief. He pushed his greasy face into hers and she ground her mouth on his, poking her tongue inside and waggling it, tasting fried food and fruit punch, as he slid his arms under her moist furry pits, lifted and carried her to one wall, pressing her against it. He groped her chest and, finding nothing, moved lower, kneading at her downy nexus through the damp shirt-dress, then reaching under to probe, not entirely sure what he was finding. She made a muffled animal sound that he felt vibrate in his throat. She unzipped him and fished around inside until she located what he thought of as The Boa, pulled it free with thumb and finger, raised on her toes and lowered herself onto it, wondering if she had found the mark. He pushed against her once, hard, made a little peep, stepped back and turned away, busying his hands with his fly. She thought he had changed his mind and wept as she asked don't you want to, then staggered through the bedsheet curtain and out of the garage.

Weeks went on and the girl felt the sting die away as she avoided Satan's Spawn in school halls and out in the air. If she saw him, she looked somewhere else. If her pains to avoid him failed and she had to pass him within earshot, she spat "Haynus" with as much venom as she had left and ignored him if he said her name back. One morning before school, as the girl's ma looked over her cigarette at her daughter pouring a bowl of generic frosted flakes and saw little curves where there had been only planes and angles, she thought she'd have to eat some crow for her own breakfast. She had said it often. "You never gon' fill out, girl," part pity, part disgust. "Some girls just don't, so you got to make yourself purty in other ways. Some's happy with just the face. Some's got other ideas when they see a girl looks more like a boy. Some just like their meat close to the bone, heh heh. Someday somebody gon' take you for his own. Just make sure he's got a job." Now, praise Jesus if her girl wasn't starting to look like one. Better late than never.

But as the girl continued to grow up front, her ma got the picture. "I get the pitcher," she said one morning. "Who left his pecker tracks in your panties?" The girl defiantly said, "I wasn't wearing none," and fingered Haynus Geasley and her mother said, "He's never gon' see you again," and the girl said he doesn't, he won't. "He ain't ever gon' see that baby neither," and the girl said he won't. Ma pulled her out of school and made excuses to the authorities and put the girl to work around the house as she continued to grow and then had that baby, a new boy to feed.

Geasley had heard the rumors and when the girl answered his door knock, holding his son, he tried a smile.

"I come to see 'im."

"Go 'way, Haynus." She spat bile with his name. "We don't wanna see you ever agin. He's not yourn."

He tried to deepen his voice and sneered. "Well, whose else's could it be?"

An angry woman shouted, "Who's that?" from inside the

house and a hand appeared on the girl's shoulder and pulled her aside and her ma took her place at the door and said, "You him?" Before he could answer, Geasley took a hard kick to the pills, doubled over grabbing at them, and was knocked half goofy when the slamming door hit him on the head.

Nights, in his lair, Satan's Spawn turned his rage to plans for recovering what was stolen from him. He thought of the infant as his property, not progeny, and no one would deprive Satan's Spawn of what was his. In darkness he began peeping the windows at the girl's house, waiting, always ready to act, until the night came when his property and the girl and her ma all slept at once and he slid in through an open window and creeped the house and wrapped his property in a thin blanket and left by the back door.

There was no other suspect, and when the cops announced themselves twice and kicked in his door, they found Haynus Geasley standing in the shuddering light of black candles. He raised his arms and held them forward and blood dripped from unenthusiastic cuts on the wrists and greasy black hair fell over his shoulders and black eye sockets and black lips and Alice grinning demonically from the walls with gory teeth and a wet red chin. Geasley's property cooed safe and sound on stained bed sheets.

No one showed up to claim Geasley at the jail or when his appointed attorney threw his client on the mercy of the court and asked only that the judge consider lowering the charge to custodial interference. A newspaper reporter sat in the back of the courtroom collecting what he needed for the end of a feature story on this strange kidnapper who stood silent as the judge threw him a bone and lowered the charge. The lawyer thanked the judge for just a year and a day in prison and another on probation and filed to collect his check.

Satan's Spawn swore there were no bars that could contain him, but they did and he served the full year and one day as hard as it could be served in the keeping of a tattooed Aryan Brother who showed a generous spirit by sharing his soft-skinned cellmate in trade for filtered smokes and weed. On the morning he was turned out, lying on his stomach in his bunk, Geasley heard rustling and turned his head to see a fat guard who held out a newspaper and said, "Satan's Spawn, huh?" and laughed gleefully. Geasley turned to look and took the newspaper from the guard's hand and read in detail of his life and crime and arrest and conviction, written by a storyteller who took his time. The writer made him sound like a weak lunatic, a punk, a loser.

When he was finished he looked back at the top of the story and read the name "Jimmy Noze." He whispered, "Fuck you. Die, you cock-a-roach, and die some more," then painfully stood to wipe away the very real blood that ran down the backs of his pale legs.

CHAPTER 4

Enough years on Detroit's streets had left Noze with a deep bench of sources, high and low, who either liked him or owed him and usually came through if he needed something. There were a few times when he regretted burning his boats by doing what he did on his last day at the newspaper, but the fact was that he couldn't bear constant reminders of a little boy's horrid demise. In the time since, his network had weakened a bit, but he still had wires all over town.

While he and Miss Bliss waited for police to arrive at the Red Oak Stables to take their report on the truck bombing, Noze used his cell to raise a jitney driver, an old friend, and talk him into meeting at the saloon to take them home. The fare was cheap, but Noze was broke and talked the driver into carrying the debt until the next day.

When the cops arrived, Noze wasn't inclined to give up his prime suspect. He'd take care of that himself.

"I just don't know," he told them. "Everybody likes me. Ask around back at the precinct. If someone there knows me, they like me." He noticed one of the uniforms kept glancing over at Mary Bliss and giving her a thirsty look. She now sat on a stool at the bar, facing the room with her right leg over the left. She held another Jack, and each time she caught the wandering eyes, pursed and sipped from the straw.

"Maybe I could understand somebody keying my ride for some reason, or sidewalling a tire, but blowing it up?" Noze went on. "Gosh, I'm at a loss, officers. I have to tell you, boys, this really makes me nervous. Gee whiz."

The horny cop peeled his eyes from Mary Bliss and turned

to Noze. "I know who you are, Noze," he said. "You've made plenty enemies. Include me."

"Oh, did I hurt your feelings some time?" Noze said. Slight smile.

"Look, asshole," the cop said, pointing to his nameplate. "Don't remember me? Fake news story about supposably padded overtime?"

Noze made a show of peering at the name. He remembered this cop on sight.

"Sorry, Officer, Spack is it? Really can't say I do. Must not have been very important."

The cop, a slab of a man with a head shaped like a mailbox, took a step toward Noze, eyes flaring with hatred. The big boy's partner told Spack to chill.

"Think hard, Mr. Noze," the partner said. "The techs say it was a pipe bomb. Somebody who hates you that much must stick in your mind somewhere."

Noze furrowed his brow and made a show of concentrating, then said, "Nope.
Got nothing." Then, "Say, Spack, you're not working overtime on this, are you?"

The slab turned his gaze from Mary Bliss's legs and shot the stink eye at Noze.

"Too bad, Noze," he said. "If we had some ideas from you, we might be able to do something. Guys like this get off on making noise. He'll probably try something again. Guess you're on your own, hot shot."

"Used to be, all the time," Noze said. "Now I've got my partner over there."

"Your partner? Telling me that little bimbino over there works with you?"

"Watch your mouth, Spack," Noze said. Looking back over his shoulder, "Miss Mary, he wants to know if we work together."

"Mr. Noze, tell him we work together like birds of a feather." She crossed her left leg over the right and shifted forward on the stool to expose the junction on her thigh.

Spack's eyes nearly popped out of his skull and his mouth formed a perfect zero.

"She's a cripple?"

"I said watch your mouth, Spack, you ignorant slob."

Spack lunged for him. Noze sidestepped and slammed a forearm on the side of Spack's neck. He reeled and got a vacant look in his eyes, then came to. "Son of a bitch," he cried, shaking his head like a wet dog. The other cop rushed at Noze and pulled out his handcuffs.

Noze sneered at Spack. "You going to let all your muscle-head friends know that you got your bell rung by Jimmy Noze?" Spack's partner looked at the lug. "Shit, forget it," Spack said, rubbing his neck. His partner put the cuffs away.

"Fuck you, Noze," Spack added.

"Officer," Mary Bliss said. "I find that language very offensive. And you hurt my feelings by calling me an impolite name." She uncrossed her legs and hooked the heels of both Mary Janes in the stool rung, holding her legs nearly together.

Spack looked at his feet, and then peered at the small space between her knees.

"I will thank you to keep your eyes elsewhere," she said. "Asshole."

Noze looked at her. She winked.

"Shall we go, Mr. Noze?"

"We shall. Partner."

They breezed past the pair of cops and out the open door, as the sharp smell of burned truck grew stronger. One of the techs looked up from her work.

"Who's gonna get this thing towed out of here?" she asked.

"I guess you guys are," Noze said. "It's not worth anything to me."

The jitney careered in from the street and screeched to a halt. Billie Holiday mourned aloud from an eight-track mounted under the dash and the driver leaned his head out the window.

"James 'B for Badass' Noze!" he rasped, grinning a grin. "Been a long time, my brother."

"That it has, Mitten," Noze said. "Last time was when you dropped me off at that triple beheading down by the incinerator."

"'ats, right, James. The stank on that trash heap was always fierce. You work the dead girl they found in the garbage there 'at time?"

"Not me. One of my esteemed colleagues covered that one. Ruined my body count."

Mitten cackled and laid out a palm for some skin. Noze obliged, laughing, and said, "Meet Miss Mary Bliss. Miss Mary, meet my old friend Mitten Lowrey."

Mary stepped out from behind Noze. "So lovely to meet you, Mr. Lowrey."

"Ooh, girl. You *some* kinda tasty."

"Manners, Mitten," Noze gently chided. "She's a lady, head to toe."

"Sorry, Miss Lady. Didn't mean nothin'. It's a real pleasure to see you. Hop in back with James." Before Noze climbed in, Lowrey leaned close to his ear. "I knows she got yo nose wide open, Noze." He heh-heh-hehed at his alliteration.

When they were ensconced in the sprung back seat, Mary Bliss gave Lowrey the name of a boutique hotel in Birmingham.

"Do you know where it is, Mr. Lowrey?"

"I knows where everything is, Miss Lady," and he hit the gas like his beater was the pole car at Indy.

She laid a hand lightly on Noze's leg, but they didn't speak. Lowrey used the drive-time for a fast-talking a monologue to explain what happened to his maimed right hand that earned him the nickname Mitten.

"You got to be curious about this," he held up his right hand, "just like ever'body is. See, I was thowin' them bones with some fellas late at night behind a Farmer Jack. Closin' time was already passed so wasn't nobody to bother us. Now, I don't know these fellas; just run across the game when I was takin' a shotecut through the alley behind the sto'. Understand, I'm a honest shooter, never throw loads. But as I'm scoopin' up more cash, this one white boy – a big Frankenstimes-lookin' fucker –"

"Language Mitten," Noze cautioned.

"Oh, sorry miss lady. He'a big ape. He grabs my cash-scoopin' hand and won't let go. 'Let go,' I says, but he keeps on. Clamps on my hand so hard I dropped the money. Then he backhands my face so hard I falls down. When I tries to get up, he kicks me in my gut and I lose all my air.

"Then," Mitten said, "seem he wearin' these shit-kickers – sorry, Miss Lady – that has a real sharp edge on the back of the heels. He stomps on my hand to flatten it then stomps again to cut off all my fingers with the heel. Least he left me the thumb. Every since I been called Mitten."

Mary Bliss gasped and thought she would be sick in the back of the jitney, but it passed.

"My God, Mr. Lowrey," she rasped. "That is one of the most savage things I have ever heard. You poor man."

"Oh, Miss Lady, I ain't lookin' for no sympathy. Just splainin' my lonesome thumb and my street name. And passin' the time."

When Lowrey pulled up at the hotel entrance, with all the dignity he could muster he turned and said, "Miss Lady, you here. Don't mind the fare. Jimmy got that covered."

"Thank you so much, Mr. Lowrey."

The hotel's liveried doorman yanked open the beater's door and offered a white-gloved hand to assist Mary Bliss. Before she accepted it, she turned to Noze and kissed him lightly on the cheek. When he turned to tell her goodbye, she kissed his mouth and meant it. She said goodnight, handed him a pearl-toned business card bearing only her name and cell number, and stepped out of the car with the doorman's help.

"Goodnight, partner," she said, stressing the word. "Please use that number soon."

Tongue-tied, Noze just waggled some fingers at her, the doorman slammed the car door, and Lowrey peeled out to take his place among the 'vettes and Beemers and such.

Mary Bliss glanced down at her left leg and told the visibly impressed doorman that she had to rest for a minute. He told her to take her time. "Have a nice evening, Miss Bliss?" he asked, and she said, "Yes, Harold, very." As she stood facing back toward the street, she was fully aware that, as always, he was enjoying what he saw. He long before stopped accepting a tip. When she looked up the street, Jimmy Noze and Mitten were gone. The doorman had called for a taxi when he saw her coming, and it arrived within minutes. Harold helped her into the hack, and she gave the cabbie instructions to her home, a dozen miles away.

When they arrived at the weathered three-story Victorian that rose from a wide lot, its borders separated from the adjacent properties by straight rows of tall, untrimmed Japanese yews, she checked the meter, opened her purse and withdrew the exact amount, and stepped out on the cabbie's side. She bent low as she handed him the fare and gave him a good look as she thanked him for a lovely ride. He drove off without complaint.

Mary Bliss went directly to her bedroom, undressed, went into the bathroom, and lit a half-dozen tall candles. She sat on the edge of the old, red-enameled claw-foot tub as she adjusted the taps. She removed her leg while the tub filled, wet a washcloth and gently wiped it clean, leaned it against the tub, swiveled on her behind, lifting her right leg and then left thigh over the water, and eased down into it. She chose an antique laudanum bottle from the tub-side shelf and drizzled rose oil into the churn of running water, breathed in the scent of the attar until the water reached her breasts, turned off the taps and scooted to the canted back of the tub, sliding down neck deep into the perfumed water.

She closed her eyes and remembered Jimmy Noze, not their conversation or the meal or the events that had preceded it, but the face with its fresh scar, the hands, the physical sense of this man. She pushed away conscious thought and the constant flow of calculations she made every day and each night to ensure the kindness and generosity of strangers. Mary Bliss breathed the warm scented air and let her hands find their way. They had been still for so long.

When she was fulfilled, she reached for one of her romance novels on the shelf and opened it at the dog-ear. They were her guilty pleasure and showed her a world she did not yet know, one where physical attraction, love, and lovemaking were limned in florid prose. She had read them since she was a teen. They described men she had never known, the good ones who seemed so rare, the kind of men like she believed Jimmy Noze to be.

She read until her bathwater cooled, unplugged the tub and stood, supporting herself with a hand on the upright that held the elongated hoop of the shower rod, its scarlet curtain gathered at one end. In the candlelight, she was a pale sylph with coppery fire perched above a graceful neck, ghostly skin shining. Water slid down her flawless back and a derriere that she objectively believed was near perfection.

She reached for a white plush towel and dabbed gently at her body, then shaped it around her hair into a long-tailed turban. Glancing out the window that framed her body, she thought she saw movement in the yews. She maneuvered herself out of the tub and hopped closer to the window.

Not certain she had seen anything, she still assumed it was Mr. LaPierre, the man who made her custom cosmetics and perfumes in exchange for a photo now and then of her in various stages of dishabille. She had once caught him peeping, but never said so, accepting it as harmless adulation that would pay off in valuable goods. Her face relaxed and the corners of her mouth curled almost imperceptibly – a modern Aphrodite. She stood remarkably erect, given her disadvantage, and raised her face, eyes closed, toward the black sky. She had another order to place with Mr. LaPierre, so she lifted a tiny hand to her shoulder and languidly let it slide down over one breast and past the gentle rise of her belly and further down, pausing before letting it fall to her side. She lowered her face to look through the window, eyes open, this time with a wicked smile, then turned away and hopped into the further reaches of the room, blowing out candles until it went dark a moment later.

Had she continued to look out from the darkened bathroom, she might have seen a figure emerge from the yews dressed all in black, including a waist-length cape and crushed opera hat that sat high on his head and showed a little of his blond hair.

Off he dashed, the cape flapping behind him as he made his escape in the manner of Mr. Hyde.

CHAPTER 5

Tito Flick picked at a crescent of green-black funk under one fingernail with the point of his prized pocketknife, a token of thanks from a satisfied client. Sometimes he took out the knife just to look at it. It wasn't big, and was largely useless because it wouldn't hold an edge worth a damn. But the cheap, chromed stainless-steel blade was large enough to clearly show the engraving on one side.

To Tito, the best lawyer I ever seen

Tito Flick never much liked his name. He'd heard so many clients squeak, "Don't tease me Tito," an apocryphal line from Michael Jackson to his brother. Flick longed to poke his blade into the eye of the next grinning cretin who said it. Worse, he'd once seen his name in all caps on the front page of a newspaper – ink was his life force – and was appalled to notice that the first two letters of his last name ran together from a distance. It looked like FUCK FREES CHILD-KILLER.

He'd have preferred a handle with the weight, historical significance, and dignity that befitted a man of his stature in the criminal justice community – the stature that he imagined for himself. Thurgood Marshall Flick had a nice ring to it.

After he graduated without distinction from the Wayne State Law School and passed the state bar exam on the fifth try, he painted his shingle on the side of a Bondo-pied motorhome and let the world know that Tito Flick *Esquire* was available to be its advocate. He added *Homicide a Speciality* in blood red as a bit of marketing razzmatazz.

But the courthouse halls, bail bonds joints, and criminal courtrooms where he stubbed around practicing his own peculiar style of law just called him Tito, a little name for a diminutive man whose personal style and unique courtroom tactics had earned him the tag "Tito Flick, BBS – Baffle 'em with Bullshit."

Another knot of people emerged from Frank Murphy Hall of Justice on St. Antoine across the street from Tito Flick's parked law-office-on-wheels. He put away his knife and withdrew a stack of business cards from his jacket pocket. Chasing down clients was beneath his dignity, but he approached those who crossed the street in his direction and offered his cards, saying to each, "Top representation is yours for the asking," smiling warmly and showing both rows of tiny teeth.

With the peripheral vision of a housefly, Tito Flick scoped Jimmy Noze walking toward him from the side before Noze smelled him. The little lawyer splashed his body each morning with an arcane blend of musk, myrrh, and cinnamon mixed by basement chemists and sold by the quart at the lucky candle and hoodoo shop around the corner from police headquarters.

"Why, Jimmy Noze, as I ... Oh, my esteemed battlefront comrade, my foe and my friend. I feared you were lost to us all, taken by the forces of an evil you have so gallantly fought – and sadly, failed – to eradicate lo these many years." Grand, the way he addressed juries when he was in full bullshit mode. "It is to my neverending relief that this is clearly not the case, and that your extended absence from the scene may be attributable to other less dire, but perhaps no less savory, circumstance." He held out his pale paw. "You, in short, are here." Tito puffed a little from the demands of his speech.

Noze shook out a Kool, lit it, and let go of the first drag before taking Flick's little mitt. It felt like a mushroom. He gave it a hard squeeze.

"I got a phone call, Flick." Right to business.

"Dear boy, would you do me a great personal favor out of our many years of mutually rugged kinship – and we are, after all, brothers under the skin – of addressing me by my given name? I perceive the acrid tang of disrespect in the way so many use my family name." He lost a little control at the end and bit down on *family*, thin wet lips drawn back over baby teeth.

"Tito, I got a call. The nit on the other end was one of yours."

The ambulance chaser and Jimmy Noze had had a long and symbiotic relationship. Noze got a source that was hardwired into the city's fusty underbelly and the justice system that was helpless to contain it. Tito got some street currency by having "a friend at the papers."

"And when was this communication?"

"Late last week. I was home. I picked up, gave my name and this guy tries to sell me woof tickets, gives me a sinister routine, blames me for losing his son. It sounded like some dialog from a bad movie."

"That could encompass many of us, dear," Tito said. "Present company excepted, of course."

"Then he said, 'You have a debt.' One character came right to mind. It was Haynus Geasley."

Flick pulled a wounded, loose-lipped face. "Are you inferring some threat from this phone call?" Shifting to mock incredulous. "He was an innocent, steamrolled by a malevolent police state whose sole purpose is to crush the rights of free-spirited, underprivileged men and women, to apply boot to neck, so to speak." Puffing a little again. "I am surprised at you, my dear, shocked, I daresay, that you would impugn the good standing of one among my many clients who enjoy their rights as free men because Tito Flick *Esquire* fought for justice."

"Guess you don't remember him, Tito. He's one who didn't get away. You pled him out."

"My lad, I recall the victims of injustice far more vividly than those whose freedom I have secured. What did you say his name was again?"

"Haynus Geasley. Head-banger with dyed-black hair past his shoulders and skin the color of a slug's ass. Called himself Satan's Spawn. There was no injustice. He confessed, Tito."

"Small matter."

"He knocked up a teenage girl, she dropped foal, and didn't want anything to do with him. He creeped her house one night and stole the baby. Still doesn't ring a bell, Tito? He was caught with the baby, copped to custodial interference, did his bit, and now he's out on the streets, bat-shit crazy and looking to blame anybody but himself. He chose me. Where is he, Tito?"

"Ah, yes, young Mr. Geasley," Tito said. "Yes, yes, a regrettable case indeed. Simply tried to exercise his paternal privilege, his natural rights, no? But the boot was on his neck, with no way to lift it but to concede some ground. Poor Mr. Geasley, I did my very best for him under the circumstances. Surely you don't think I have a clue as to his current whereabouts. I have had clients in the hundreds, perhaps thousands, yes, certainly thousands, and you think I am conversant with them all, that they keep me apprised of their situations, their comings, their goings?"

"Not much gets by you, Tito, not at street level. Or below."

"Dear, dear, Jimmy, you credit me over generously. I am of course flattered by your assessment, though undue. I value our friendship, your banter, and even your always good-natured teasing over our many years in these concrete valleys. Can you think that if I was aware of this young man's location and any enmity harbored toward you that I would not forthwith inform you of such if there was even the slightest possibility of misdirected revenge?" He caught his breath. "You hurt my feelings, Jimmy."

"Keep your ears open, Tito. Let me know if you hear from him. I've got business with this guy."

Flick reached up, squeezed Jimmy Noze on the shoulder, and offered his other spongy mitt. "Of that, you can rest assured, my brother. I remain your humble servant and your loyal friend."

Noze shook his hand, squeezed it until Flick winced, and walked away. He needed a drink.

Late that night, Tito Flick lounged pleasantly, if a tad warily, on his comfy chaise. He favored shiny polyester robes, cool on his damp flesh, and if he allowed himself to nod off on the slick synthetic surface of the chaise, he could slide right off, again.

Most often, he confined his lounging there to phone work. It had taken some practice to prop the receiver between his ear and shoulder. The French provincial-style telephone, the landline he trusted over any cell, had a teardrop base with a rotary dial and the handset rested in an upright cradle. Its gold tones were nicely offset on white faux porcelain. The gift of another satisfied client, the ornate phone made Tito feel like pampered Gallic royalty. He didn't know it was a princess model.

"Dear man, with respect to your concerns, I have made inquiries," he said, lapping a stray droplet of honey from his lower lip. Shouldering the phone kept his hands free to snack. He had a primal love of cheese. He also had a well-developed sweet tooth, and had it been tangible, it would have dwarfed the rest of his runty choppers. He dipped another Cheeto into a double-shot glass of orange blossom honey. It was the only type that met his exacting tastes.

"Yes, yes, I consulted associates, certain denizens of the streets we both know so well, a few friends in law enforcement, eh? Rest assured, dear fellow, that in spite of your unkind skepticism, Tito Flick Esquire does indeed have certain amiable acquaintances among the guardians of public safety.

"If you'll allow me to continue." He reached up to pull the headset away from his little ear, smearing oily orange dust on the faux porcelain handle. "Please. Please permit me to continue." Munch. "I am, after all, making these efforts in your service. Yes." Dip, drip, into the maw. "I assure you that I was as thorough in my inquiries as if my own kin were in your place." He smiled a blowfish smile.

"In short, there is no trace of the subject anywhere in our environment. He seems to have gone poof, vanished. I was able to question the gentleman who tends to his probationary requirements and he too has lost track of the young man. Yes, truly. He informed me that he recently heard a scandalous rumor that the lad was somewhere far out of state selling ersatz cannabis to unsuspecting youth. Had our Mr. Geasley consulted me before embarking on such folly, I certainly would have advised compliance with the court's orders, if indeed the rumor or any part of it is true."

As he listened to Jimmy Noze's reaction, a muted belch escaped from Flick's innards. "Oh, dear," he said, and then pretended it hadn't happened. "Let us cut, as they say, to the chase. If Haynus has remained in this jurisdiction, he would be terribly foolish to raise his head above the hidey-hole. He has made an ill-advised choice, breaking communication with the authorities. He is, in short, a wanted man. I suspect his telephonic communication with you was a melodramatic venting of the proverbial steam. My thought is he will have the good sense to either admit his mistake and behave according to the strictures imposed on him, or stay deep underground so as not to risk his continued freedom."

Dip, drip, met halfway with outstretched tongue. He chewed, holding the receiver away from his ear. "Now, Jimmy, my dear colleague. Indulge me for just another sec. There. Good. Please take me at my most solemn word. Tito Flick has investigated, pondered, and believes you have no cause for concern. This is my well-considered judgment.

"Is there any other way I may serve you? No? Then I am pleased, bid farewell with respect and deep personal warmth and fervent hopes for your continued well-being. I remain your servant." He replaced the receiver on its cradle. "Hmmm. Even a modicum of gratitude would have been welcome."

Tito Flick reached into the folds of his mandarin robe and idly scratched at his balls, leaving an orange smudge on his white polyester briefs. "Now," he said, as he sniffed his fingertips and looked across the room. "I do hope that satisfies your request. Let's turn our attentions to my needs. Come, sit with Tito."

Haynus Geasley drained the rest of the Asti Spumante, dropped his cigarette into the glass, stood and walked slowly toward his benefactor.

“I must say,” Tito said, “prison seems to have changed you.”

CHAPTER 6

"Do you drink coffee?"

"Who may I ask is calling?"

"Jimmy Noze."

"I love coffee, Mr. Noze," Mary Bliss said. "Hot, black, and very sweet."

"What would you think if I swing by, pick you up, and we'll get some?"

"Swing? Swing by where?"

"Your place."

"But your truck. Have you found alternative transportation? Mr. Lowrey perhaps?"

"I have another friend who manages the cops' impound auctions. He let me have a Taurus for a song. Runs OK."

"Pick me up at the hotel, in front. I shall stand with the doorman so I am good and safe until you get there. Let us say five-ish. If the coffee is yummy, maybe some dinner, seven-ish? If that goes nicely, who knows?" She giggled, throaty.

Noze was sorry he had waited so long to call. "Five-ish," he said, looking at his watch. "Better hustle." He heard the line go dead.

He quickly showered, dried himself, and left his face wet to shave. This was always a contemplative time. Any time in which his mind wasn't active was contemplative time – self-centered, introspective, most always resentful contemplation. His counselor said it was the way of drunks, a role that Jimmy Noze was only beginning to accept, this center-of-the-world victimization that encouraged more drink, irrationality, and misery. One fed the other and on and on in a mental drain around which anything of value circled and eventually fell in. Noze started working at objectivity in his self-examination, trying to stop the eddy around that drain, to plug it and let things settle where he could pick them over and deal with each in its turn. If he could manage that, he thought, maybe he could keep drinking. The thought of quitting terrified him.

Though he usually ran an electric razor over his face, a hit-and-run style of shaving that made short work of a tedious and annoying chore but left his face rough with short stubble, he covered his beard in foam and went for the razor. He wanted his face smooth for this date, if that's what it was.

He felt an anticipation that was unfamiliar, one that had been replaced long ago by relentless dread, without reason or specific cause. He knew it as foe, the beast that lived in his head, a shit-covered ferocious thing, smothering and immense, even in the face of a pharmaceutical arsenal. He took stubborn pride in facing it down and functioning, with varying degrees of success, to confront each new day. He was strong and unafraid in waking hours. It might have the power to beat him, but not without a fight.

So why did he hesitate day after day to call Mary Bliss? He had her card. She gave it to him. Name and phone. She asked to see him again after a cheap dinner and some chat. She had taken the next step.

Approaching women, girls, had always been difficult. He had no opening patter and little patience for small talk. He could hold up his end or better on many subjects – news, politics, writing and literature, music and art, food, movies, painting and sculpture, history, woodworking, forensic pathology, street fighting, theater, and a range of other disparate topics in which he had some level of expertise and for which he thought of himself as a low-rent renaissance man. Within the highly clannish world of newspapering, such broad knowledge wasn't unusual. He was entirely comfortable with people in the business, especially the drinkers. Outside of it, he felt like a bad fit.

Talking with Mary Bliss was easy, mostly, and he didn't attribute it to any skill on his part. As he ran and reran the reel of their evening together, he realized that she was in control of the conversation, that she led it, and she did so by focusing on him. Her eyes rarely strayed from his face. She reacted to nearly everything he said, and nearly always responded with a question, trying to get to and inside him, interviewing with the easy skill of a professional, but never making it feel anything but personal. She was graceful but forthright in showing that she was attracted to him, or so it had seemed. Still, she was overtly sexual every time he had watched her.

It confused him. Her remark about relying on the kindness of strangers. Her story about the Viking and how readily she had gone to his home. The way she worked a room, just by entering and sitting alone. The subject of money had never come up, but she was clearly attracted to it. He couldn't shake the notion that she was a hooker, a stunningly beautiful working girl. Is that what the calling card was for? He felt ashamed, unjust, following that line of thought. But Jimmy Noze had been around.

He finished dragging the razor over his face, with the grain and against it, until the skin burned shiny red. He rinsed his face, dried it, filled his palm with rubbing alcohol, slapped it on, and waited for the sting to go away.

As he dressed, Noze fought back the ragged feelings of dread, tucked them into a compartment, and concentrated on the anticipation of seeing Mary Bliss again. However things worked out, he would have had that excitement, a relic of a past he could barely remember.

As Noze neared the tony hotel, he saw her chatting with the doorman, right where she said she'd be. She didn't recognize his car, and it pulled up in front of her before she saw him. She touched the doorman's shoulder, said something without looking at him, and began walking toward Noze.

He had thought about how she might look, what character

she would play for a coffee date and who knows. Her bright hair was pulled back into pigtails. There was no lusty red on her lips or nails. She wore a blue gingham blouse and loose white low-rider denims, with a belt of Indian silver and turquoise. One hand rested on a plain tan shoulder bag and as she came closer, she stopped, cocked one hip, and held out her thumb, a gorgeous country hitchhiker.

"Need a lift?"

"You would not believe it," she said. "Hi, Mr. Noze."

He walked around to the passenger side of the wheezing Taurus, helped her in, and closed the door. As he crossed in front of the car, he saw her scoot over. When he climbed in, she kissed his cheek and said, "Know what? I missed you. So where are we going?"

He put the car in gear and pulled away from the curb. "Where do you want to go?"

"Truth? I want to see where you live."

"Not a great idea."

"Why?"

"I'm not set up for entertaining."

"I don't want to be entertained. You told me you like to cook. Do you know how to make coffee?"

"If there's one thing I know, it's how to make coffee."

"And I want a simple dinner. A piece of fish would be wonderful. Do you know how to cook fish? Maybe you could teach me. I do not know a thing about cooking. I am really helpless. In the kitchen."

"I know a place with the best fish and chips in the city. Their coffee's good too. It's not far."

"I eat out all the time, Mr. Noze. I want to know you better, fast. You can make coffee. You know how to cook. I think you told me you even enjoy it. Seems to me there is only one place to go." She stopped his heart with a wicked smile. "Whip something up for me, Jimmy Noze."

He tried to think of a way out. "There's nothing in the fridge."

"Still early, no? We can stop at the market, pick out what we need, make a nice quiet evening of it." She waited, but he said nothing. "Do you have any windows that face west?"

She could throw a curve. "Yes," he said, glancing at her. "Why?"

"I think the evening light has special properties. Do you know a good market? We will make it quick."

Noze drove to one of his favorite food stores. The prices were right, quality was high, and it had a liquor license. Mary Bliss insisted on joining him in the store, and insisted again that she would choose and pay for drinks. As she wandered off to the wine section, Noze went straight to the seafood counter, chose six jumbo shrimp and four chubby fillets of mahi mahi. He hustled up and down the short aisles and picked up small bottles of mirin, light soy, basswood honey, and two packets of ramen noodles. He grabbed a pint of heavy cream from the dairy, then on to produce, beside the liquor counter, and chose four flawless fresh shiitake mushrooms, a small hank of scallions, two perfect freestone peaches that yielded to his touch just enough, and a small scoop of salted and shelled pistachios. He looked up to see Mary Bliss walking toward him, beaming, while she pulled two wine bottles from her hand basket.

"Champagne?" she said. "No. A simple, fine option. Spanish cava, crisp, dry, and earthy," stretching the word. "This is not as delicate as Champagne, but it has the tiny bubbles I love. They tickle. This is to drink with dinner, and after." She laid the wine in her basket and withdrew a quart of Jack. "And we must have Mr. Daniels for our pre- and post-prandial needs." She looked into his basket. "Interesting. What in the world are you going to make with that?"

"A surprise. I hope you like it."

They rang out, and Noze lost a small argument when she again insisted on paying for the drinks. He was relieved, but enough of a codge to feel that it all should be his treat.

As they pulled into the driveway of his apartment complex, Noze said, "Welcome to the projects," though it was better than that. There were bright flowers in border beds and window boxes, the lawn was well tended, and the parking lot fairly clean.

"Do not undersell, Mr. Noze. It looks lovely. Be proud of where you live. And you are with me. Lose the gloom."

He carried the groceries and hovered while she climbed the two short flights to the second floor, led her down a long hallway, and unlocked the door to his rooms. "Do me a favor?" he asked. "Will you wait out here for five minutes while a straighten up a few things? You'll be safe here."

She agreed, and he hustled in, dropping the groceries in the kitchen and trotting to a small closet to grab a quilt for the couch to cover its grunge. He ducked his head in the bedroom door, confirmed that the bed was still made with fresh linens because you never know, and gathered up fast food wrappers and dead soldiers, stuffing them in the wastebasket under the sink. He fired up two squat, half-burned candles in the living room, and fetched Mary Bliss.

"Candles," she said, taking in the sights. "How nice. You do not strike me as the candle type."

"Sometimes they help me relax. How about I make some coffee?"

"I have changed my mind on that point. I especially enjoy coffee in the morning."

Noze hoped he caught her meaning correctly. She went on.

"The paintings, are they yours?"

"Mine. Not so good, but I like the colors."

"Do not undersell, Mr. Noze," she said again. "They're good, very good. And a fortuitous surprise, considering the one I have for you. You told me you painted a little, but I had no idea. And the charcoals are stunning. You have a fascinating eye. Where do you paint and make your drawings?"

"Well, the riverside scene I did at a riverside," he said, chuckling, self-conscious, and hot to know about her surprise. "It's a place I used to fish. The farmhouse is from a photograph of where my mother grew up. The watercolor, the guy with the beard, is an old road buddy, dead now."

"And the nudes?"

"From a pretty good memory and a pretty good imagination."

"The poses as so languorous, sensual, unashamed. My, your imagination must be quite a place." She moved through the room, and into the smaller of the two bedrooms. "Will you fix us a drink?" she said over her shoulder. "Oh, I have found it."

Noze used the small bedroom as his library and studio. Board-and-brick shelves overflowed with unsorted books for what might appear to be an undisciplined mind, on topics from Japanese wood joinery and the Old West; fat biographies and how-to manuals on engine repair, home wiring, and plumbing; journalism theory and oversized art and photography tomes; hundreds of novels and short story collections; and at least as many cookbooks. To one side, Mary Bliss saw an artist's easel and a side table crowded with paints and brush jars and solvents, pastels and charcoal sticks, plastic palettes, and an overflowing ashtray. A small davenport for two sat beside one wall. The tall windows along another wall faced west.

Noze brought the drinks, two double Jacks on bar ice he always had in the freezer, handed one to Mary Bliss, and tinked his glass on hers.

Tink. Tink. One after another, an emergency room doc plucked bloody popcorn kernels out of the little girl's knees, like buckshot, dropping each into a metal basin with a loud tink. With each extraction, she moaned or keened with the added pain to her already ravaged little knees, the result of a terror campaign by her meth-crazed simpleton mother who threatened her with fire until she peed herself and was forced to kneel all afternoon on the raw popcorn strewn for that purpose in the corner of a tiled kitchen floor.

"Mr. Noze? Mr. Noze! Where did you go?"

His eyes cleared and he remembered where he left off.

"To you," he said, and sucked down the opening swig.

She met his eyes and said nothing, leaving it alone, and turned toward the windows. "Do you see what I mean about the light? It will not be long before it is gone. If you do not mind, can we eat a little later, when night comes and your candles will have their own special quality? I want you to do something for me while we still have this luscious light.

"Paint me, Jimmy Noze."

Noze wasn't ready for that one. "The light, there's only another hour or so. It takes a lot longer than that to make a painting."

"I know that. But you can start the sketch."

"I just do this for myself."

"Then it is high time you shared," Mary Bliss said. "You really are very good. Maybe better than you know."

Noze caved and busied himself with finding a clean painting surface, picking through various sizes of Masonite panels coated with gesso leaning against the wall next to his easel. "How do you want to pose?" he asked.

"Standing. You have a way with nudes, but they are all reclining."

He turned and saw she had removed her blouse, and her jeans were now puddled around her feet. She leaned one hand on a bookshelf and stepped out, kicking the pants aside with her right foot. "Won't it be fun not to rely only on your imagination?"

Noze was struck dumb by Mary Bliss and how she presented herself to him. He had had no expectation of seeing her like this, giving new meaning to the old "in all her glory" cliché. Glorious indeed. He had no other words.

The evening light did have special qualities he hadn't seen in it before, playing on her skin and contours, and bringing bright fire to her hair. She turned away and stretched her pale arms above her head, turning a little at the waist. She was preening.

"Someone, a gentleman friend, once said I was 'preternaturally beautiful.'"

"That's quite a word," Noze said.

"Do you know it?" She turned again to face him and rested

her little hands on the perfect little dome of her belly.

"Words are what I do, or used to. Yes I know it. And yes, I agree with the other guy's use of it." He clumsily tried to change the subject, and didn't know exactly why. "You'll get tired standing."

"I will rest if I need to. Let me worry about that." She turned away from the light, giving him a three-quarter profile, feeling the warmth on her back. She loosed her hair and rested her hands on either side of her neck, tilting her face up. "This should be nice. Do you like it?"

"I'm guessing you already know the answer to that," he said, feeling his imagination pull his attention from the miracle that stood before him. He turned and chose a white panel and clamped it vertically in his easel.

Mary Bliss broke the pose and said, "Could you find my drink? It will help." She smiled, the evening light glinting in her eyes. "I fear I may feel self-conscious."

Noze left the room, found their glasses, added fresh ice, and topped them off. The beast was working at the back of his skull, worming around and working on a way to screw this up. He quieted his mind, pictured the foul thing looking for an escape, and shoved it back.

She resumed her pose and Noze went to work with a sharp "F" pencil. He slashed straight lines to set the angle of her head, arms, shoulders, waist, hips, and legs, and then returned to each to make small adjustments. Noze hadn't intended to draw on the gesso surface, but it was going OK. He roughed in the shape of her head, drew ovoid shapes for her torso and limbs, and sketched sweeping curves to connect the geometrics.

"Is your hand steady?"

"As a rock. Where did you come from, Miss Mary?"

"How do you mean?"

"Who are you? You're very good at controlling conversation, at focusing on the other person, on me. My turn now. I want to know all about you. Who are your people? Where, how did you grow up? What gives you pleasure? What do you hate?" He sketched, refining lines, lightly adding details, scrubbing with art gum to correct error. "What kind of work do you do?"

Mary Bliss dropped one hand to pick up her glass from the windowsill, and sipped. "Have we not already answered that?"

"The 'kindness of strangers' thing was a little vague." He looked up at her, took a slug of Jack, took a chance. "I mean, here you are, without a stitch. But you've shown me nothing."

She stretched, arching her back, relaxed, and turned her face toward him. "You still worry that Miss Mary may be a pay-for-play harlot, just another crude, cold-blooded seller of her own flesh?"

"You're hardly just-another anything, Miss Mary. But I have to say, I've seen you sort and choose men to spend your time with. You went home with that Viking, and then he manhandled you like he had some claim. You've mentioned other 'gentleman friends.' You have no visible means of support. You dress provocatively, but not cheaply. I know cheap. You live uptown in a fine hotel. How do you do it?"

He saw a hardness pass over her face, and fade. "How do I do it? I have a little bit of family money, enough for necessities. The niceties are provided for me. Gentlemen of means give me gifts. There is nothing unseemly about that."

"And what do they get?"

Mary Bliss dropped her arms to her sides, palms turned out. She slowly began to turn, taking small steps, some a little awkward, until she faced him.

"They get this, Mr. Noze. The same as you." She resumed her pose. "We have almost lost the light."

"I think I've done all I can do before finishing this in paint."

"I relish your company, Mr. Noze. Posing again would give me another opportunity to spend more time with you."

"You don't need an excuse for that, Miss Mary. You're already my favorite person."

"I want to teach you something, if you don't already know

it," she said, raising one arm straight over her head.

"Come to me." Noze moved to stand beside her. "Now, lean in and sniff my neck." Noze did as he was told. "And what do you smell?" Mary Bliss said, wearing a small smile.

"I – it's – I smell something sweet. Is it perfume?"

Mary Bliss smiled a full, satisfied smile. "I made a point of not wearing any scent today. And now, do the same under my arm." He looked at her quizzically and, noticing that her armpit was so smooth it must never be marked by hair, he touched the tip of his nose to the flawless skin and took a deep draft. "Sweet," he said, and a mystery to me."

"Good," she said, and pointed to one breast. "And here?" More of the same, Noze said.

"And finally," she said, gently holding his head in both hands and directing him to the warmest part of her body. He dared not touch her there, but breathed deeply and said, "Still the same with a little more of your, um, inscrutable musk." She raised his head and lightly kissed his ravaged brow, then unhanded him.

"As well," she said, "due to our pale skin, anything pink on our other-haired counterparts stands out in higher contrast on redheads, on me. Nipples. Our mouths and nether lips, as you have just seen. It is part of our allure, and throughout recorded history, contributes to our reputation as the most sensual, the most desired in all womankind. Many men have made assumptions that this means we are wanton, lustful, lascivious, sexually available, that we are X-rated. Certainly, that is not always the case. But sometimes, at the right time with the right person," she gave Noze a meaningful look, "we are.

"And so, let me see how you have portrayed me. I am dying to see myself through your eyes."

She walked to the davenport and sat, entirely at ease in her nakedness. Noze removed his drawing from the easel, and sat beside her. He was not nearly as unmindful of her state as she, and was befuddled by the exercise in scent.

"Before I show you, please tell me why you had me do what

I just did."

"Well, I thought you might enjoy learning something unique about natural redheads, and as you can see, I am one. We are distinguished by a natural scent, sweet and with a touch of ambergris. Do you know what that is?"

"I know it has something to do with whales, but that's it."

"It collects in the stomach of the fecund-sounding sperm whale, which gets its name from a waxy substance that collects on its enormous head, having nothing to do with sexual function. Ambergris is excreted from the bowels of the whale, smelling like where it came from until it bobs in the sea for many, many years, when it is transformed into something with the sweet musky smell that I trust you have enjoyed rising from my body. It is very rare, illegal to sell in some places, and extremely expensive. A mere drop of it can enhance a quality perfume, which was first done for Marie Antoinette. In case you are not aware, she was not just a blonde but a *strawberry* blond. Do you take my meaning?"

"I do, my queen," Noze said, chuckling.

"My personal perfumer and cosmetics maker, Mr. LaPierre, enjoys varied and valuable contacts in Europe and has obtained enough to use in my custom scents, and only in mine. He does this so the scent does not clash with my natural aroma.

"One more thing. Even Mark Twain had something to say about those of us with natural red hair. He said something like all the rest of humankind is descended from apes, but redheads come from cats. I like that.

"And that concludes my lecture for the day."

"I'm so glad you gave it," Noze said, and handed his sketch to Mary Bliss.

"Oh, my," Mary Bliss said. "Oh, my, my. It is remarkable. You have made me ripe; the nymph lusted after by all satyrs. You see me as an air spirit, but still earthy in some respects. Clearly you see me as worthy of desire."

"You're all those things. I'm very pleased they come through."

"Just one thing. I have to ask, why do you show me only above my thighs?"

"I wanted to capture you as a goddess, and I suppose I thought that such a being would be without flaws."

"Flaws? I see."

Noze was immediately chagrined, sorry that he had not drawn an accurate, full-length image. He struggled for words to apologize, but she spoke first.

"No matter. I understand your point. I do not know how I will be able to wait very long to see it as a painting. You truly do have a masterful touch, Mr. Noze. Such a fortunate man, skilled in both words and pictures."

Jimmy Noze tried to suppress a sigh of relief and was very surprised, once she mentioned it, that she was not hurt or angry or both when she saw the three-quarter-length portrait.

"I know what I see when I look at you, and you describe it so accurately. You never fail to surprise me, frankly, about almost anything. So I'll ask again. Who are you Miss Mary?"

"Why, Mr. Noze, I thought you knew. I am art."

CHAPTER 7

He threw the empty Taco Bell bag over his shoulder onto the trash heap in the back of the ancient Geo Metro, quarter panels rusted through, tires bald, broken window replaced with a black trash bag and duct tape, the entire body painted matte black with a few shoplifted cans of spray paint.

Geasley didn't move his eyes from Noze's window framing most of Mary Bliss's body as she stood very still a couple of feet from the glass.

"The maggot's gotta be so fuckin' happy," he continued, speaking into a small digital recorder swiped a couple of weeks back from the table of a Hardee's customer who was at the counter getting a Coke refill. "How she serves Noze is an offense to Lord Satan and his Spawn. He don't deserve her anyways. Fuck. *Fuck*! Where'd she go?"

Geasley was nearly panting with hatred and lust. He paused the recorder and fingered a roach out of the ashtray. Fitting it into a paperclip, he lit up and sucked at it until it burned out. It was only a little dope, and it calmed him only a little. He continued to gaze at the empty window and unpaused the recorder.

"Is she just lettin' him look at her? Why don't she move much? Why'd she stand like that so long? Where's Noze? What's he doing? What's that rat-fucker up to with butt-nekkid quim in that room?

"Mental note. Gotta know her, learn more about her so she can't resist me." He kneaded his crotch.

"Mental note. Come back tomorrow, same time, see if she's back.

"Mental note. Watch Alice on TV interview tonight.

"Mental note. Call Tito and tell him to get me summa his poppers, and more bud and papers. No more dirt weed.

"Mental note. Get rope, duck tape, lumber, nails and shit, mask, bucket, soap, awl, birthday card for Mama, poster board, straight razor, Gatorade, zip ties, ball gag, lube, snacks.

"Guess she ain't coming back. No sign of life and only about 9 o'clock. Start up notes again later."

Geasley clicked off the recorder and dropped it on the passenger seat. He breathed in the grassy, bleachy smell of his fresh emissions and shifted in his seat. "What'll you think when Satan's Spawn pumps you fulla his hot jizz, bitch? What'll you do when he takes that body, slow, tasty slow, doin' this-and-that to all your these-and-those? Best-lookin' cooze I ever seen. We'll make us some videos. Some'll be just for us. Prolly they'll all be just for us. Satan's Spawn ain't stupid enough to show to nobody else. You'll be my little dirty movie star, a whore in scarlet, loads'a scarlet."

He laid his head back on the seat, closed his eyes and imagined scene after scene of himself with the stunning bitch. Nobody knew that he was watching her, following her when he could, making notes on everywhere she went. For now, he was The Eye, and anytime he wanted, he would capture her, take her to the room and do whatever he wanted. Before it became too much of a mess, he would have her, over and over and again, in every way he could think of. He would make her feel what it was like to be taken by a real man, not sorry slime like Jimmy Noze. Then he would make her feel other things, because she must be cleansed.

His reverie was broken by the thought that, in full regalia, he was easy to spot and memorable. Tito meant as much each time he asked him to "clean up a little." He wasn't performing anymore and he affected many looks when posting on his blogs.

Satan's Spawn would be allowed to rest for a while.

Haynus Geasley would disappear into ordinariness.

He opened his eyes, sat up and started the car.

The lust had drained out of him. The hatred remained.

CHAPTER 8

After Mary Bliss stepped away from the window, sat, and looked at Noze's sketch, she picked up her shoulder bag, reached in and withdrew a cropped white T-shirt and pink briefs. She pulled the top over her head and adjusted it, then pulled the panties up to her thighs and stood to finish putting them in place.

"Let us eat, Mr. Noze."

"It'll take just a little while. Top off our drinks and I'll get to it." He chuckled. "You and your appetite."

While Mary Bliss brought his drink, Noze got to work in his tiny kitchen, turning on the oven, laying out doubled squares of foil and placing a brick of ramen on each. He topped each brick with the fish, then the shrimp and sliced mushrooms, and formed the foil into bowl shapes. The dry ingredients were mixed together and divided between the two bowls. He combined the liquids next, squirted in some Vietnamese fish sauce from his pantry – "For umami," he told her, "the fifth taste" – and poured half the mix into each bowl. He gathered the foil and shaped it into small steam chimneys, placed each packet on a cookie sheet, and slid it into the oven.

"I have never seen anything like that, but I get the idea," Mary Bliss said.

"A spiffed up version of a hobo's dinner. It's a recipe from one of the food shows."

"Another surprise. I know you like to cook, but you do not seem to be the food show type."

Noze reddened a little, set a timer and tinked glasses with her. He winced, waiting for it. When it didn't happen, he said, "Here's to everything coming out OK."

"Here is to us," she responded, and Noze reddened more. He didn't know what she meant, but liked the sound of it.

"Let's sit at the table for a little while until the fish is done," he said. They took their places and each sipped some more Jack. Noze had never seen such a healthy looking person who could handle as much booze as Mary Bliss.

She turned to one side of her chair and said, "Mr. Noze, do you mind if I remove my leg?"

That qualified as one of the strangest requests Jimmy Noze had ever heard. He'd heard a lot.

"Of course not. Does it get uncomfortable?"

"Just a little after I have used it all day." She fiddled with something near the top where it attached to her thigh, then gripped it in both hands and held it to the floor as she pulled her thigh back. It emitted a small fart as the suction was released. "Is that not funny?" she said. "Would you like to hold it?"

He was afraid to say no, reached out and gently took it by the ankle. It was nearly as smooth as Mary Bliss's skin and had a slight give. Odd as it was to hold the leg in his hands, it was odder still that he found it to be lovely, stunningly so.

"Do you know what that is called?"

"Um, a leg?"

"No, the technical name. It is a cosmesis, the pinnacle of the prosthetist's art. It is a silicone skin, tinted to precisely match my own, fitted over an ingenious prosthetic leg. That includes a clever array of hinges and swivels to allow it to move almost like a real limb. I can dress it as I like and can even paint the toenails. It is waterproof, light enough for a full day of use, and costly. Fortunately, I have a very good gentleman friend who made it for me as a gift."

Noze thought better than to pursue that line. He ran his hand up the calf, and handed it to her.

"Amazing. Nearly as exquisite as you."

Mary Bliss cast her eyes downward and smiled coquettishly, a master of her craft.

"I have to know, Mr. Noze, because of the sketch," she said, raising her eyes to his. "Does this or my stump in any way repel you?"

"God, no, Miss Mary, no. I'd think you'd know that much by now."

She sipped and sipped some more, thinking.

"You know, we have not talked about the mystery creature who bombed your truck."

"There really isn't much to say. Haynus Geasley. He's a cowardly, demented putz who thinks of himself as a sinister prince of darkness. He's really just a dumb little Alice Cooper fanboy. I wrote about him a while back when he got popped for stealing his son from the teenage girl he knocked up. Excuse me, impregnated. The charge was reduced and he did a year, losing his son in the process. He says I owe him."

"Was he violent when you were writing about him?"

"Not that I know of, so I can't really say if he's stepped up his game with the bombing."

"Are you sure it was him?"

"No doubt."

"Are we in danger?"

"I'd have to say it would be prudent to feel that way, to have a little extra caution. But you should trust that I could take care of both of us. I'll find him."

The kitchen timer sounded and Noze stood to fetch their meal. He shut off the oven, took a bottle of cava from the fridge, and carried it to the table with two cheap flutes.

"Would you mind opening that and pouring?"

"Of course, Mr. Noze. It should pair perfectly with fish."

He plated each foil packet and carefully opened them, avoiding the rush of steam.

"Oh, it smells scrumptious," Mary Bliss said, handling the cava as he asked, while Noze set down their plates. He sat and raised his glass toward her. "To the most fascinating person I've ever known," he said. She raised her glass. "To our partnership."

He drank. The cava was bright, crisp, delicious, a little citrusy, and with a distinct note of pear. He thought for a second that his sense of taste might have been enhanced by the presence of his visitor.

"Partnership?" he asked.

"When we talked to the police officers at the restaurant, you referred to me as your partner several times."

"Oh, right. That was just to talk smack to Spack."

"You did not mean it? The idea excites me." Sip. Forkful of fish and noodles. She didn't continue until she swallowed. "My, that is yummy. Now tell me, what do you do exactly?"

"As I said, I was a newspaperman for a long time; mostly worked the street. Got fed up with the way the editors butchered my copy. I believe the violence we do to one another should be described in detail, so people know it's nothing like the movies. One editor told me plainly, after hacking pieces out of my latest story, 'Noze, nobody wants to read that shit with their morning eggs.' And I quit right then, burning my bridges." He didn't tell her the real reason he quit, the darkest night of his life, played out in rain and mud.

"How do you mean?"

"I cussed them out, dropped my pants, showed them my pink and white butt, invited a smooch, and walked out. Never returned, and I don't think they'd have taken me back anyway. Fortunately, I had a Scottish grandfather who pounded into my head to bank part of every paycheck, so I had some savings and still do. I'm a good investigator after years as a reporter, so now and then I pick up piecework finding bail skips, doing deep-dive research for defense lawyers, writing a freelance piece every now and then, and whatever else I can scrape up. I don't see how you'd fit in any of that."

"Well, Mr. Noze, I am a very good researcher and I think my interviewing skills are also well above average. I am also aware that I am a distraction, which can be a positive."

"I've noticed that. I don't know, Miss Mary. I run into trouble now and then and don't know if you could handle it."

"I can take care of myself. I like the idea of being Jimmy Noze's partner."

"Well then, that's another way you're unique."

They ate and drank in silence for a time, Mary Bliss occasionally moaning with pleasure, Noze keeping their glasses full.

She broke the silence. "Mr. Noze, when we clinked glasses earlier, you paused for a moment with a pained look on your face and seemed to have gone, I do not know exactly how to describe it, to another place I could not see. I am guessing it is something personal, so do you mind if I ask where?"

He thought about it while clearing the table, poured the last of the opened cava, and excused himself to go to the kitchen. "You might want to save the other cava to go with dessert. It should be perfect."

He put a dry cast iron skillet on high heat and hand-whipped the heavy cream while he waited. Deftly skinning both peaches, he cut them in half and removed the stones. When the skillet was nearly smoking, he added a pat of butter and lay in the peach halves flat sides down. He carefully lifted the edge of one with a spatula, and continued to check it for a few seconds until it came free. The peach faces were nicely caramelized.

"My," Mary Bliss said in the dining room, modulating the word into two notes. "What is that enchanting smell? It is almost erotic."

"You'll see in a minute. Patience."

He placed two small circles of chopped pistachios on each of two plain white plates and nestled a peach half on each circle, face up. A dollop of whipped cream followed, then a heavy drizzle of honey over all with a garnish of whole pistachios.

"Erotic?" Noze said as he set her plate before her. "Some friends told me how to make it, a Persian dessert. They told me it's an aphrodisiac."

"Aphrodisiac? What are you up to, Mr. Noze?" She said it with a mischievous smile.

"The final touch is mine." He brought out a small jar of clear liquid with what appeared to be freshwater pearls on the bottom. Unscrewing the lid, he held the potion under Mary

Bliss's nose.

"What in the world?" she said. "It smells like almonds."

Fishing out six of the pearls, Noze carefully arranged three on top of each of the desserts. "The French call these *noyaux*," he explained. "I save any peach pits I might have, let them dry a little, then fold them into a dishtowel and smack them with a hammer. When they break open, each has one of these *noyaux* in the core. I let them marinate in quality vodka in the jar for a good long time. Sipping shots of the vodka while munching on one or two of these makes a fine digestif. But tonight, we'll have them with dessert. They're a little bitter, which goes great with the sweets. They also contain a very small amount of cyanide, which I think gives them an arousing sense of danger. I hope you enjoy."

Mary Bliss took a bite, munched on one of the pearls and quickly followed it with another. She licked cream from her lips. "Ooh. Oh. I think your friends are right." She spooned in another bite, chewed and swallowed, rolling her eyes to the ceiling in what certainly looked like ecstasy. "I think you are right too. I'm going to take my time savoring this marvel, but I can eat and listen. You were going to tell me about something."

"I've never talked about it with anyone but my counselor. I'm sorry you were concerned. It's my cross to bear."

"Please, Mr. Noze, I want very much to know everything about you."

"Why don't we finish?" They took their time with the rest of dessert, and Noze relished watching Mary Bliss in her enthusiasm for the confection; it was part of his own dessert. She picked up the final bite with her hand, slid it between her lips, noisily sucked it in and licked the stickiness from her fingers.

"Did you enjoy yours?" she asked.

"Much more than I can say," Noze replied.

"Now, tell me the story."

So he relented, and told her the tink of their glasses took him right back to the little girl's popcorn torture. Mary Bliss put one hand over her mouth in dismay and her silver-gray eyes grew wide and moist with tears. They were for the little girl, and herself. It was a secret she had told no one, not even Miss Ruby, who would have killed some or all of them if she knew what they did to her granddaughter.

Noze told her more.

He related the story of a small airplane crash he covered, and detailed the appearance of the victims, including three kids who survived the emergency landing but burned alive in a pile while trying to escape the plane through its small door. He described the scene, the posture of the bodies after the flames had shrunk the skin at every joint, leaving the dead tucked into hellish defensive poses, and he told her about the smell, fuel mixed with roasted meat.

Marry Bliss's eyes brimmed.

He recounted a story he covered about the latest in a string of prostitute killings, describing body-shaped hollows in the dirt floor of an abandoned two-car garage, lined with the slightly phosphorescent waxy soap that is the form a human body takes if left to decompose long enough during summer days and nights.

He told her of the old man he had found one morning while responding to the police scanner he kept in his car. He went to the scene, getting there before the cops, saw feet sticking out from behind the garage and found the old guy lying on his back on the grass, a shotgun clutched on his chest, holding two shells in the other hand as though he might need to reload. Most of his head was gone, bone, gore, and brain matter splashed far across the yard. When Noze talked to family later, they told him the old man had seemed fine as usual, but was terrified of going to the dentist the next day, a first in his life.

Mary Bliss stopped him.

"Please, Mr. Noze. No more. I do not know if I will ever get those images out of my head. How do you do it?"

"I don't. Reporters at least try to be dispassionate about the things they see, distancing themselves a lot like news photographers do, seeing the horror through an imaginary viewfinder as though they're apart from what's in front of them. They park the sights in the back of their minds and figure they'll stay there. But sooner or later they show up with a vengeance. I've had chronic severe depression for a long time, and the memories feed it sometimes. I take a strong anti-depressant at night and one in the morning. And I see a shrink when I can afford it. Sometimes it wins, though.

"You won't hear many news people talk about it, even among themselves. It's a tough-it-out macho type thing, with the women as well. Eventually I realized that was bullshit. Sorry for the language."

"You are forgiven, dear man. Can I help?"

"Directly, no. When you have this, you're really on your own with it. But just being with you, looking at you, does help."

She stroked his cheek with the back of one hand, and then gently traced the scar on his eyebrow. "What is this about?"

"It's embarrassing. There's a place down on Third Street where the ragged people go, as the song says. It's a good place to get in trouble, and sometimes that's just what I'm looking for. Called Big Chigger's Bar and Grill. He added 'and grill' to his sign after he bought a George Foreman rig to make burgers on the back bar. The last thing, the only thing, I remember on this particular night was Chigger's yellow teeth and grin as he swung a foot-long leather sap my way.

"Chigger's got a rep for tolerating verbal abuse and crackpot monologues so long as the big mouth keeps calling for more and paying cash. But he doesn't like his joint to get loud, won't take anybody swinging on him or anyone else, and enforces his rules with the sap."

"Sap?"

"Know what a blackjack is? Not the card game."

"Yes, it is a weapon used to beat someone."

"A sap is the same thing. Chigger's is old, a solid lead bar sewn inside leather attached to a spring-loaded handle. He got it from a longtime customer, a street cop who drank on the cuff during work hours and sometimes reminisced about the days when he could freely use the sap to keep the peace on the streets. He claimed he once bent it on the skull of a huge, rampaging dust head, right between the eyes. The giant was terrorizing a guy selling fruit from his pickup. The cop said the hulk just looked at him, grinned, and crushed an apple in one mitt. It took five jumbo uniforms and one dick – one detective – all of them swinging saps, sticks, or fists to bring in the guy, and all of them got their own injuries.

"The cop told this story as he gave the sap to Big Chigger to enforce order inside his joint, and later looked the other way when he used it. He told Chigger, 'Hit only where the bone's thickest,' and that's why I took it across the brow."

"The reason?"

"I have no idea. Can't remember. Chigger knows me and we get along fine, so I'm sure I earned it."

"How could that be?"

"Oh, easy, I guess. You've never seen me blind drunk, and I'll try to keep it that way. One thing for sure, I won't ever take you down there."

"But what if I want to see it?"

Noze ignored the question. "Now tell me about you."

"You keep asking for that, but I do not like to talk about myself. My training keeps me focused on the man I am talking to."

"Maybe so. But you need to explain what you mean by training."

"I told you about Miss Ruby. She raised me alone in a big Victorian house after my mother and father left one day and never came back. When she was young and very fetching, she made her way by enchanting men and enticing them to part with things she needed or would make her happy. She said no harm came of it, though she had what she called some close scrapes with several of her suitors.

"She trained me in her ways, how she studied men and learned what they want and how to persuade them to give her what she needed. I was tutored to understand that men are visual creatures, very much so, and how fulfilling their deep desire to look at me as so many had looked at her could be a powerful way to provide for myself."

It briefly occurred to Noze that she could be doing the same to him, but that didn't make sense. He had nothing of value to give her.

"How about you, Mr. Noze. Are you highly visual?"

"Well, for my paintings."

"No, not for that. Do you sometimes feel transfixed by the sight of an alluring woman? Do you imagine more than what you can see? Do you fantasize about what may be under her clothing? Do you imagine having her?"

"Guilty," Noze said. "It seems harmless and natural to me."

"So you see, men are like that. I learned from Miss Ruby how to accommodate it to my own advantage.

"She told me I was a natural beauty, as she had been, and meticulously demonstrated how to apply makeup and scents to enhance without overpowering. She taught me how to care for my skin, which is quite delicate, and many methods of styling my hair and dressing seductively like the characterizations played by an actress. And then there was my stump."

"What could she have told you about that?" Noze was confused, mystified.

"You see, as we went along in my lessons, she naturally educated me about sex, the mechanics of it, the physical and emotional hazards, and the vital importance of recognizing when my wooers will not settle for a generous look. Some of their desires stray far from what most people would consider acceptable. She warned me that there are those who would be aroused by the sight and the thought of doing unspeakable things with my stump. I was horrified. She assured me it is true, and I have found during my life without her that she was correct."

Noze was not shocked by this, having himself learned just how perverse sexual attraction can be. "Is that why you chose such a lifelike substitute, to avoid these freaks?"

"Only in part. My primary reason was to present myself as a complete picture, with two pretty legs instead of my own right leg and a clumsy, obvious substitute, a plain prosthesis with very limited motion. I wore those for a time, even a modern version of a peg leg, and never stopped receiving unsolicited stares, which I most certainly did not want. I want only those that are solicited.

"You, Mr. Noze, quickly established yourself as far above the freaks, as you call them. You should understand that I do not hate men. Generally I like them. But you? In truth, sir, I am most fond."

The candles had guttered for a few quiet moments, then snuffed themselves out. Mary Bliss yawned, and put the back of one hand over her mouth to cover it.

"I have to say, even with your intensely stimulating company, I am getting weary. Would you help me to the couch?"

"If you're ready, I'll take you to the bed. The couch gets a lot of wear and tear, and there's a butt divot where I always sit. I'll take the couch. To be honest, I sleep on it most nights. I just don't like to sleep in the bed. It feels really empty."

"I can do something about that."

Mary Bliss started to stand, but Noze stood and scooped her up in his arms, holding her like a dear little child. He took her straight to the bedroom and set her upright on one foot.

"The linens are fresh. Just let me turn down the bed right quick." He did, and picked her up again, his breath catching at the feel of her, and laid her gently on the fresh sheet. She looked at him, and in the dimness her silvery eyes seemed almost to glow with their own light.

"Would you lie with me and hold me while I sleep? I have never been with anyone I trusted to do only that." She rolled on one side.

Jimmy Noze was again confused. He padded to the other side of the bed, stripped and got in, lying on his side facing her back, and pulled her body snugly against his.

He couldn't help but move his hips against her bottom, and the rhythm of it began to have an effect on him.

"There is one thing I left out of my story that I really should inform you about, Mr. Noze. You may have heard me say I *only* want to be held. I have never made love except in my imagination.

"You see, I am pure."

CHAPTER 9

Finding and tracking Noze had been almost too easy. The dumb fuck still had a landline in his apartment, and his address was in the phone book. Tito knew some of his downtown daylight hangouts. Haynus Geasley followed him at night. It wasn't hard to keep that ratty pickup in view, even hanging back a half-block in traffic.

Geasley watched him off and on for weeks until he found what he wanted. He had taken his usual post, parked on the opposite side of the street and a dozen storefronts down from the Train and Tunnel, which seemed to be a new favorite for Noze. Not the kind of place he usually favored, too fancy for such a beat up, worn out asshole. But there he went, night after night, among the pretty boys and the bitches who came and went, laughing and posing and dressed so nice. The sparkly people. Noze must have been a turd in their punchbowl. When he came out of the place, walking stiff-legged and picking his steps carefully, Noze was always alone until one night when Geasley watched in wonder, grinning, as a glowing redhead walked out in front of him, rocking her hips in an unusual way, and got into his truck. The bitch was hot.

He cranked up the Geo Metro – a gift from Tito, who had accepted the dinged ride in trade from one of his other clients, it ran good, not too bad on gas – made a uey and tailed the pickup to a rundown restaurant in downtown's neglected warehouse district. The Geo blended right in with the other cars in the parking lot. He chose a slot at the fence, backed in, shut it down, and slouched low behind the wheel. He had a good view of the door.

Haynus Geasley had nowhere else to be and plenty of patience in his quest. He sat for hours, swigging Dr. Pepper and gin from a brown paper bag, smoking and flinging the butts under his car so he wouldn't leave a pile beneath the driver's window. On TV, tails always got spotted because they leave that conspicuous pile of butts beside the driver's door. Noze and the hot bitch were inside for hours and by the time they came out, cover in the parking lot was getting thin. He watched Noze steer the truck in the direction they came, and wheeled in behind it after a safe interval.

During the ride, Geasley could see her move closer to Noze, then rest her head next to his. Good, very good. She never ducked her head out of view. No suckie. Nice girl, maybe. So it was strange, after the truck stopped and she gave Noze a grinding kiss, that he just dropped her off and left. A cab arrived almost immediately and he watched her get in. This time of night, even in this suburb, there weren't a lot of cabs, so it was easy to tail all the way to the house where it let her off. After she was inside, Geasley wrote down the address in case he forgot his way.

He made the house part of his regular surveillance. When she appeared, he recorded detailed notes on the times he saw her leave and return. She was always alone. One night he hung back for a while after she got home to see if she left again. She didn't. But he watched, fascinated, when a hooded tubby guy, who just seemed to be passing by, turned off the sidewalk and hurried into the trees beside the house. Tonight might not be as boring as others. He sipped his brown-bagged cocktail, smoked, and watched until the fat man reappeared and hoofed on down the line, empty handed.

Geasley followed him, lights off, as he walked several blocks then hoisted his big ass into a parked Land Rover SUV and drove off. Big ride for a big slob. Geasley had no problem keeping it in sight as he drove outside the city and pulled into the driveway of a small house in one of the classy suburbs. Rich fucks. Dude has coin, Geasley thought. What's he need with creeping a hot bitch's house in the middle of the night? He noted the address and the plate number on the Land Rover, and called it a night, heading back to Tito's place.

Of course, Tito was waiting for him, pretty drunked up and pissed. He was always pissed when Geasley rolled in late stinking of cigarettes, weed, and sweat.

"Any reasonable inquiry is made in vain," he said, huffing and stomping around in his shiny tasseled babouche slippers. "This I know. My feelings, my anxiety, are of no concern to you. This I know. My kindnesses and solicitousness and generosity mean nothing to you. This I know. You make that abundantly clear with your sneering and demands, your rude language, your defining cruelty." He stopped and turned to face the accused. "Nevertheless, I ask, I insist that you tell me where you go on these forays, a sneak under cover of night. What do you do in these absences? Where..." Geasley liked this part, when the lumpy little perv lost it.

"What the fuck, Haynie, you ungrateful shit. What the fuck, you ignorant, self-important prick. Fuck you, Haynus. Get the fuck out of my home. Go see how you do on your own, you cocksure little prick. Where would you be, now, this night, without Tito Flick? On the stroll, peddling that ass. That's where you'd be. You have only one marketable skill, only one. Your pretensions to musical talent are pitiable. Yes, on the stroll, or behind bars, perhaps? Back under the brutal tutelage of the unwashed, back to being anybody's and everybody's, back to tossing salads – yes, I know what that means – back to being a mere commodity with a value measured in cigarettes and skunk weed." Tito sprayed gummy spittle with his fricatives. He shone with perspiration and the fleshy folds of his pallid midsection and stubby legs rippled as he raged. "That is your preference?" he shrieked. "Begone, wretch. Leave this place and do not return to Tito Flick's embrace." He glared, silent, eyeballs popped, his flabby chest heaving.

Geasley smirked and reached into his shirt pocket for a smoke.

"I told you, Haynus. Cigarette smoke offends my nostrils and inflames my lungs."

Geasley stuck the smoke into the corner of his mouth, pulled out his Zippo and fired it up. He sucked hard and blew a cloud in Tito's direction. "Y'all done, Frito?" Flick's nostrils flared with the smoke and insult. "How's about you go fill up the tub?"

Tito opened his lips to speak, thought better of it, and sagged with relief and gratitude. He padded into the bathroom, turned on the taps, adjusted the heat, and shook a few drops of sandalwood essence into the water. He sat heavily on the floor and watched the water rise, regaining his composure and gathering his remaining strength. A surge of anticipation stirred him.

When he turned off the taps, he heard Geasley enter the room behind him, and turned to see the slightly muscled young man sit on the dressing stool and hold one booted foot in the air. Tito scooted across the cold tile on his ass and gripped the boot with both hands, straining, then pulling it free. He began to hum a gospel tune and didn't look up as he unbooted the other foot and peeled off the socks.

"Forgive my outburst, Haynie," he said, as Geasley stood, raised his face to the ceiling and held both arms out to his sides. "Sometimes your negligence is just too much for quietude and forbearance. Nevertheless, I am embarrassed and ashamed by my histrionics. Regrettably, *in vino veritas*."

Tito raised himself to his knees, unclasped Geasley's belt, freed the waist button of his jeans, slowly lowered the zipper, and helped the pants drop to the floor. Although he thought it a bit savage, Tito was pleased that the young man's custom was to wear no undergarments.

"My, my, my," he said, "Your prison yard bodybuilding was an unqualified success. Michelangelo himself could do no finer." He hoisted himself to stand, and unbuttoned Geasley's shirt in the next step of what had become ritual. Geasley shook his head vigorously, the greasy tendrils of his hair slapping either side of his face. He pulled the shirt open, shrugged it off his shoulders, and let it fall to the floor. Then he opened his eyes, lowered his gaze to Tito's twitching face, and fixed him with his best malevolent gaze.

"Ah, yes, yes," Tito said. "You are a menace."

Geasley climbed into the hot water, sitting erect, face forward, eyes again closed. Tito went to work with a soapy washcloth, asking his ward to stand at the appropriate moment, then dropped the washcloth and lathered his bare hands, tending with particular fastidiousness and energy to the part that Tito believed was most subject to careless hygiene.

It responded to his slickened caresses. Geasley gripped Tito's pomaded hair, pulled his face close, and buried The Boa in it.

CHAPTER 10

Why couldn't she just have left it at Prince?

If his sainted mother hadn't been such a rabid baseball fan, she might not have given Tug Prince LaPierre a name he deplored. It was the one thing in all their years together for which he was not grateful. He never forgave it.

Eunice LaPierre studied the players she admired, and once she learned how Tug McGraw got his nickname, it was a done deal. And she delighted in telling the story anytime anyone asked. Dramatically clapping one hand over a withered breast, and beginning her response with an appalling grin, then a sigh and "Oh my, my, my," Mother always explained in detail about her infant son's aggressive nursing.

"I used to have very pretty titties, but oh, he sucked them flat with all the tugging, clamped down on my nippys with his little gums," she said, telling the same story every time as though it were scripted in her mind. "I had bruises and, my dear Lord, chafing that never healed. He drew blood, the little tick." A hideous laugh.

"That boy, it warmed my heart with how ferocious he went at me from the very first suck. I remembered reading about Tug McGraw's mama and how she called him that for the same reason. So right there, after the first time he was on my tit, I named him Tug too. Made his first name of Prince his middle name." Little Tug's father had no say in the matter, having vanished at the first whiff of paternity. "I took it as long as I could but had to cut him off right after he turned six." She always ended with her cackle, enjoying the mixed response of her listeners.

By anyone's standards, Tug's life as a child was one of tribulation. Mother worked hard to tend to him before catching her bus to work each day where she constantly handled or simply was around industrial chemicals, maintaining metal turning lathes and saws. She made certain he was clean, adequately clothed, that his brogans were brushed if not perfectly shined, and that his socks matched. She had always admired patterned male hosiery and favored argyles, but none too loud. She smeared skillet cornbread with oleo and brown sugar syrup, wrapped it in waxed paper and put it into a sack with 15 cents – sometimes all pennies – for milk money, a ripe apple because it was one of the most nutritious of fruits, and a 200-for-a-dollar picnic napkin. Often, when he was down, she penciled "Remember Mother Luvs U" on it to remind her boy that he was not alone. She stopped adding an exclamation point because her pencil tore the napkin.

Tug was a big boy with a small voice, meek and averse to physical competition, so he was soft. Looking back later, he thought of playground as yard time, the way it was portrayed in the prison movies he enjoyed. On the yard he was called Tugboat and Tug It and The Tugger.

He had a recurring nightmare that would follow him into adulthood after a dirty boy from the retarded class, whose ashy skin cracked and peeled in patches, launched himself from where he leaned on the chain link fence around the playground, and ran screaming into Tug's chest and belly, knocking him flat onto the gravel and clinker and using his knees to pin his victim's shoulders to the ground and leaning over his face with gaping mouth and sharp teeth and hot breath that smelled like stale popcorn and milk gone off and lowering his mouth over Tug's nose and growling, "Yum! Yum! Eat 'em up!" Tug wept and opened his own mouth in horror but could make no sound. Other boys, and some girls, stood by and laughed and pointed and shouted look at what Lizard is doing to the Tugger and no one tried to stop it until Miss Collins the nappy-haired gym teacher pulled Lizard off and tossed him aside like the piece of trash he was. She ordered Tug to stop crying and walked away, her whistle swinging from a braided plastic lanyard around her thick neck.

Even that memory was overshadowed by the time in high school after swim class when the other boys took their usual locker room observations about penis configuration an awful step beyond. “Look, it’s a giant anteater,” and, “Hey, it’s an army helmet,” and, “Aw, there’s a mushroom cap.” Tug did his best to keep his back to the commentators, but one day they pumped themselves into a tribal frenzy and spun him around from where he faced into his locker and some of them pinned him against it and chanted, “Can’t see it can’t see it can’t see it” and a Bic lighter was produced and fired up and brought low and close and closer until it burned and he shrieked a terrible shriek and they let him go and returned laughing to the task of getting dressed for the next class.

He left school without permission and limped home where he fell onto the couch and stayed until Mother was back from work and found him in such a state and whimpering and sobbing with snot flowing and hardly able to breathe but finally managing to blurt, “Mother, they’ve hurt your boy.” He showed her where it was red and a little blister had been raised and she wept as she found the salve and gently rubbed it on with a thumb and two fingers. Tug calmed and looked at Mother and her hard little hands and thought she was the most beautiful thing he had ever seen. Neither of them acknowledged his little erection.

Tug never toughened as he matured and was, as he had always been, drawn only to passive recreation. He considered observation a teachable, valuable skill, and spent hours consciously honing his abilities, often taking voluminous notes that he would review repeatedly to train his memory as well.

His favorite subjects were women, and his notes about them were his preferred late night reading material. He observed them in public, which as a practical matter was his only opportunity, as they sat, stood, walked, ran, danced, jiggled, stumbled, fell, and stood again. He observed them when they were among themselves and when they were with men. He observed how they dressed, but except in the movies had never seen one put on or take off her clothes, the closest being when he set up a folding chair at a public swimming pool or beach and watched as they wrapped themselves in towels or gauzy pullovers or other light apparel to tame their goose bumps or protect their skin from the sun, and better still when they removed those coverings. No girl or woman had ever in his life approached him with any interest. Tug's relationships with women were the stuff of vivid musings.

Always an above average student of the arts, Tug also discovered a special ability with science and math. He had studied hard enough to earn a small scholarship to a community college, one that focused on the practical application of knowledge, much of it in the trades. Before entering, he carefully looked over the various curricula, repeatedly, with an eye to finding something that would put him in classrooms with more young women than men. His epiphany came when he saw an ambitiously wide range of classes in cosmetology.

Over the next two years, he enrolled in them all and excelled in each, including perfumery. He was a novelty in most of the classes and even became a favorite of many of the girls, who most often practiced the makeup techniques they learned on themselves and one another, but clamored for the chance to pair up with Tug, who from the first class began to introduce himself as Prince. He also changed the family pronunciation of his surname from "lapeer" to the standard Gallic "lah-pee-air." He was never critical, always gentle in proposing what he believed would be the most complimentary makeup choices for each face – the cheeks and chin, the eyes and brows, the nose, and the lips. They found that he was invariably right, and he declared each of his subjects in turn as gorgeous or darling or daring. They might have been surprised to learn that he adored them as they came to adore him. They confided in him and gossiped with him and commiserated over small tragedies and believed he was safe. Prince LaPierre, by his kindness, good humor, increasingly affected mannerisms, and seemingly deep understanding of the nature of women, was almost universally regarded as gay, like the few other young men who studied among them.

He did not foresee a life for himself of simply working behind the cosmetics counter of a department store, or even as a freelance makeup artist who depended on occasional assignments from brides, boudoir photographers – although he certainly would accept such work if it was offered – or morticians. Prince LaPierre's driving ambition was to meet and spend time with the most discerning and, by his rosiest theory, most attractive women who would seek him out to buy his own custom-created, unique handmade cosmetics, soaps, lotions, and scents. The name T. Prince LaPierre would be the platinum standard for personalized beautification and intimate pampering.

He bolstered his classroom studies with outside research into the ingredients and techniques, both time-honored and innovative, used in the creation of cosmetics and toiletries. He practiced the craft late into the night in Mother's basement, and she tolerated his insistence on testing his creations on her, though she routinely commented, "You might just as well try softening gator skin," or, "Still trying to make a silk purse out of a sow's ear," or "It's just like painting an outhouse wall like a Chinee temple."

When Mother simply did not wake up one morning, he wept and convulsed and vomited and screamed and gave full vent to his grief for a day, a night, and most of another day, then washed her body, dressed her in the only dress she kept for rare social occasions, the one in which she was married, pulled new white cotton gloves over her ravaged hands, did her face to the best of his abilities, and called the authorities, who were surprised by the appearance of the body but suspected nothing unusual about the death. They carried her off to be incinerated the next day. He accepted her remains packaged in a twist-tied black plastic bag inside a waxed cardboard box and put it away until the day he could afford a proper receptacle.

To fill the void, he focused more keenly on sharpening his skills until he emerged as the fully formed character, T. Prince LaPierre, perfumer and maker of fine cosmetics and beauty potions. He carried his creations in a sample case door to door in tony neighborhoods, persuaded the women of these houses to let him transform their faces into visions they had never imagined, and found enough moneyed converts to stake him in opening a small shop in Clarkston, a northern suburb far from his Detroit home. Within three years of hanging his shingle, T. Prince LaPierre was free of debt and serving a deeply devoted clientele who paid him well for intimate, quality time in beautification and gossip, and kept his handwritten ledger backed up for months with orders for his small-batch product lines. As soon as he could afford a two-bedroom house near his shop, he bought one and moved.

He had his favorites among his clients, and sometimes kept others waiting past their own appointed times as he indulged himself in the warmth of their company, their attentions to him as a special but always unthreatening companion, and the contact with their faces or necks or arms or hands as he applied his cosmetics and lotions. Some thrilled to the sensation when Mr. LaPierre lightly powdered their liver-spotted chests with a high-end, hand-tied NARS Yachiyo brush, its exotic Japanese appearance adding to their arousal.

But he had never been as moved, as delighted, and as lascivious as the uncommonly slow afternoon when he looked up from his Victorian desk to answer the tinkling of the dainty bell over the shop's front door and saw a radiant redheaded woman who walked in with something prettier than a limp. She wore a thin white sundress printed with bright tropical blossoms in reds and greens and yellows that bared milky shoulders, clung to her body and fell just below her knees. A light spray of adorable freckles spread lightly across her nose and chest, and her coppery hair moved like liquid on either side of the most singularly alluring face yet encountered by T. Prince LaPierre.

She took the chair across from him without being invited. "Are you the proprietor?"

"I am he, T. Prince LaPierre, a wizard of the cosmetic arts. May I say at risk of offense that you are the most stunning woman to ever have set her bottom to that chair. How may I be of service?" She ignored the compliment, having heard such things so often.

"I have very specific requirements in makeup, soaps, body lotions, and other emollients to tend and adorn myself. You see my skin is quite delicate. I want you to make some things for me and nobody else, and I am just as particular with my scents."

She opened a cigar-box purse and withdrew several pieces of pastel peach notepaper and laid them on the desk.

In a tiny hand, she had written an extensive list and he thought her quite clever not only for identifying each hue by hex code and color-chart reference, but even describing the container she required for every lip gloss, powder, blush, shadow, and perfume, as well as the size and shape of a variety of brushes and natural sponges.

"You have a reputation for work that exceeds excellence. I do not require your advice, but I expect you to draw on all of your powers in creating and providing these things."

When T. Prince LaPierre looked up from the list, he saw that she was studying his face as intently as he had studied hers. Then it softened and became almost flirtatious.

"Are you a homosexual?" He was momentarily startled not by something that so often had been presumed about him, but by the fact that she so forthrightly put the question into words.

"No," he said with a self-conscious chortle, "no I am not."

"Well, I do have one thing that you may be able to advise me on." He was stunned to see that she had begun to unbutton the top of her sundress as she spoke, and he had to call on his learned behavior not to gape.

"There is a color that I want to match exactly, and I have been unable to find any standard reference to it." She never moved her eyes from his, which were struggling not to stare at her fingers. "It is perfectly all right," she said. "Look." She spread the front of her sundress and bared one breast, then pointed to and touched the tip. "This. I want you to match the color precisely for rouge, lip gloss, eye shadow, and nail enamel."

T. Prince LaPierre had never, until this moment, seen a bare breast, certainly not one as immaculate as this. For a moment, he feared he would weep in gratitude, but knew he must maintain his professional aplomb. "I, I pledge to you, Miss ... I'm afraid I didn't catch your name."

"My name is Mary," she said, pausing for a beat, "Bliss."

"What a wonderful and perfect name. Well, Miss Bliss. I pledge to you that I will not rest until I've met or exceeded your expectations."

"There is just one more little thing," she said, folding her hands in her lap, and looking down at them, the breast still bared. "To be candid, I am afraid I have very little money." She looked up and he raised his eyes to hers. They are not just gray, he thought, they are shot through with shards of glistening silver.

"Still being candid, Mr. LaPierre, I have very little means but pray we can reach some understanding. Do you have a camera?"

"Only an old Polaroid."

"Does it make color photographs?"

"Yes."

"Perfect."

He produced it from a desk drawer.

"Even an artist such as you should not entirely trust his color memory. I have read this is our weakest recollection, yes? Take a photo and use it in your work. Get close." He did.

They sat silently while waiting for the "instant" photo to develop. When it was done, she held it next to her nipple and judged the color to be accurate.

In that moment, Mary Bliss and T. Prince LaPierre, maker of fine cosmetics, sealed their arrangement. He told her to give no more thought to something as unseemly as cash. His labors would be as artist for model in the service of the exquisite. She asked if he used email, and he handed her his embossed business card with all the necessary contacts.

"If I have any more questions or requests," she said, "might I send you another picture?"

CHAPTER 11

Dick Sloane was used to being treated like what he was intended to be – a golden god – and he was goddamned if he was going to let a little cunt like Mary Bliss tell him when things were over.

He had been raised to godhood first by treatment as a little lord, always being dressed up in little suits and little hats and little boating outfits and little riding breeches and having his portrait made by professional photographers with expert lighting assistants. His lavish birthday galas brought supplicants for his father's friendship and business largesse from near and far, each bearing a gift to lay at Little Dick's feet and be measured against those that came before and those yet to come. Little Dick examined each, sometimes thrilling the offerer by turning it in his hands before tossing it aside to call for the next until all were collected and all abandoned. He attended only private academies, though from pre-school through prep school and business school his father had to use a well-practiced combination of threats and cash endowments to gain his son's admittance and keep him there. His father insisted Little Dick did not do well on tests because the tests were flawed.

Dick Sloane wafted through life on a downy cloud of privilege. He never worried about money. His place in his father's waste disposal empire was secure – "There's always trash and shit, son, and we sit on the mountaintop." – and he spent his workdays looking important for the female support staff, firing and replacing on a whim or because he tired of how they looked, taking three-hour drinking lunches and six months of vacation, and looking forward to the day when the old man died, he inherited all of his holdings, and could really cut loose and live as he pleased. Dick Sloane, with all that he had, always wanted more.

"Have you ever heard about the most powerful aphrodisiac?" he liked to ask when breaking in a new personal trainer, always a shapely female and not equal even to Sloane's own sluggish intelligence. "It's money, honey, and power. Do you think that might be true?" As an adult, he was tall, golden blond, blue-eyed, and blessed with a metabolism that burned off all of his excesses but a little booze-fat around the middle. The personal trainers were hired to tone and define his muscle groups, and do what they could with his gut. They never complained about his frequent lunges for a little grab-ass.

Women flew to him and said, "I could eat you like candy" and other come-get-me's and he smiled preening self-satisfied smiles and could be choosy about who he took home. He prowled every night in the trendiest bars and clubs, entering alone and sitting at a highly visible table to let his magic work. He paid with his Amex Black Card, and kept it on the table where it could easily be seen. He never left alone, and he never failed to score until he took home Mary Bliss.

She was mesmerizing, both hot and cool, and seemed to radiate her own light in a low-cut, knee-length mint green sundress that eddied around her perfect body when she walked. Her hair was the color of a new penny, and she wore a delicate necklace with a ruby-studded blunted fishhook pendant.

Sloane had never seen her before in the Train and Tunnel, so she presented him with a first-time conquest. As she neared him, she watched his eyes and the smallest changes in his face as she gave him plenty of time to look. It was easy to see that he was vain and preening and confident in his appearance and she had already noted his superior demeanor in the way he treated the servers. She made intricate calculations and settled on an angle of attack when she stopped at his table.

"You look like you are never lonely, but I am. Could we have a drink together?"

"It will be my pleasure," he rasped, then discreetly cleared his throat. She ordered Champagne, just a glass she said, and he chose the same, sending back an almost untouched glass of wheat beer.

"What's your name, lovely lady?"

"Mary Bliss," she said, smiling prettily and showing her teeth as she pronounced the ess. "And yours?"

"Dick Sloane, just Dick."

"Oh, and what do you do, just Dick?" He thought she blushed just a little, but maybe it was just his imagination.

"It isn't very glamorous. I head the country's largest waste disposal concern and," after a dramatic pause, "with our other worldwide holdings some people call it an empire. If that's so, then I'm the emperor."

She widened her eyes and pursed her candy apple lips in a perfect circle.

"Oh my, I think that is clever really. Emperor Dick. I do not imagine you are ever short of raw material." She giggled and looked down so he might think she was a little embarrassed by her own turn of phrase. No woman had ever enchanted Dick Sloane, but this one came close.

And not that he cared but because polite conversation seemed to be required by this woman before moving on to something more on point, Sloane asked, "And what do you do?"

"I do my best to take care of myself and my needs," – she paused to show him a superb naughty smile – "and earn my way by doing a little of this, a little of that, a little of other things. I hope you do not think me too bold asking to join you. I do not want you to get the wrong idea," and again the naughty smile.

Sloane ordered two more glasses of Champagne. "Just to keep our whistles wet," he said with a wink between conspirators. He talked about himself until she finished hers and said, "I know a place where we can eat a pile of caviar and slurp some ice cold oysters," drawing out the word slurp, "and enjoy whatever kind of wine or cocktails you like, way better than anything we can get in a place like this, and where we can be more comfortable than anyplace you can imagine."

Mary Bliss again formed those bright red lips in a perfect circle and asked, "Oh, where might that be?"

"My house, but it's more than a house and you don't have to worry, I'm a true gentleman. Let me entertain you as you deserve."

She looked hard at his eyes so he might think she was taking his measure, and tapped the candy apple fingernails of one hand on the tabletop for one beat then two then a third and said, "Are you really a nice man?"

"As nice as you'll ever find." He showed his pearlies in a boyish smile and Mary Bliss said, "Let us go see this place that is more than a house. I am hungry. And I adore oysters and caviar. I find them very – how shall I put this? They arouse certain senses."

Dick Sloane ordered his car brought around and excused himself to go to the restroom where he phoned home and told the butler who answered, "There better be a big can of Petrossian in the fridge and the oysters better be fresh and open on ice. Beat it when you're finished and take the others with you."

Outside, he watched closely as Mary Bliss lowered herself into his Mercedes E-Class, which he liked to use not so much for its cachet or its speed or its handling, but because it sat just inches off the ground. The seats were low too and even the most mindful of his dates could not avoid showing an extra length of leg and sometimes more when they settled in.

As he drove he glanced over at her profile and was emboldened.

"You have to be pretty good with a stick to handle this. Maybe I'll let you try it someday. Are you good with a stick?" She ignored the oafish innuendo and just smiled.

Sloane could plainly see her imitation leg next to the console that separated them, and asked before he could help himself, "What's that all about? Sorry, but it's right there."

She showed no reaction but said what she always said when they asked. "I was born this way. It was hard to accept when I was little girl and even an older girl because the prosthetic devices always looked like prosthetic devices until I was grown and found the means to have this one created. It is as much my leg as the right one and it is beautiful, do you not agree?"

Sloane rasped, "Oh, yes," and reached over to touch it. Mary Bliss brushed his hand away, saying, "I thought you were a nice man." While he apologized, she shifted both legs closer to the console and smiled that naughty smile.

After a bit of a drive, they pulled up to the gate of Sloane's mansion in Barton Hills Village, and he opened it with a few quick taps on the touch pad. He helped her from the car, again peering to see what he could see, and led her through the massive, studded oak front door.

Mary Bliss quickly took in the grand foyer and what could be seen through the doors of adjacent rooms and judged that it was not as tastefully appointed as other oversized houses she had visited, but it was indeed huge compensation for what was almost always the same shortcoming. Still she began a mental inventory of all she saw and estimated the value of each thing and held her eyes wide and her mouth open as Dick Sloane suggested a tour of his humble abode before they ate.

He offered one arm to escort her down the first hall, but she ignored it and walked ahead. Sloane held back far enough to watch the movement of those hips and told her when to turn this way or that so she followed the right path. He showed her through most of the house, wowing her with its enormity, the professional kitchen he never used, and the climate-controlled wine cellar reached by a hand-wrought iron spiral staircase, which he helped her maneuver, and where he poured the first drinks – a 2004 Perrier Jouet Belle Époque Fleur Blanc de Blancs Champagne. He supposed the fine vintage was lost on her, but knew she would love it and perhaps overindulge.

Moving on, with stops en route to open doors and reveal such expensive gadgetry as the compact dry-cleaning machine he also never used and stores of one hundred percent silk bed linens in dozens of colors – "Confidentially, they feel like cool fluid on your skin" – and the mahogany-paneled elevator between the basement and fourth floor. He offered his arm for an escort into his Art Deco movie theater with oversized plush recliner seats and a popcorn machine and a well-stocked mini bar, and he poured them each another full glass from the bottle he carried.

"Do you enjoy elegant erotic cinema?"

"Do you mean pornographic films? No, Mr. Sloane. That is not to my taste."

"Please. Call me Dick."

"I am ravenous, Dick. May we have the oysters and caviar you promised?"

"Immediately. What garnishes do you like with each?"

"I appreciate purity," she said. "Just ice cold oysters with the smallest squirt of lemon, and caviar is glorious unadorned, on its own." She giggled, adorable. "I like it best right out of the tin."

They returned to the kitchen, where Sloane opened the Petrossian and settled the can into a deep silver bowl of crushed ice. He took two dozen oysters-on-the-half from the massive refrigerator, and arranged it all on an intricately carved ebony service cart with a dish of lemon quarters, a bottle of Tabasco in a silver cozy, and two mother-of pearl caviar paddles.

"You might not know, but any metal makes the caviar taste off and real gourmets know you should only eat it with these," Sloane said.

"Well you learn something every day," said Mary Bliss, who had many warm memories of eating caviar from mother-of-pearl. Her host pulled a fresh bottle of Champagne from his wine cooler, opened it with a loud pop and a wasteful gush of foam, leering, and nestled it in a silver ice bucket that he added to the cart with two cut-crystal flutes.

"Please follow me, my lady. I promised you a comfortable place," and she followed him down a long hall and stopped at the door as he wheeled the cart into the master bedroom.

"Oh," Sloane said, looking back at her. "Don't worry, I just wanted you to see it and the genuine polar bear rug in front of the fireplace. There's no more comfortable place for a snack than on the bearskin." Mary Bliss had already taken in the Alaskan king bed with a gaudy array of pillows. It looked more like a stage than a place to sleep. A tiled Roman tub and open shower had been built as part of the room, and an enormous canvas print of a period Orientalist slave market scene hung on one wall.

"Well, you have been very nice and if you promise you will still be nice ..."

"Oh, yes, of course I'll be very nice." He parked the cart at one end of the bearskin. "Make yourself comfy." She hesitated. "Really, it's like nothing you've ever felt."

"This is awkward; I have some difficulty lowering myself to the floor."

"Oh, because of the leg," which he fixed his eyes on and felt a sexual reaction he didn't really understand. "Don't worry, just relax. We're all family here. You can take it off and I'll help you settle." Mary Bliss smiled her well-practiced naughty smile and said, "I thought you would never ask. Excuse me." She turned away.

Sloane watched intently as she removed the cosmesis. He felt lightheaded, but snapped to when she said, "Well?" and he took the leg from her and let it drop gently on the other end of the bearskin, took both of her hands and helped as she lowered herself onto the virginal white fur.

"Ooh, you were so right," she cooed, and he looked at all of her as she leaned back on her elbows and stretched her right leg luxuriously on the fur. In an entire life full of wanting, Dick Sloane never wanted anything so much.

"Before we eat, will you excuse me? I have to use the little boy's room." He went in and closed the door, and a few minutes later emerged fully naked and proffering his angry member in one hand.

"No. No, please. Put that away. We will have none of that. Maybe another time. If you are nice."

She turned her face away and scooted on her butt toward

the end of the rug to retrieve her leg. Sloane ran to it with his phallus bobbing, scooped up the leg and threw it hard across the room to the bed. "Let's play," he said, grinning demonically.

Mary Bliss reached down to cover her stump. Sloane grabbed a handful of her silken hair and jerked her head up. "You wanted to be comfortable. Take off that dress." It was an order.

She made intricate calculations and lowered the straps from her shoulders, then peeled the dress down to her waist. She let him have a good look. He again grabbed a handful of her hair and pulled her face-to-face with his member. Mary Bliss spoke, with a new chill in her voice.

"You are a voyeur, are you not? Let go of me," and to her surprise, he did. "Has anyone ever cried rape?" Her eyes had gone dead and she stared at his.

"You want it as much as I do. I know you do."

"No, you are very wrong, and whatever you do to me will be described in great detail to some very good friends I have in law enforcement. They will believe me, and they will come to arrest you and will have a search warrant. They are very good at what they do, and because I will tell them you are a voyeur, they will find the cameras and recorders that I know without any doubt are hidden throughout this house-that-is-more-than-a-house and you will be stopped. Hard.

"Believe this. None of your girls is anything like me." She pulled the top of her dress back into place. "If just watching were enough for you, we could have started a nice arrangement. We could have seen each other again, and who knows where our relationship might have gone. Now bring me my leg!" She saw that Dick Sloane's penis had flagged, and he did as he was told.

As she arranged herself and stood with his help, Dick Sloane begged. "Please, Mary, I'm so sorry. I misjudged what you want. It was a mistake. Please, I have to spend more time with you – your rules. Could we see each other again, at a restaurant or something? Wherever you like."

"To you, I am Miss Bliss. Now cover yourself, you awful man, and call me a cab." He did both. "Go wait at the door and tell me when it arrives," and he obeyed.

When he called to her, Mary Bliss tucked a mother-of-pearl spoon into the caviar, picked up the tin and cradled it in one arm, walked out of the bedroom and out of the house, settled herself in the cab, and he watched as it drove her away.

The vivid memory of this encounter steeled Dick Sloane in his resolve to do something about it. Like it or not, she will be with him again, and not by her rules but his. He hadn't shown her everything in the house. Next time, things will be very different.

CHAPTER 12

She rolled over and kissed him awake, once on each eyelid and firmly on the lips.

"I'm glad you woke me up," he said. "I was getting very tired."

She laughed, and he thought it sounded like music. She cut herself off when she realized he might not be joking.

"What do you mean you were getting tired? Do you not have restful sleep?"

"To be honest, almost never. There's a landscape in my dreams full of broken buildings and rubble and people without faces who live in the rubble. Sometimes the stories staged there are frustrating. Sometime they're terrifying. Wherever I am, I can't find my way out and no one will help. Everything is sepia. They're intense nightmares and prevent me from waking fresh."

"Oh. Now I do not know if I should tell you how I slept."

"No, please, go ahead."

"I have never felt so safe, so appreciated, or so cozy as when I fell asleep in your arms last night. It was pure, dreamless sleep, and when I awoke this morning still in your arms, I was very pleased. I am still very pleased to be here with you. But, Mr. Noze, I believe we have work to do."

He wanted to lounge all day, looking at her, talking with her, just being with her, but Jimmy Noze knew she was serious about their partnership. He agreed; there was work to do. But there was time to relax and chat over fresh coffee.

Mary Bliss, like Noze, did not eat breakfast. Strong coffee was a morning necessity, often as a curative in Noze's case. Waking with her in his arms was glorious.

"It is a fresh day, Mr. Noze, and I must say starting it with you is a new experience. You can take it as a high compliment that I simply do not spend the night with anyone. It speaks to my trust in you."

"I hope I'll never lose that, Miss Mary," he said, letting her rise first and savoring the chance to watch her stand, steady her right leg against the bed, and stretch.

"I will wait for you to finish in the lavatory. I suspect I will take longer in there, and you can prove to me in the meantime that you are as skilled at making coffee as you say."

"Fair enough," he said, getting out of bed and trying to cover himself with his hands as he started to leave the room.

Mary Bliss giggled, this time a sound almost like birdsong. "Do not be shy," she said. "You have seen all of me you can possibly see, and turnabout is fair play. And I must say, you have nothing at all to be ashamed of in that, um, area. All in all, you have a very handsome form." He moved his hands and, turnabout being fair play, she gazed at what he uncovered and repeated, "A *very* handsome form."

He kissed her forehead and purposefully walked to the bathroom, trying not to scuttle. When he brushed his teeth, shaved and otherwise finished, Noze came out and Mary Bliss walked in carrying her shoulder bag, her left leg in place. Noze busied himself with the coffee, scooping dark-roasted Jamaica Blue Mountain beans from a bag he kept for special occasions – there were few – and pulverizing them in a burr grinder. The aroma was intoxicating. He arranged an unbleached filter in his six-cup Melitta pour-over drip funnel, drizzled in some boiling water to moisten it, discarded the water, and added the ground coffee. He kept the kettle on medium heat, waiting for Mary Bliss to rejoin him.

"That smells wonderful," she said as she left the bathroom and Noze poured the steaming water over the grounds. He turned to greet her. "It'll be ready in a few minutes," he said. He took in the sight of her. She was dressed again in the white jeans and gingham blouse, this time leaving it unbuttoned and knotted at the bottom. Her hair flowed freely, and she appeared to be wearing no makeup. Miss Ruby's opinion was dead-on perfect: Mary Bliss was a natural beauty. Maybe even supernatural. As before, he did not recognize her perfume, and it seemed to be different this time.

"Speaking of smelling wonderful, what's that perfume? It's not like another you've worn before."

"It is plumeria, a special treat for you. I do not wear it often because my perfumer, Mr. LaPierre, can make it only in limited quantities. It is a painstaking job to obtain the fresh blossoms, which have to be flown express from the source. They are used for garlands in Hawaii, and also grow in parts of Mexico and the Caribbean. The name I have given this scent is Lei, L-E-I. It is meant as a double entendre. I am told it is provocative." She offered her neck, and Noze breathed deeply, immediately feeling a bit lightheaded.

"Now where is my coffee?" she said with faux impatience. He helped her settle on a chair at the table, and brought out the pitcher of fresh brew and two mugs. After pouring, he sat cater-corner to her, offered raw sugar, which they each took, sipped and said, "Now it's your turn."

"My turn? For what, Mr. Noze?" She sipped. "Goodness, this is ambrosial."

"Please call me Jimmy."

"What is it my turn for, Mr. Noze?"

"I think you still know far more about me than I know about you. Why don't you tell me what you most enjoy?"

"Well, let me see. I love fine art, and am an avid student of it. It has taught me many things as I have defined my own ideas about womanhood and sexuality. Would you bring me my bag?"

He did and she withdrew a calfskin notebook tied with plum ribbon. "It happens that I have taken careful notes in my studies. This is the result, which I have assembled as a handbook on male desire. It is not a sex manual. It is a manual on innate attraction. As a practical matter, I have included notes on love. Let us see. Here is one of my first notes:

"It is called *A Young Girl Defending Herself Against Eros,*" she continued. "The girl is a woman in bud, still fleshy with baby fat and unmarked by life, according to my notes. Her hair is black and her skin olive. She sits on a cold stone block, almost naked, just her legs covered with a rich cloth. The baby-god Eros has a knee on her lap, trying to climb on, but she holds him off with straight arms. The gleeful little horror tries to infect her with a dart he holds in one hand, not strung in a bow. This gently smiling maiden fights the erotic impulse, and in that we are alike. I prefer to think of myself as a master of Eros, not as his target."

Noze chose not to think too hard about what that meant for him. He returned to the subject of their partnership.

"Tell me how you see your role if we are to go partners."

"If? I thought we had settled that."

"OK. Let's say it's a done deal. I know we have talked about your power to distract, which can no doubt come in handy. But I also know there's more to Mary Bliss than sex appeal. What do you do when you're not distracting?"

"Are you saying I am not just a dumb redhead?"

"After talking with you as much as I have, that goes without saying."

"Say it anyway."

"Without question, you aren't a dumb redhead."

"That is the first time anyone, besides my Miss Ruby, has remarked on my intelligence. It gives me joy. If that is truly your belief, you may be surprised that my formal education ended before I finished high school."

"Why?"

"As my body became more womanly, I began to attract more attention from both girls and boys. The girls were terribly mean to me. The boys behaved like filthy little scoundrels. While I use my looks to my advantage now, at that time the attention was unwanted and crushed my spirit. Much of it focused on my leg, but most of it on my developing body. So I left, with Miss Ruby's blessing."

She sipped her coffee and Noze refilled his mug. He glanced at her, and saw that her face was downcast in thought. He was sure he hadn't yet seen her look sad, and it broke his heart. She shook her head slightly, and raised her eyes to his.

"I became an autodidact, determined to refine my knowledge and practice my intelligence. Most of what I now know I learned on my own. Oh, there is one exception. I learned to play the cello with a very patient teacher. I tried watching online videos to teach myself, but the cello does not lend itself to an autodidact. Not I, anyway."

"Hold that thought. First, would you care for some more coffee?"

"It is the finest coffee I have ever had. But as you know, it has a strong diuretic effect. So I will say no, thank you so much. I learned the word 'diuretic' in my medical studies."

"Excuse me?"

"Oh, I certainly am not a doctor or a nurse, but I found medicine fascinating for a time and studied until I knew I would never be a professional. Still, I picked up a lot of knowledge along the way. I would say I am fairly expert in first aid, and maybe a little more."

"What are some other things you 'picked up,' Miss Autodidact?"

"Hmm. I am fluent in French and Spanish, and know quite a lot of Latin, which helped me learn the other two languages. The first computer I owned was a PC I built myself, in preparation for becoming adept at its use. There are few things I cannot find with the computer."

"Including people?"

"Yes. A suitor who treated me badly due to his slovenly drinking habits moved away when I filed a sexual assault complaint with the authorities. A short time later, they told me they were unable to locate him and just dropped it. Within two days I found him in a halfway house for alcoholics in West Virginia. I phoned it in the middle of the night and asked for him by name. The night attendant woke him and told him to come to the phone.

"When he answered – he was very angry – I told him my name, that he could not run anywhere that I could not find him, and to prepare for a visit. Then I called the police down there, gave them the information about my sexual assault case, and the address where he could be found. They went right out and took him into custody. It was not long before he was returned to Michigan and is now about two years into his fifteen-year sentence for second-degree criminal sexual conduct. It was the most the court could give. I was satisfied with that."

Noze didn't like the story as much as she expected.

"So you've been put in danger by your activities. Besides the Viking, I've wondered about that."

"Yes. Why do you bring that up?"

"Because I worry about you. I'd think it would be obvious."

"You are a dear, but you should not worry. I have taken self-defense classes and know some tricks, like punching the Viking, as you call him, in the throat. I also even know a move I can perform with my cosmesis. Stomping down with it on an assailant's instep works wonders."

"Even so, why do you do it?"

"Do what, Mr. Noze?"

"Entice men with an unspoken promise and turn it to your advantage. Someone as intelligent as you can find any number of jobs. So why do you do it?"

"The first reason is simple. It is much easier to support myself this way than having to meet all the requirements of an ordinary job. The other reason is that I feel it is payback for all the ways I was mistreated in school. They hurt my heart. I think of it every time I successfully gain control over a man. Does that make sense to you?"

"I guess I can't argue with it, is one way I can answer."

"Miss Ruby taught that all women have power over men, but many of them, maybe most, do not know how to gainfully draw on it."

"I'm still going to worry, you ..."

A loud knock at the door interrupted them.

"Excuse me, Miss Mary." Noze stood and answered the knock.

Standing outside the door was a young man with short-cropped blond hair and wearing khakis and a long-sleeved plaid shirt. Noze thought he looked like the kind of guy who would sprain his ankle kicking somebody in the balls. He held a square box with a printed label addressed to Noze.

"This dude in the parking lot give me ten whole dollars just to bring this up here," the stranger said. "Easy money. Here's your package." He looked past Noze and said, "That's some sweet piece you got there."

Noze took it and said, "Nobody asked you," and then, "Have we met before? You look kind of familiar."

"Must be one of them coinkydinks," and he turned and walked away down the long hallway.

Noze went back to Mary Bliss at the table, thought better of it, and excused himself. He took the package into the bathroom, laid it down on its side in the tub and took out a penknife to slit a narrow opening to look inside. Better safe than sorry.

"Jesus Christ!"

Mary Bliss gasped. "Mr. Noze! Are you alright?"

As he slit the top of the box open, she rushed in and looked over his shoulder. Noze turned bright red with rage at what was inside.

"My God, is that supposed to be me?"

"Please, don't look at it anymore," he nearly shouted. "Go back and sit."

She did as he asked.

Inside the box was what appeared to be a woman's head with blood streaking a pale, comely face and clotting in the long red hair that cushioned it in the carton. Laying on top was a note in a child's hand that said, "I'm coming for her."

Noze raced to the west-facing window. He scanned the parking lot for any sinister presence and saw only his nearest neighbor walking to her car, and the delivery kid trotting off.

"Goddammit," he said turning back toward Mary Bliss. "This seems like the kind of thing that piece of trash Geasley might pull. If I could have caught him it would make our first task unnecessary."

"What is that, partner?

"We have to find Haynus Geasley and make sure he doesn't graduate from being a pain in the ass. Let's get on it." Mary Bliss, just now, thought silence to be a better choice than scolding him for the profanity.

CHAPTER 13

T. Prince LaPierre didn't get nearly enough Polaroids of Mary Bliss to quench his painful thirst for the sight of her. He texted her several times to ask if there was anything she was running low on, trying to prompt new photos from her. They went unanswered.

She had returned to his shop just once, with a request for lip gloss that would match the color of her blazing red hair. It would be a difficult formula, she was sure, but she had no doubt that her personal cosmetologist was up to the task. She allowed him to take a small tuft of her hair from a discreet spot, but she offered no nakedness as part of the transaction. So, losing his rigid self-control, T. Prince LaPierre became a highly focused peeper.

Rather than try to tail her everywhere she went, as he did after her first visit, he returned night after night to hide in her yews and peer at the bathroom window, hoping she would stand there while toweling off. He had watched her several times and, seeing her pause in what she was doing to stare hard out the window, LaPierre entertained thoughts that she knew he was out there and was all right with it. Still, he took as much care as possible not to be seen.

As he drove past Miss Bliss's stately home, he saw a nerdy-looking blond kid hustling toward her yews. LaPierre continued to drive to the place a block away where he usually parked his car before walking back to the house. On this night, he watched carefully as he approached the house and saw no sign of the nerd. When he skulked toward his customary dense green hiding place, he saw movement directly across from the bathroom window and quickly backed into the foliage.

Miss Bliss was not in the window, but the light was on and she may yet appear.

When she did, she turned her back to the window and dropped her filmy dressing gown. With fluid grace, she gently rolled her hips – favoring the right for balance – while unpinning her fiery hair and combing it with her fingers before letting it drop around her neck. She turned her face to the window and slowly swiveled around to look out. She saw slight movement in two places among the yews, and wondered about a new peeper. She'd caught a glimpse of the needy Mr. LaPierre several weeks earlier and assumed he was one of the two spies now in the evergreens. She couldn't imagine who the other was.

As she pondered that, there was sudden movement, and a skinny blond boy burst from the yews and ran off. Mary Bliss thought for a moment that he looked like the boy who delivered that dreadful package, then dismissed the thought as too unlikely.

That left Mr. LaPierre, and she wanted to please him to keep their commerce open. She steadied herself on the side of the tub, and reached in for a big soapy natural sponge, leaving it loaded with water. She stood and faced the window and squeezed the sponge down the front of her body, using her free hand to languorously spread the suds on her skin as they slid down. She dipped the sponge into the soapy water, reloaded it, and stood with her back facing the window. She slowly squeezed the sponge over her shoulders and let the foam slip down over all. Then, show over, she sat in the bath.

As she luxuriated in the steamy, scented water, she let her hands explore under the water and thought of Jimmy Noze in her stimulating reverie. Perhaps he was the one to take her purity.

Noze was thinking of her at the same time, but with a decidedly different effect. She had kissed him goodbye, lingering as their lips responded to one another, before the arrival of the cab he had called to return her home. He tried to hand her carfare, but she refused it saying she knew she could work something out with the cabbie. The comment triggered a few moments of frustration. Noze was quite sure he was in love with her.

He watched her go as her last comment also beckoned the wet brown thing that seeped from its cave at the back of his brain and enveloped him, coloring the world like a tintype, thickening the air and making it hard to breathe. The thing had teeth, but no sharp bite. It was like being gnawed at with molars.

He returned its hatred, and tried to force it back into its lair. Still, it sucked at him until it swallowed the last spark of energy, deflated him until he felt like an empty bag of skin. At such times, everything, every least movement, every thought and intention, was accomplished by stubborn will, a strength he learned by example from his old man, who'd suffered with his own beasts and refused to lay down at their feet.

His pride in that was peculiar, much like Detroit, which seemed to constantly congratulate itself on being able to take a beating. Few cities had taken as many. And Detroit raised its progeny in its own image. Noze never missed a day on the job, when he had one, because of depression or drink. He sometimes toyed with thoughts of stopping, purely for economic reasons, but had not yet learned that quitting drink was not an act of will, but of abdicating it. As long as booze offered obliteration, whether he leaned on a bar or sat at home relentlessly draining a bottle of Jack, his thoughts of quitting were purely academic, he told himself, as were his thoughts of suicide. When he once said as much to his social worker, the recovering drunk got a good laugh. "Academic?" Noze laughed with him.

He cracked the seal on a fresh bottle of Jack, and pulled out a joint to bolster its effect. He had obtained a state medical marijuana card for his physical pains and crushing depression. Plodding to the fridge to fill a tumbler with bar ice, he headed for the couch, scooping up an ashtray and lighter along the way. After he settled into the ass divot, Noze fired up the fat spliff and inhaled deeply. He held it in his lungs as he filled the tumbler with Jack and took the first long pull. When he blew out the vaguely skunky smoke, he felt a little rush from the combined intoxicants. He continued that way until the ultimate desired effect overtook him and he slumped sideways onto the couch. Jimmy Noze dreamed his usual dream of a sepia-toned, rubble filled landscape where this night, armed with only a pellet gun, he fought another faceless enemy. He had hoped for dreams of Miss Mary, but she was nowhere to be found.

Jimmy Noze remained on Mary Bliss's mind as she snuggled into her posh bed. While he struggled with his nocturnal horrors, she dreamt only of him throughout the night. She unconsciously smiled at her adventuring in dreamland.

CHAPTER 14

There was no shortage of abandoned buildings in Detroit. They were spread throughout the city, from the heavily industrial riverfront outward through the neighborhoods that grew along with industry, through pockets of light industrial zones, and on once-thriving commercial strips.

Haynus Geasley inspected many of them before settling on a massive, rotting edifice that was once the Eternal Life in Good Hope Baptist Church near 12th and Clairmount, where the deadly, destructive riots in the summer of 1967 jumped off, sparking waves of white flight to the suburbs, including much of church leadership. Later, after the effects of the civil uprising worked their way throughout the city, "ruin porn" became a thing, one that photographically documented the physical decay that befell the once great city. People traveled long distances just to shoot pictures of Detroit's decomposition.

The deciding factor for Geasley was the life-size crucifix he found leaning against a wall in a basement storage room. Its statue of the tortured Christ was gone, but the cross was nearly as good as new. He was already thinking about using this place as his lair because it had very little water in the basement, setting it apart from all the other ruins he investigated. It also had long been stripped of everything that could be sold by the city's hyperactive army of scrappers, so unexpected intruders were unlikely. And the cross, which Geasley didn't know he needed until he found it, was just what his plan required.

The basement also held the church's baptismal tub, now filled with trash. It too would be handy. Graffiti covered everything, and included several large representations of the goat-horned Satan. Haynus Geasley was amused that whoever the taggers were, they might be alarmed to know that this was now the home and workplace of Satan's Spawn in the flesh, the real deal. For the time being, he cleared out the tub and replaced the trash with army surplus blankets for his bed. This would now be his home and staging area.

The storage room was dank, but held no water. Dank was a plus in Geasley's mind, and it was big enough to hold his abattoir, though he didn't know that was the word for it. He also chose the old church because a boarded up door in back was big enough to admit his car. One dark early morning he pried the thin plywood door off its frame and tested it to see if he could prop it up over the opening without its nails. It worked perfectly and he left undisturbed the tall weeds that grew along its bottom.

Over many nights he brought loads of materials for his project into the loading bay, pulling the detached door closed behind him. He was careful in his use of a penlight to show his way inside the building, holding it in his mouth when his load required both hands. It was hard work, but he was inspired by visions of what the storeroom would become and what would happen inside its dripping walls.

He used several of the two-by-fours he'd brought in to make rough sawhorses, four of them, on which he mounted the cross horizontally. He toenailed spikes through the sides of the cross into the sawhorses to prevent it becoming dislodged during energetic use. It was the centerpiece of the room.

Geasley assembled a first aid kit in a workman's tin lunch box, containing rolls of gauze, adhesive tape, packaged sutures, ammonia inhalants, rubbing alcohol in the small Thermos stored in the lid of the lunch box, sharp tweezers, baby oil, tongue depressors, lube, disposable scalpels, surgical clamps, eye speculums, and saline eye drops.

While looking over the materials he had, Geasley pulled his tiny recorder from one pocket and switched it on.

"Mental note: Paint or posters?

"Mental note: Buy two construction lights, most brightest.

"Mental note: Work on welcome speech for Satan's Spawn's lair.

"Mental note: Long black wig and makeup

"Mental note: Dildo?

"Mental note: Bring boom box and CDs.

"Mental note: Grand Guignol."

Geasley wished he had taken a camera while peeping the yummy redhead at her bathroom window and in the one at the maggot's apartment. He had not intended it, but he too was now in the bitch's thrall. She was so beautiful that he couldn't put it into words from his limited vocabulary.

"Girl, you obviously want it. That's written all over your body and red hair. Until I made my own luck finding you posed all nekkid, I didn't have no chance of studying you. I had big, scary plans for that body, but now I'll just make you mine. I'll prolly have to sell you on that deal, so that might get wet.

"I'm gonna send you on a great trip, and whisper in your little ear while you ride. You'll become Satan's Spawn's own bitch. You'll do anything I order you, and smile. With you beside me, we'll get jealousy from all boys and men, and the lumpy horny girls, with wanting to be you and to be taken by Satan's Spawn in any way he thinks of it."

Geasley had it that bad for Mary Bliss, and he didn't even know her name. He'd never had any opportunity with a woman as beautiful in face and body as she – or any woman, for that matter – and despite his physical yearning and evil intent and encompassing need for power, had never turned to rape, although his momentary coupling with his son's mother was just on the legal side of statutory. He did not believe he was a fag because his dalliances with Tito Flick were just to get off. He never allowed Flick to take him in the way he had been in prison, and his new obsession with Mary Bliss was proof in his own mind.

He was sure she wouldn't like him at first, but trusted his

plans for persuading her to become his own once she saw his dark majesty. It might take some time in this special room, but he would come around under his attentions.

He was Satan's Spawn, and she would become his piece, his bitch, his Lilith.

CHAPTER 15

After two days at home on her laptop, Mary Bliss ran out of ideas for finding Haynus Geasley.

The last address that he'd used for a lengthy period belonged to his parents, before he went to prison. When he was released, he might as well have vanished from the face of the earth. Mary Bliss was chagrined and disappointed that, after claiming a special skill at finding people, she came up nearly empty. The only thing she found was a mug shot of Geasley on the Michigan Department of Corrections roll of prisoners and their status, which confirmed that he was no longer a guest of the penitentiary where he served his full sentence and was released under parole the year before. At least now she knew what the horrid man looked like, that his full name was Haynus Bedford Geasley, he was 5-feet-10, 148 pounds, had brown eyes, and myriad scars on his back.

When she finished, she phoned Noze, gave him her address, and told him it was her house.

"I am so sorry, Mr. Noze, that I have been unable to locate our target. Please forgive me."

"No need, Miss Mary. I know you gave it everything. What I'd like to know now is why you pretended to live at the hotel when you have a home."

"I was tardy about letting you in on my ruse. I trust you implicitly, but I have never trusted those gentlemen who would woo me. So many of them go away disappointed or even angry with me for not giving them everything they want. It is simply a matter of personal security." She paused. "Are you upset with me?"

"Of course not. I get security. But you talk about those guys in the present tense. Do you still entertain them?"

"I have not since I began spending time with you. Will I ever find a need that can be filled by the right gentleman and give him a reason to help me? I hesitate to make a vow that I may be unable to keep."

Disappointment, jealousy, dread, and a touch of anger hit Noze with an unexpected lurch of the stomach. Without discussing it, he had assumed that he and Mary Bliss were more than partners.

"I thought that was all over," he said. "I just assumed that because of all the time we've spent together and the affection you've given me that you might have feelings for me. The idea of you seducing these so-called gentlemen with the sight of your body is so hard to take. I might sound like a sap, but I thought you were my girl."

"Oh. Dear Mr. Noze, I feel that too. Any rendezvous I might have with another man would simply be a business transaction, nothing more. I believe that these wealthy and powerful men can help me provide for myself, as Miss Ruby taught. Please don't be offended, but are you able to do the same?"

Noze reddened, already feeling low because his finances were limited and he now feared that in time it might lead Mary Bliss to abandon him because of it. He must work harder to take care of her.

"Well, I can't compete with rich slobs like the Viking or any others who have the money to do pretty much whatever they want, including giving you what you want. Giving yourself to them is just too..."

"Giving myself? I never do any such thing. That thought repels me. I have never spent a night with any of those who woo me, nor have I ever even kissed them. Kissing is very intimate and I kiss only you. I do not let them touch me in a familiar way, or pretty much any way. All I am doing is satisfying their innate voyeur, the male need to look at beautiful women and fantasize about them. It is as innocent as being an artist's model, just as my posing for you was. Did that make you happy? Do you fantasize about me?"

"Of course it did. And I do."

"What is your favorite fantasy, Mr. Noze?"

"I'll ignore for a second that you're trying to divert me from the issue."

"Will you please tell me your favorite fantasy?"

"I'm talking to her."

"I am not letting you off so easy. Tell me."

"I've read about a place way down in Mexico called Zihuatanejo. It's a little fishing village on the Pacific coast where tradition still lives and you can get the freshest possible seafood almost directly from the boats. One tradition is walking on the beach at dusk with your *novia*, who has adorned her hair with live fireflies. It is said to be beauty without comparison. When the fireflies glow, they're making love talk to each other. I fantasize about you with fireflies blinking neon green in your fiery hair, walking beside me on white sands as it gets dark."

"*Novia*," she said. "So in this fantasy, too, I am your girl. You thrill me. I had no idea a fantasy could be so luscious, and so chaste. When other men told me their fantasies, it always involved my body and what they wanted to do to it."

"What gets to me," he went on, "is not only your physical beauty and allure. It's your grace and even your way of speaking. It's formal but sounds natural coming from you. Your persistence in educating yourself. Your self-taught skills, which I think I've only started to discover. You delight even in small things, like a cup of coffee. You're very sophisticated and, I'm thinking, much smarter than most people you meet, including me. Maybe especially me. I don't mean to discount your beauty. You are without a doubt the most gorgeous, sensual woman I've ever seen. There's just so much more to you."

"That honors me, partner. Here is how I see you. When I am awake, I know you as a very capable man who has been made deeply sad by experience. I know you as tough and gentle, especially handsome and strong, a force, and someone who needs to be cared for. I will admit that I dream of you quite often, when I fantasize about what I won't allow for myself – you, the skilled and gentle lover who is quite smitten with me. I do not think I have ever dreamed of or felt that way about anyone else. I am your girl, as you so quaintly and adorably put it."

"So how do you suggest I get over you showing yourself to other men, tempting them with whatever they imagine, pretending that you're up for grabs?"

"Do the same as I do. Treat these encounters as bloodless necessities that mean nothing to me but what they can do for me. You really must believe that my heart has nothing to do with it, nor does desire, except on their part. If this helps, think of it as acting a role for the entertainment of an audience of one. It is all they ever get. And if they wish the play had another ending, well, if wishes were horses, beggars would ride. Miss Ruby loved that old saying."

"I don't know if I can do that."

"Try."

Noze's chest hurt and the brown beast was oozing out of its lair in the back of his skull. He took a moment to steady his breathing, saying nothing.

"Mr. Noze?"

"I'm still here. Just thinking about our next step."

"What does that mean?"

"How we're going to continue our hunt for the little prick."

"Language, please."

"Time to hit the streets and try out this new partnership. How much time do you need before I pick you up?"

"I know early afternoon might seem late for me to still be in my nightwear, but so I am. I need to tidy myself up and look pretty for you. I have not even had coffee yet; I've been so busy at the computer. Can you give me an hour?"

"That, I can give you," Noze said sourly. "I'll bring the coffee."

"I am anxious to see you again. As I said, I am your girl, Mr. Noze."

"See you in an hour," he said, and hung up the phone.

CHAPTER 16

When Mary Bliss heard the knock at her door, she thought it was too soon for Jimmy Noze to arrive. She opened it to find Sloane standing there. He shoved her back into the house, slamming the door behind him.

"If you scream or fight me, I'll wring your lovely little neck right here."

She was wrapped in a short robe and wearing her cosmesis.

"I told you I do not want to see you again. You are mean. You do not know anything about how to treat a woman. You repulse me, you awful, awful person."

"It doesn't matter anymore what you want. You'll do as you're told and do it with a smile. You're much prettier when you smile."

"That is not very original. Now get out of my ..."

"Drop the robe," Sloane commanded, angry and flexing his big hands.

Mary Bliss was calculating her next move, running various past scenarios through her head looking for a way to stop this. She would not give in to the fear that was settling in her stomach.

"Goddamn it, I said drop it. Now!" He raised one meaty hand as if to hit her. She did as she was told. A lupine grin split his face as she exposed herself. "Ah, hah. Turn in a circle now. That's a good little slut. This is the first time I've seen all of you. You're flawless. My God, don't you see it? We're a perfect couple."

Mary Bliss gagged and the fear overcame her. "Please, sir," she said, barely above a whisper. "Do not hurt me. I will obey."

"Obedience is just the start. When we get to where we're going, you'll find out more. My car is at the side door. You won't need clothes. Put the robe back on and we'll leave that way." She did, and he gripped her left arm until it hurt. "Lead the way."

Dick Sloane had backed his Mercedes up the drive and left just enough room by the side entrance to allow her to get into the passenger seat. Mary Bliss tried to hold her robe in place as she bent to get in. Sloane shoved his hand under the hem of the robe and squeezed. She instinctively lurched forward and fell into the seat, the robe again askew. She arranged herself and clutched it closed.

"Man," the Viking said. "I'll never say 'smooth as a baby's ass' again. From now on it will be 'smooth as Mary's ass.'" He thought that hysterical, laughing as he slammed her door closed, got in the driver's side, started the car, and drove out.

Less than a block away, Haynus Geasley watched from his car, where he had been surveilling his Lilith's house for several hours. It looked like a hulking man shook her like a rag doll and roughly shoved her into the Mercedes. When it pulled out, he saw the red-haired quim inside, and held back for several car lengths before tailing it.

He didn't recognize the car and had caught only a glimpse of the driver. It was enough to know that whoever it was had the red-haired goddess, his Lilith, *his*! Tail them to their destination, and then do what has to be done to free her.

Sloane gave a running commentary to fill in Mary Bliss about what he had planned for her. "I have been shopping for you, dresses that even you wouldn't wear in public, and lingerie and more. In my house, you'll wear them comfortably." He told her he would swim with her in his rocky indoor grotto where they would frolic like innocents in paradise. He suggested that she'd enjoy it nude, as so many of his girls did, but added that he had a large showroom just off the grotto filled with lifelike mannequins displaying swimwear she could use. Sometimes he sat in that room and fantasized about each model. "Most of them are what Brazilian girls like to almost wear on the beach.

You can be the girl from Ipanema, you know, Ipanema Beach? They're all so brown and cute, but sometimes a bit much. Your body is more to my taste, and believe me, I will be tasting," he chuckled, "whatever I choose. The suits are tiny, but if you insist on wearing one, so be it. I'm already wearing my Speedos to join you in the pool. I really fill them. But after last time, you already know that, don't you?"

Mary Bliss listened in silence. He roughly grabbed her hair. "Don't you?" he snarled. She was now terrified, an emotion she had experienced only once, so many years ago, with those other students. "Yes," she managed.

"I don't know if you saw it during our first date, but there's a large canvas print in my bedroom. Somebody said it's an Orientalist picture. It shows some A-rab poobahs dickering over the price of some bare-ass slave girls. *Tres* sexy. You'll see. And there's a hidden switch to raise the painting and show what's behind it. It's a very colorful and specialized collection of love toys for my playthings. To be honest with you, Mary, sometimes I even surprise myself with the things they allow me to do to them."

His ugly laugh made Mary Bliss's stomach lurch. She tried to push back. "What makes you think I will go along with any of this?"

Sloane remembered the last time he had taken her to his mansion, and her threat to tell some cop friends what he had tried with her. In the time since, he decided it had been a bluff.

"Oh, you don't have to agree, *cunt*," he snarled. "One way or another, I'll see that you experience the entire pleasure palace I've built. I believe that even if you fight me, as I tend to you and play with you, it's likely you'll give in to that pleasure. There's so much of it; it's very hard to resist. As I'm sure you've guessed by now, I'm crazy good in the art of sex. And as you correctly guessed during your last visit, I have many cameras to record all of our lovemaking, although some of it will just be fucking, you know, without tenderness." He grinned a hideous grin. "I can be an animal and I bet you can too. We'll enjoy the videos later in my comfy movie theater, clothing optional." Again, the frightful grin.

Mary Bliss thought she might vomit. Her stomach somersaulted, her heart pounded, she trembled at the image of Sloane the animal and what that might mean. She imagined being split in two by that unholy log in his pants.

But she talked herself into getting calm and clearheaded. He was worse than she knew, a monster, and she'd need all her faculties to deal with him. She gulped, swallowing her fear, and tried a different tack.

"You keep referring to pleasure," she began. "I present myself as a pleasing sight, something to be enjoyed in the abstract. Of course many men such as you expect physical pleasure, and I have always dismissed that as something bestial of which I want no part. Perhaps I have not been open-minded enough to give it a fair chance. To be candid, the way you describe it all is beginning to stir something – dare I say – naughty in me. Fucking, as you say, does not appeal to me. But the gentler sound of 'lovemaking' is something other. If you are nice, we may both be in for a memorable encounter."

"Don't try to mess with my mind, bitch. I know what you're up to."

"No, no, you are wrong. I am starting to think that I was badly mistaken about you all along, though you have to admit you have been a little brutish to me. As you may guess, I have had much thrilling and varied sex," she lied. "I am almost a living, breathing Kama Sutra. But none of it compares to what you are describing. And yes, I did see your impressive member the last time I was in your pleasure palace. I reacted badly because I did not know enough about you. It seems you are a thoughtful and generous host. We will drink your Champagne and nibble snacks throughout our adventure, especially those that heighten desire. Do you have more oysters and caviar? Do you have chocolates? You know what they say about chocolate. Strawberries? Is it fig season? Have you ever used the tip of your tongue to lick out the warm, wet, red heart of a fresh fig?"

"No, but I plan to use the tip of my tongue for many things. I already have most of the stuff you mention. After we've been together for a while, I'll be sure to get the others. Believe me, over time I'll give you as much as you can handle, in ways you can't even imagine."

Mary Bliss was washed with fear again when she heard his talk of time.

"If I may ask, Mr. Sex Machine, what do you mean by being together for a while?"

"Just what it sounds like. You're going to be my pet, pampered and adored, there for me whenever I want."

"What if I choose not to be your pet?"

"Well, there's really no choice. I've set up a big room for you with every comfort you can dream of. I can lock the door from outside, but I know you won't mind once you settle in."

She didn't react, but felt her underarms drip. She didn't speak because she was sure her voice would give away her terror. She dared a glance at him, at the side of his head, and he looked ever more bestial. When seen straight on, he was the Adonis he thought himself to be. But from the side, his bottom lip protruded, as did his brow, giving him a primitive look, and exposing the beast inside. Lost in his thoughts, he unconsciously let one hand rest on his crotch, moving his hips to push against it. "Mmm, Mary."

They were silent for a few moments as he turned onto a street lined with mansions, and Mary Bliss recognized it. Remembering a mistake she'd made during the first visit to his house of horrors, she looked at the street sign and the address, repeating them to herself over and over until she was sure she'd remember, as he drove up the long driveway and stopped.

Sloane got out of the car, walked to Mary's door and waited for her to open it.

"Would you please help me get out?" she asked. "This automobile is so low."

He took her outstretched hand and when she started to rise, her robe again fell open and she intentionally gave him a good look to distract him. She was sure he'd detect her fear.

Looking toward the massive front door, she closed the robe and said, "Well, my Priapus, shall we begin?"

"What did you call me?"

"It was a compliment. Priapus is the ancient god of male genitals. He boasts an enormous, permanent erection."

"Almost," Sloane said. "Better believe it, lady."

As they entered the mansion, Geasley followed a service road until he was at the back of the estate. He parked and opened the trunk to retrieve a black ski mask and one of the tools in the collection he was assembling for his special lair at the old church. He also grabbed a pair of WWII German army sun goggles – he swiped them from a military surplus store to add to his collection of Nazi playthings – to cover his eyes. The lenses were metal-rimmed yellow glass mounted on a cracking black leather mask with a wraparound elastic band. They covered the entire eye opening in the ski mask. He was already dressed neck to toe in black, including gloves. He pulled on the ski mask and fixed the goggles in place, then climbed the wrought iron fence that enclosed the property and dropped down inside. Satan's Spawn squatted inside the fence and waited for a reasonable time until he was sure no alarm had been tripped.

Crouched over, he scuttled to the back of the house and looked for a way in. When he tested a service door, it was unlocked. "Stupid-ass servants. Gotta be nigras." He assumed that his beloved's captor had sent the help home until further notice. He didn't know this, but trusted his skills to elude if need be.

Geasley crept in and found himself in a hallway outside the kitchen. It was where mops and buckets and trashcans and cases of wine and canned goods were stored and kept handy. There also were cases of booze and he paused for a moment, considering what he might cop on his way out. He continued to low-walk his way toward the sound of voices, including musical tones that must be from Lilith. *My* Lilith! Moving through the kitchen to another hallway and following it right as the voices grew more distinct, he came to an open door and laid flat on the tiled floor to sneak a peek inside. It was a well-lighted room big enough to hold a single bowling lane, several full-size digital arcade games, a pool table and plenty of exercise equipment. Instead it held racks of garish dresses and at least 50 realistic mannequins, all displaying tiny bikinis in a full spectrum of colors. They were arranged around a low podium that commanded its own pair of spotlights. Sloane was in the showroom, sitting on a stool and leaning toward the podium, where Mary Bliss was trying on a blood red number. She took her time, stalling, and a pile of discarded swimsuits lay at her feet. Geasley maintained his prone position and watched her, enraptured.

"You are smiling," she said, winking at Sloane as she pulled the string bottom up her thighs, wiggling, and in place between them. "Do you like? I'm afraid it barely covers my lady parts." She turned her back toward Sloane. "And it does not cover my fanny even a bit. I must try on another suit for size.

"No, no, no, no!" Sloane cooed, sounding pained. "You've tried on enough. This looks like it was made just for you. And as I'm sure you're thinking, red is the color of passion."

Mary Bliss turned a clumsy pirouette, a last desperate move to delay whatever was next. She tried to stop shaking before the Viking noticed and was onto her charade. "Do you really like it?"

"I could eat you," the twisted ape-man said, "and I will." He stood, stripped off his clothes, and proudly stood facing her, hands on hips. "You like?"

She feigned awe. "You were right about filling your little swimming pants. Oh, my, is it my imagination, or is it growing? It is very intimidating to a smallish girl like me. This may be challenging."

"Don't worry, I'll make it fit, wherever." Sloane smirked and pointed to the other door in the room. "Out there," he said. "I want to see you wet." Mary Bliss walked past him and out of the strange room. Her host followed.

When they were gone, Geasley rushed through the back door to the showroom and through it, and again took a low posture to peek out the one they had just used. There was a swimming pool made to look like it was in an underground cave. His Lilith removed her left leg and slid into the water like an otter.

"Almost as I imagined," Sloane said. "I'll join you in a sec, but as good as your little red nothing looks, would you take it off? I've already seen you in the altogether, so why not?"

Mary Bliss cringed inside and turned away, pretending modesty. She began to slowly remove her top, teasing, and then flung it to one side of the pool where it landed with a wet fwap. "Halfway there," she said. "Now you will get what you want."

Geasley thought he'd wait until she slipped out of the bottoms and he could catch the view, but thought better of it and burst into the grotto. He jumped on Sloane's back, wrapping his legs around the giant and putting one arm around his neck in an attempted stranglehold.

"What the fuck?" the Viking shouted, and before he could break the annoying neck hold, Geasley raised his other hand and slammed a long awl into the top of Sloane's skull. It was harder than he expected. He used one palm to hammer it through.

Sloane shivered, grunted, and stiffened a little before Geasley started working the awl like a stick shift, back and forth and back and forth, then side to side and in circles, scrambling the big man's eggs until he dropped to the cold stone floor. Geasley withdrew the awl and drops of blood oozed slowly from the wound.

He saw Lilith standing still in the middle of the pool, mouth open. She didn't make a sound.

Disguising his voice, he rasped, "Your name?"

Petrified, she was barely able to get out, "What?"

"What's your name, cunt?"

"Mary Bliss."

"Get outta there and find somethin' to put on. Call the fuckin' cops if you want. Find this asshole's wallet. Take all his cash. Call a cab and go to your crib."

"There are hidden cameras everywhere," she fairly screamed. This demon terrified her, covered as he was in black with sinister-looking goggles. Not an inch of his skin or the color of his eyes showed. "Who are you?"

"Do what I said. Now git."

When she left the room, clutching a towel around her, Geasley returned to his work.

The blood still dribbled out of the small hole in Sloane's head. Geasley guessed that meant he was still alive. He pulled a folding knife out of his pocket and opened it. The blade was curved like a talon and had a serrated edge. He placed it on one side of Sloane's neck and pulled it back, pressing hard. Blood spurted from the severed carotid, as it did when he dug in deep and slashed the other side.

This was his Grand Guignol! Geasley remembered the days spent in a library carrel, poring over old books on the French theater of blood. The feigned torture and murder and sex shows titillated him. Now he was the director of his own play, and the star. Inspired, and feeling a thrill that seated in his crotch just as it had in the carrel, he watched the blood flow let up and decided to leave a clue that would throw off the dumb cops.

He rolled the big man onto his back and, using just the tip of his knife, began to carve letters into his chest. When finished, the ragged incisions spelled, "HE MAKE ME DO." Next, he cut the Speedos open, grabbed the guy's cock in one hand, pulled it taut and slashed. It came free. He stuffed it in his victim's mouth.

"That'll do 'er," he thought. "Cops'll figger it was a fag fight."

Geasley panted while he wiped the bloody blade on Sloane's little underpants, closed the knife and returned it to his pocket. He heard the big front door slam, and remembering Mary Bliss's warning about the cameras, ran through hallways and up and down stairs until he saw a room set up like a movie theater. This had to be it.

He hustled around the front of a projection booth at the

back, found the door open and went in. Shelves filled with hundreds of DVD cases covered one wall. A long table held a dozen DVRs, all of them humming away. Satan's Spawn ripped open each recorder in turn and removed the DVDs to take with him. For good measure, he yanked out every wire he could find. After one final scouring of the small room, he found no separate hard drives or servers.

With that, Geasley left the way he came in. His legs still wobbled from adrenaline withdrawal. It would pass. His first kill went good, real good. Satan's Spawn felt more powerful than ever. He could get used to it.

CHAPTER 17

Mary Bliss searched through a closetful of clothing in the room with the outside lock that Sloane had prepared as her posh prison cell. She couldn't stop her hands from violently trembling as she looked for the most modest of the dresses, which wasn't modest at all.

She dropped the towel and shimmied as quickly as she could into a turquoise Spandex mini dress that hugged her all over, cut nearly up to her bottom in back and scooped low and wide in front. Her cosmesis was fully displayed and her breasts nearly so. All the shoes in the closet had dangerously high stiletto heels, which she couldn't wear. Walking barefoot in this costume would likely draw attention in Sloane's obnoxiously affluent neighborhood. But because it was in the middle of the day and all the houses were set far enough back that they could hardly be seen from the street, she hoped she wouldn't be noticed anywhere near his mansion. If she was, she hoped the slutty dress to keep eyes on her torso instead of her identifying left leg and hair.

She thought for a moment of looking for Sloane's cell phone and using it to call Jimmy Noze. Then it occurred to her that his number would appear on Sloane's call history, and her fingerprints would be on the phone itself, making them both suspects. The landline was likewise useless.

She avoided the grotto to find her way out of the mansion, and slammed the heavy front door behind her. Moving as quickly as she could manage, Mary Bliss walked down the long sloped driveway and made her way several blocks to the main street. She didn't think she had been seen.

But once out on the busy main drag, her appearance drew attention from men who slowed their cars when they saw her.

"Where you off to, sweet meat?"

"Howzabout climbing in here and doing your thing?"

It went on and on. She ignored them all until an older man in a dinged Chevy pickup pulled over to the curb and stopped beside her. "Do you need help, miss?" He seemed sincere.

"Do you truly want to help, sir?" She could barely get the words out and tried to cover her chest with crossed arms.

"Yes, miss. I don't mean no harm. If you don't mind me sayin', looks like somebody done you wrong."

Mary Bliss concentrated hard to speak clearly. "Do you have a cell phone?"

He picked it up and handed it to her. Her hands and fingers shook so badly that she couldn't use it. She handed it back.

"Please call this number," and she slowly recited it as he punched it in. "Tell him his partner desperately needs him to pick her up. Oh, dear, I do not know where you can tell him to find me."

"How's this?" he said. "There's a filling station about two blocks ahead. I'll drive you there and tell him where it is. I'll stay there with you until he shows up. You can sit in my truck. It's pretty clean and I won't try anything."

"Promise? I do not think I can take any more. It has been a horrible day. I am not what I appear to be just now. I am a good person."

"I'm sure you are, miss. I'm very sorry if you been mistreated. And yes, I promise."

He got out of the truck, looking for traffic, hustled around to the passenger side and helped Mary Bliss inside. When he gently closed her door, she let out a fluttery sigh of relief. She felt as safe as she could hope to be.

"Here," he said, rummaging behind her seat. "Cover yourself with this blanket. It's clean."

"Thank you, sir."

As they rode to the gas station, she asked his name. "Early," he said. "Most ever'body calls me Earl."

"Oh, sir, thank you for everything you are doing for me, Mr. Earl."

He nodded while pulling into the station and parked to one side in the shade of an old maple. Turning on the radio, he found a classical music station, lowering the volume to a gentle level. The number he'd punched into his phone was still there and he hit dial. He tried to hand the phone to Mary Bliss, but she declined, thinking her voice might alarm Jimmy Noze. She listened as the old man calmly told Noze that he was with his partner, she was very shaky, but didn't seem physically injured, and that's all he knew. He said she desperately needed him to pick her up, gave him the address and a description of his pickup.

"Get here as fast as you can, but don't drive like a nut. She needs you bad, in one piece."

CHAPTER 18

"Sweet God, Mother! *They're hurting your boy!*"

It was so dark. To start, he was blinded with duct tape and silenced with a ball gag and God knew where it had been. He retched when it was stuck in his mouth, and he immediately tasted something salty, sweet, and thick. He forced himself to fight his nausea, fearing he'd vomit, suck it into his lungs, and drown like a drunken rock star. His arms were pulled painfully behind his back and bound with a heavy zip tie, and his ankles were crossed and secured with two others. Each end of some kind of spreader was heavily duct-taped to his knees, holding them far apart. Loathsome depravity joined his dread.

T. Prince LaPierre didn't know his tormenter, but the sadist knew him. Haynus Geasley despised the tubby, gentle man. More than once, Geasley saw him scoping Mary Bliss – *his Lilith!* – from the yews outside her house before following him to his own place. He'd had no reason to go there again until he murdered Sloane and mutilated his body. He knew it was genuine blood lust he felt when the deed was done, and not the theatrical blood lust and arousal he'd enjoyed in his studies of Grand Guignol. This needed to be slaked and fast. He could hardly stop himself from panting like a beast in at the kill.

In the middle of the black night after the day he'd taken the horrific step to becoming worthy of the name Satan's Spawn, Geasley drove to LaPierre's home and parked behind the chain link fence around the backyard. He opened the trunk and pulled out the black clothes, goggles, and ski mask he'd worn to Sloane's mansion, standing in the open and changing into them. There were patches of crusted blood on the shirt and pants, and he was sure he could smell them. He licked one patch, savoring the taste, and immediately had an erection.

Walking through the gate in the middle of the fence, he approached the back door and pounded it. When no lights came on in answer, he pounded again and LaPierre opened the door. "What's this?" he said, then seeing the figure in black, "Who? Who are you? What do you want?"

Geasley showed his talon-shaped knife and stepped toward his personal fatted calf. "Party time," he snarled. "Come with me, or I gashes your throat." He grabbed LaPierre by the collar of his wine-red robe and pulled him out the door. Stepping behind the trembling cow – he was more fatted cow than calf – Geasley shoved him through the gate and to the back of his car. He opened the trunk and ordered him to get in. When LaPierre hesitated, Geasley shoved him hard. Falling partly into the trunk – filthy with spilled motor oil and stage blood, mud and horseshit-encrusted muck boots, mold – LaPierre banged his head and passed out. So much the better. Geasley lifted the cow's legs inside and slammed the trunk closed.

When he awoke, LaPierre's robe was gone and some sort of ritual had commenced with his blinding, binding, and gagging. He wept behind his duct tape blindfold, where the tears had no place to go. He was left for what felt like a very long time to contemplate his victimhood and horror.

There was an overpowering stink he could not name, comprised as it was of black mold; fouled water; intense, almost tangible, body stink; his own urine; a revolting sexual funk; something cloying, like rot; stale food; and feces, not his own.

Not a word was spoken, so he didn't know how many tormentors there were or why, oh why, they were doing this to him.

There were long minutes of inactivity that heightened his terror with anticipation of what might be next. When it came, it was a pinprick on one fleshy breast that made him wince. Then another on an inner thigh. And another and another until he lost count as he suffered them over his entire body, including the soles of his feet. But this he could bear, if this is what was to be.

Then he smelled sweet and sour repulsive breath very close to his face, and heard a voice that sounded like that of a movie demon. "I got grudgements agin you. She's mine forever and ever." Then, "Time to get real. Let's start over. Take it from the top this time."

Who was he talking about?

Again, the voice.

"You know the Chink thousand-cuts thing, dontcha? Here's how she goes."

LaPierre felt a terrible sting on his forehead and recognized that he was cut. Then he felt another near the first, and others until his brow was covered with them. He panted behind his gag and squealed deep in his throat. He felt blood running into his eyebrows and down his face.

"Oh, those look fearsome," the voice said. "Can't let 'em get infected." LaPierre briefly smelled rubbing alcohol and nearly passed out when it hit the cuts, including those already on his body. Snot burst from his nose in a torrent.

"You is nasty, boy."

The slitting began again on his fleshy chest. "Don't know if we got time for the whole thousand. Let's just see how far we get."

LaPierre finally passed out from his pain and nausea. He returned to consciousness with a splash of stinking water on his head.

"I'm bored," his torturer said. "Let's try somethin' else."

He was roughly rolled onto his face, and in a moment LaPierre felt something new. With the sawing motion of some kind of blade, he shrieked inside his gag as a strip of flesh was sliced from a buttock.

"Mother! Dear God! *Mother, they're skinning your boy alive!*"

He couldn't scream, but an animal sound escaped from his nose.

"Big as you are, this might could take all night," the demonic voice said close to one ear. "So relax." An ugly chuckle.

“What else you gon’ do?”

CHAPTER 19

Noze felt like his heart was being crushed in a vise.

Since Mary Bliss had collapsed in his arms when he helped her out of the old man's pickup, she couldn't stop crying. He had never seen her cry for any reason, and he could hardly bear it. While she shuddered in his embrace, Noze asked the old man if there was anything he could do to thank him, and Mr. Earl said, "Just get her safe to home. I don't know what's got her worked up in such a fright, but I wish I could find whoever done it. Then we'd see about it." Noze reached out and shook his beefy hand. Mr. Earl gave him the blanket from his truck to wrap the girl.

When he tried to help her into his own car, she clutched him tighter, sobbing.

"Miss Mary, partner, you have to get in so we can go to your house. We need to get you cleaned up and fed and pour you a bracer or two to calm you down. You need to sleep in your own bed and I'll be right with you all the way. Don't try to talk now."

She held on while Noze backed her to the passenger seat and gently sat her down. She hugged herself as he lifted in her legs and faced her to the front, buckling her in. And still she wept.

"Please, Miss Mary. Take deep breaths. Try to clear your mind. We'll do whatever we have to once we get you home and rested."

"S-S-Sloane," she managed.

"What?"

"Viking," she spat.

"That son of a bitch?"

She sobbed, and stopped trying to talk.

Noze wanted to get at the Viking right now, take him apart and let somebody else clean up the mess. He felt he could kill the smug prick, and shoved that somewhere in the back of his mind.

When they arrived at the Bliss house late in the afternoon, he helped his partner inside through the unlocked side door, sat her in a chair and told her to wait while he trotted to every room, every potential hiding place inside. It was clear.

He returned to Mary Bliss, picked her up in his arms and took her to a plush davenport in the parlor. He loaded the fireplace with newspaper, kindling and split timber, lit it, and hoped the warmth would help stop her violent shivering. He took the blanket from her and replaced it with a thick comforter. There was a small bar at one side of the room holding crystal lowball glasses and several bottles, including Jack. He poured three fingers in a glass and carried it back to Mary Bliss, whose trembling prevented her from holding it. Jimmy Noze sat next to her and gave her small sips.

"I don't want you to even try to talk. There's time for that later. Once we get more of this sedative in you, I'll clean you up."

Twenty minutes later, he carried her into the bathroom, where he again sat her down and removed her cosmesis. He'd seen her do it enough that he knew how. Then he had her stand and steady herself on the back of her chair while he peeled off the hooker rig.

"B-b-burn ... it!" Mary Bliss spat when Noze dropped the garish dress on the floor.

"Are you OK to stand there for a minute?"

She nodded.

Noze went to the bathtub and shoved the stopper into the drain. He ran the taps until they poured tolerably hot water and let a few inches fill the tub before he again picked Mary Bliss up in his arms, kissed her on the forehead, and gently set her into the rising water. He scanned the bottles and jars on the shelf beside the tub and chose one labeled Voluptas in a hand-painted script with Bath Oil in smaller letters beneath. He uncorked the antique apothecary bottle, smelled a floral and citrus scent, and poured a little into the running water.

"Lay back, sweet girl," he said. "Close your eyes, empty your mind. If you can't think of nothing, think of something sweet. A field of, I don't know, let's say gardenias or any sweet flower you love. Maybe the plumeria you told me about. Or anything you love. Soak. I'll be right here." She did as she was told and Noze let the water run until she was covered to her neck. Her trembling disturbed the surface of the water for several minutes until, blessedly, it subsided.

Noze soaked her natural bath sponge in the water and slowly squeezed it over her head, once, twice, then carefully ran his fingers through her hair until it untangled and regained its fiery sheen. He tenderly massaged her scalp and neck and, to his surprise, she sighed a long, sweet-sounding sigh.

"Ahh, Mr. Noze, I ..."

"Don't talk now, beautiful. Please just go with the flow."

So Mary Bliss thought of something she loved, concentrating on Jimmy Noze's face when she first saw it. Again, she sighed.

When the water cooled a bit, Noze ran in more hot and helped her sit up. He used the sponge to carefully clean her face, neck, chest, and back, and then soaked it to squeeze warm water over all. She raised her face toward the ceiling, eyes still closed, and he continued for a time to squeeze more water over her hair and shoulders. It seemed to soothe her.

Her face was relaxed, and his crushed heart began to beat quietly again.

"Do you think you can stand for a bit, Miss Mary?"

She nodded, and he helped her up in the tub. Her shining eyes opened and she reached her left hand to grip the upright holding the shower curtain rod. With her right, she cupped the back of Jimmy Noze's head and pulled his face to hers, kissing him deeply. He returned it.

Then he soaked the sponge and gently ran it down the

contours of her back and backside, her chest, her tummy, between her thighs, and down her legs. Her skin glistened. Without question, she was the most transcendently lovesome sight he had ever seen or imagined. He pulled the stopper to let the water drain while he patted her dry with a thick white towel.

A plush robe hung on the back of the bathroom door. He took it, helped her into it and carried her in his arms to her bed in the next room. He left her there for a minute, then returned with another glass of Jack and handed it to her. She was able to hold it and sip on her own. When it was empty, she handed the glass to Noze.

"I have to tell you. Sloane. The Viking."

"Don't," he said, imagining her violent ravishment by the goon, though he hadn't seen a mark on her. "Whatever he did to you can wait."

"He is dead," she said. "I saw him murdered before my eyes."

CHAPTER 20

Haynus Geasley forgot to keep a souvenir from the Sloane killing. He made up for it with his selection from the nearly completed murder of the fat man.

He decided to keep the entire, gleefully mutilated body as a reminder of his unstoppability and dominion, of his Emerging.

Once he'd finished flaying the fat man, he stuffed a sticky piece of the guy's own flesh up each of his nostrils. While Geasley worked, LaPierre had managed to stay alive through every assault during his slow torture. His tormenter, or a team of them, had stripped the skin from his entire body.

LaPierre knew he was in shock, very cold, beyond pain, and felt his body floating in a sharp-edged white light. He'd lived through it all by concentrating on praying, pleading for Mother, trying to focus on the beautiful sights Mary Bliss showed him, thinking of Mary Bliss. Thinking of Mary Bliss. Thinking of Mary Bliss, his *idée fixe*, who he would never have anyway.

He was *so* weak, he assumed from blood loss. The tangy smell of it offended him. The ball gag was still in place, so he had no choice but to inhale and exhale through his nose. Then something sticky was crammed tightly into both nostrils. His chest lurched with the effort of his lungs howling for air. He tried to scream and could only hear it behind his eyes.

As his will faded and death loomed, he stopped struggling. His last thoughts were of "*Mother!*" And then, "Mary. Mary. Mary. Mary. *Bliss*."

Satan's Spawn regretted that he couldn't listen to what was going on inside the fat man's noggin. It would have been really something.

He wiped his gore-covered hands and wrists with a filthy rag. Despite all the wet work, nothing had spurted or splashed anywhere else. He gripped the hem of the plastic sheet he'd butchered the fat man on. He dragged the limp, heavy corpse out of his ghastly workshop, down a hall and to the side of the baptismal tub, now cleared of trash. He left the drain unstoppered, and pulled on the pair of disposable plastic gloves he'd found in a livestock supply store Downriver. They covered his arms up to the shoulders. Farmers used them to reach inside a mother cow having a difficult birth. Geasley thought he'd really like to see that.

He cut out pieces of a black trash bag to create a vest, and pulled it over his head to cover his torso. First, there was the skin. He scooped up pieces with both hands, over and over, and distributed them on the bottom of the tub. Then, pulling the corpse into a sitting position, he reached under the arms and around the chest, and with great effort hoisted it up and dropped it into the tub. He arranged the body face up. He had intended to use quicklime to preserve his kill, but found it cost too much, and the bags were too big to shoplift. So he bought four 50-pound bags of rock salt from the same livestock supply where he found the birthing gloves.

Lifting one to the edge of the tub, he sliced open the top and slowly poured it in a thin layer over the body from head to toes, and the skin tatters around it. He repeated with the second bag of salt. If it worked the way he thought, the body wouldn't stink and eventually might dry like a mummy.

It would be very satisfying to occasionally brush aside a small patch of salt to gaze at what had been the face, or anything else that he took a notion to see.

If this wasn't enough to finally transform him into the devil's own son, he'd find new ways to make another blood offering.

CHAPTER 21

Noze didn't question Mary Bliss about the killing she thought she saw. She may have been confused, too frightened to understand what was going on. Now, most of all, she needed rest.

It was night. He lay down next to her, pulling her body in close as she turned onto her right side, facing away. He shushed her when she tried to talk. "You have to rest for as long as you need. We'll have plenty of time to talk about what happened to you." When he was searching for Mary Bliss, he'd nearly lost it. Noze taught himself long ago never to panic, ever; it makes you useless. And he never did, despite all the hairy situations he'd been in. So he allowed fury to squeeze out the near panic, and it had not diminished.

As he gently shushed and stroked her brow and hair, Mary Bliss finally calmed enough to drop off into deep sleep, helped along by the sour mash. She even snored lightly and, as always, it charmed Noze, sounding like a kitten's purr. He lightly kissed the back of her head between strokes, lingering to sniff the flowers and lime that scented her from the bath.

He allowed himself to drift off, caressing the warm, porcelain skin of her left arm. He had always been a very light sleeper, and trusted that he would come to if she stirred. And he did, having no sense of how long they'd both been out. When he checked his watch, he was surprised to find that it was a little past four o'clock. Judging by the daylight behind the bedroom curtains, it was afternoon.

Mary Bliss turned toward him and kissed his cheeks, his nose, and his brow before finally reaching his lips, lingering there. "Mr. Noze," she whispered. "I am safe."

She sat up, turned to the edge of the bed and stood on one leg, steadying herself against the bed as she removed the robe. "I have to dress," she said, as he reached to stop her. "I must feel normal again, if I can."

"Wait a sec," Noze mumbled. He clambered off the bed to fetch her cosmesis. She sat then and watched him return with it from the bathroom. "Please, Mr. Noze. Clean it gently with a warm washcloth and a little soap, all over and inside the cuff. It was fouled by my travails, just like the rest of me."

He took it back into the bathroom and did as she asked, as meticulously as if it had been her natural leg, dried it, and took it to her, squatting to fit it in place. She stood, embraced him and kissed him again, then walked to a closet to choose something to wear. Noze, obsessed, allowed himself to watch. A description from one of Henry Miller's gaseous streams of consciousness flickered before him as he gazed at her. She was "pink as a fingernail." As Miss Mary had told him, she was art.

"I do not wish to go outside," she said softly. "We can lounge here and enjoy our own company while I rid myself of terrible, horrible things. Unfortunately, Mr. Noze, I will do this by telling them to you, already so tragically experienced in too many abominations."

As she spoke, Mary Bliss stepped into a black cashmere jumpsuit and slipped the top over her arms and shoulders, tying it closed. Noze had yet to see her wearing black, and he thought it made her hair even more brilliant. She caught his gaze and said, "Do you approve?"

"Of course." Noze believed she was either astonishingly adept at pretense, or was truly beginning to step away from whatever nightmare she'd experienced.

Barefoot, she walked to her dressing table and sat, picking up her brush to return the luster to her hair. As Noze watched, she brushed to a count of 100, set down the brush and stood, turning to face him. "Miss Ruby taught me always to put on an alluring face, but I am just too tired for makeup. Am I taking your approval for granted?"

"No way," he said. "You're perfect, just as you were made."

"Would you please fix us goodly portions of Mr. Daniels with ice? You will have to go to the kitchen to find the rocks in the freezer. Take the ice bucket with you. May as well fill it while you are there. When you return, you will find me on the davenport in the parlor. After a few minutes of our refreshments, I will be ready to talk."

When he returned with their drinks, he saw that she had arranged a large crystal ashtray, a silver lighter, a pair of granite coasters, and an erotic ivory netsuke holding a smoldering cone of gardenia incense, all on a squat side table of hand-carved African blackwood.

"The incense is lovely and calming to me, just as your cigarettes are to you," she said. "So please feel free to smoke them as you wish."

Craving one, Noze took a Kool from his shirt pocket and lit up.

"This is how it began," she said, her voice flat. She described her kidnapping and debasement, the manhandling, and Sloane squeezing her bare bottom. She hastened to add that it was the only physical sexual abuse she suffered during the ordeal.

"I want to kill that prick," Noze said, his suppressed rage making his hands tremble.

"Language, please. Mr. Noze, just let me tell it."

Jimmy Noze reddened, his brow furrowed.

She was sure that Sloane would have used her as a sexual plaything, "but he was interrupted."

Mary Bliss held her poise as she continued to speak in a low voice. She told him that Sloane intended to keep her in a room that locked from the outside. He forced her to put on a skimpy bathing suit and enter the pool in a manmade grotto. The Viking was staring at her as she stood in the water when a figure in black burst through a door behind him and leapt on his back like a simian demon. Her voice quavered for a few seconds as she described Sloane's murder, how he fell to the floor grunting, and then was silent.

And so was she. She scooted next to Noze and laid her head against his shoulder, reaching up once to stroke his face and run her fingers over his mouth. She rested like that, snuggling hard against him and lightly sighing a few times as he pulled her close to settle her.

Then she told him the rest, about the demon croaking terse orders at her to effect her escape, her choice not to use Sloane's phones or take his cash for a cab, wanting to leave no trace but the fingerprints she could say she left in her first visit to the mansion, if need be. She spoke briefly about the harassment she suffered as she walked the avenue in the awful stripper dress she took from Sloane's whorish collection. And she ended at her reunion with Noze, for which she would be forever grateful to the old man in the pickup.

"If you don't mind me asking, why didn't you call the cops?"

Mary Bliss tried to move even closer to Noze and said nothing.

"Miss Mary?"

"It doesn't matter. Something happened a long time ago that left me feeling like the police were useless, or worse."

"What was it?"

"I said it doesn't matter, Mr. Noze."

"I don't much care for secrets."

"That is odd," she said. "You seem to be full of them."

Noze dropped it. He didn't know what it would do to him if he spoke about the little boy and the wet day by the railroad tracks. He hadn't shared it with anyone, not even his counselor.

Neither spoke for several minutes. Then Mary Bliss asked, "Did you burn that horrible outfit?"

Noze stood immediately and went to retrieve the dress, then threw it in the parlor's fireplace to help feed a blaze he was anxious to light.

CHAPTER 22

They didn't leave the house for two full days and nights. Noze found enough ingredients and snacks in the kitchen to keep them well fed and satisfied. Mary Bliss had a new toothbrush and razor for him, as well as a hotel robe to wear while she laundered his clothes. He was a little surprised that she had domestic skills. Somehow, when he thought of it at all, he had assumed that Miss Ruby didn't cover such things in her training.

When she handed him the neatly folded, warm stack of clothes, Noze said, "I appreciate the laundry." She said, "It is simple enough. You have cared for me so well, it is nothing really."

On the second night she had him stand in the warm tub to bathe him after he had gently washed her. She lingered over his body with the sponge until it responded in what should have been a predictable way; she finished rinsing him quickly so as not to be unkind. They didn't speak.

They watched local TV news, in spite of Noze's marked distaste for such shows, and on the third day over coffee heard an almost breathless report that the body of a well-known businessman was discovered by a domestic worker in his Barton Hills mansion. Several dismayed neighbors were interviewed, all saying they didn't hear or see a thing out of the ordinary. Then a detective faced the mike and said Dick Sloane was murdered in a very unusual way, and that his body was extensively mutilated in a manner that suggested a lovers' quarrel. He left out that investigators suspected it was a gay beef, and that there was no evidence of the killer's identity.

"But we're pretty sure about this," the dick said. "This was personal, and the murderer enjoyed killing, no, *destroying* the victim. We believe he will strike again."

Mary Bliss was momentarily shaken. "I did not see any mutilation, only the attack with the heavy icepick thing. It alarms me even more that the man in black was capable of such savagery."

Noze was concerned that she might sink back into shock, but when he asked if she was OK, she replied, "Yes. Do not be concerned. I have regained myself."

"In that case, do you think you're ready to get back to work?"

"Oh, yes," she replied. "Are we still looking for that awful Geasley person?"

"Yeah," Noze said. "I was about ready to write him off. Figured he'd show up sooner or later. But after that stunt with the note and the head in the box, it's even more important to find that grub. He directly threatened you. Blowing up my truck was one thing, but the note – he has to be stopped before he makes a move on you. We have people to see who might shed some light on where he is. I know I said I'd never take you to Big Chigger's, but things have changed. If you're looking for a bottom feeder, you have to check the bottom. If we're partners, we're partners through whatever."

Noze was pleased and a little surprised to see Miss Mary, his partner, was eager to get to it.

"I must attend to my morning toilette," she said. "How can I dress properly for two such different places?"

"Go with your instincts, partner. You'll figure it out."

While Mary Bliss moved about between the master bath, the dressing table, and her closets, Noze went upstairs to use the guest bathroom, where he kept his own toiletries. Fortunately, his clothes were fresh, though they were his usual street threads – Hawaiian shirt and black jeans.

He went back downstairs to find Mary Bliss fastidiously applying makeup at her dressing table. She wore nothing. When she noticed his expression, she had an explanation.

"I just wanted to give you a little treat," she said. "I once saw a painting of a naked red-haired, pale-skinned woman at her own dressing table, leaning toward the mirror and highlighting her little bottom, and thought it beautiful. Am I equal to that?"

Noze simply nodded, and knew he wanted to make another painting once the first was finished.

"That is enough now," she said. "I think I have a proper outfit in mind, and want to surprise you with it. Will you excuse me while I finish?"

Noze nodded again and went to the kitchen to wash the dishes while he waited. He was drying the last one when he heard, "Please tell me the truth. Will this do?"

He turned to look at her. The gorgeous coppery hair fell around her neck, and she wore subtle makeup, with peach lipstick and matching eye shadow – the color supplied by LaPierre after she asked him to match that of her nipple. She had chosen a white business shirt that buttoned nearly to her throat, a coal black lace bolero jacket, a black pleated skirt cut to the knees, and a burgundy leather belt with a simple silver buckle. A burgundy choker fashioned like a shortened necktie was around her neck. On her feet were black-and-burgundy women's wingtips with two-inch block heels. And she carried a burgundy leather document bag for her laptop and a file on Geasley.

Noze thought that a toned-down Mary Bliss was as stunning as ever. "You are the very picture of propriety for today's work," he said. "As always, you're a wonder. With me in my usual rig, we'll present quite a couple. You still up for this?"

"Mr. Noze. Partner. I can scarcely wait to see what kind of team we make. You and me. Together."

"First, there's something I've been meaning to get done so you don't always have to rely on me for transportation."

"Oh, I have no problem hiring a taxi if I need to."

"You need your own ride," Noze said. "Let's go to the cops' impound lot and see if my friend can fix you up."

They went, and when Noze's friend saw Mary Bliss and was told she needed a reliable car, he walked down one of the rows of impounded vehicles, got in a Mazda Miata the color of a ripe tomato, and drove it to her. It was in almost pristine condition and Noze once again marveled, and felt a twinge of jealousy, at Miss Mary's power over her male observers.

"It's yours," the cop said to her. "Been waiting for the perfect person to give it to. You're perfect, Miss Bliss."

"You're giving it to her?" Noze said. "Why'd you charge me for the Taurus."

"Because you look as raggedy as that car does. It fits you, like the Miata fits this lady."

After arranging to leave the Taurus at the lot, Mary Bliss drove them off, fully set to take care of business.

CHAPTER 23

Big Chigger was behind the bar on his stool, all five-feet-four of him, legs dangling, a stinking black Parodi cigar clamped between his stained teeth. He had things arranged around him in a prescribed way that allowed filling most orders without climbing down from the stool. There wasn't much call for cocktails, so there weren't many fixings beyond the basic booze and beer, some ancient olives in oleaginous brine, and wizened lemon peels. A yellowed clear plastic jug of pickled pigs feet off to the side on the back bar looked dangerous enough that nobody had asked for one in years.

Chigger took pride in the fact that if you wanted to find out anything related to Detroit's underbelly, he was the guy to know. He had a small army of rumdums and winos who hung out beside the building, sitting against a fallen tree trunk, passing brown-bagged sneaky Petes and grenades of Mickey's malt liquor, always ready for an assignment from Big Chigger, who rewarded them with more of the same.

Once, at the request of a precinct dick, they were sent looking for the missing piece of a headless body found at the back of a vacant lot, rolled up in a filthy rug. It was winter, and the crew was reluctant to leave their comfy burn barrel. But they spread out, asked around, and in a couple of days found the noggin under the ice in the James Scott Memorial Fountain on Belle Isle, several miles away.

If he was in the mood, Big Chigger liked to explain how a guy his size got the street moniker. "See, a hunnert years ago I was called just Chigger on account of my size. One time, I was working in the back of a crummy diner washing dishes, and this

A-rab cook kept fuckin' with me. Comes the day I had enough, grabbed a pot full of bubbling oil, and threw it in his mug. Had to find work somewheres else, but every since then they call me Big Chigger."

He was drying glasses with a grimy rag when the door opened, and he smiled when he saw the new scar that cut through one of Jimmy Noze's eyebrows. Then he turned his eyes to Mary Bliss.

"So, Jimmy, all's forgiven?" he rumbled. "You had it comin', you know. All that booze makes your mouth stupid. Who's the broad?"

"Good to see you, too, Chigger," Noze said, without asking why he got clocked with the sap. "No hard feelings. And she's not a broad. She's my new partner."

"Partner? For what?"

"Investigations."

"When you get into that?"

"When I found my partner. Been doing a little research for lawyers and skip tracing for PIs who lay work off on me when they've got too much going on. Won't do the sleazy window-peeper stuff, though." Noze felt something lightly hit the back of his head. He ignored it. "Now we're going to handle our own cases. Meet Mary Bliss."

Chigger's eyes hadn't left her. He stuck out a leathery paw. "Pleased to meet ya, girl. How'd a loser like Noze land a fine piece ..." Noze cut him off as Miss Mary shook his hand.

"Mind your manners, Chig, if you can remember them. She's a gentlewoman."

That caused a stir behind him, where the regulars perched.

"What the fuck you think *we* is?" a flamboyant blonde tranny roared.

Big Chigger's Bar & Grill was on Third Street, the end-of-the-line hooker strip in Detroit's notorious Cass Corridor near downtown. Noze had covered the padlocking of two joints as public nuisances when the county prosecutor invited the press for a show of fighting crime there, saying, "We have now cut prostitution on Third to its irreducible minimum." Noze spoke up. "What does that mean, John?" The prosecutor testily said, "Hell, Jimmy, I don't know. Thanks a lot."

Chigger's had remained untouched by the camera-loving crimefighter for reasons that could only be guessed at. After the bulky barkeep appeared in court for the only time he was threatened with closure, and prevailed, Chigger told reporters, "I don't bar out them girls. How do I know what they do outside? None-a my beeswax." He grinned. "Their money spends just fine, like any of my customers."

If there was an average example of how "them girls" presented themselves, it was overtaxed Spandex and torn fishnets and crop tops that barely contained their dugs, and as often as not they had open sores on the insides of livid forearms. The air around them was cloying with the smell of mouthwash, which they gargled after spending as few moments as possible taking care of business in the alley out back.

Then they returned to their mocktails and primping for men who came to drink and deal. Many of them were tourists who asked their cabbie to find some action. All the hacks at Metro Airport and throughout the Detroit area knew about Chigger's. One liked to say, "You can get a decent *beef* burger there too," and laughed until he coughed every time.

Chigger's "regulars" had long since given up trying to bum drinks from Jimmy Noze or hit him up for a few bucks. But out of camaraderie they sometimes threw balled-up paper napkins at the back of his head and teased him obscenely. "Jimmy, gimme!" they screeched, or, "I gots somewhere you can bury that nose, Noze."

They eyeballed Mary Bliss like she was new competition.

She stood at the bar and locked eyes with Chigger. "We need your assistance locating a person," she said. "His name is Haynus Geasley. He destroyed Mr. Noze's truck with a pipe bomb. He sent a bloodied mannequin head to his home. It looked like me, and he put a threatening note in the box saying he was coming for me. He kidnapped his son from the baby's teenaged mother and went to prison for it. He wears long black hair and black clothing and fancies himself a star of rock-and-roll." She reached into her bag. "This is his mug shot from prison." She handed it over.

Chigger looked it over hard. "I'd remember a prick like that," he said, handing it back. "I don't."

"Please mind your language, Mr. Chigger. It offends me, and reflects badly on the person who uses such gutter talk." She took a paper napkin from the bar and wiped off a stool, scooted onto it, put both elbows on the bar, and rested her chin in her hands. "I had taken you for a gentleman, Mr. Chigger."

"Oh, Mary. You sure pegged me wrong. But I'll see what I can do." He grinned at the bit with the stool. Fancypants, he thought.

"If you do not mind, sir, I prefer Miss Bliss. We are doing serious business here. Maybe one day we will become friends. Perhaps then you can call me Mary." She sat straight. "Now, tell me about the men who come here. Be forthright. As yet, I have no reason to believe Mr. Geasley was ever here. However, I am told you have an encyclopedic knowledge of every miscreant who treads the streets outside and who comes in here, and an eerie skill at finding those who do not want to be found. How do you manage to be such a savant?"

"Well, Miss Bliss, it's this way." Chigger went into great detail about his bums-on-a-log secret weapon. And he told her about successes he'd had both with and without them, exaggerating some to pump up himself in her eyes.

As she continued to probe, Noze was approached by one of the girls.

"Come over here, Jimmy," she whispered in his ear. "I might got somethin' for you."

"I'm not playing, Beyoncé," he said to the mighty bleached blonde.

"I ain't neither, Noze," she replied, pulling him away from the bar to her table. "Looka here. Sounds like a guy used to come around. I dated him once, and he wasn't a power playuh, ya feel me? And he paid me with greazy singles and pocket change. You don't need no details, but he was a stone freak." She had Noze's attention.

"Called himself Satan somethin'-or-'nother. Punk ass. His breath stanked worsen mine's after I did him. Didn't want to see him again, but he shows up one mo' time jus' a little while back. Didn't know him at the git until he hit on me. Hair was cut down short and blonder than mine's. Tol' me something he wanted to do to me, somethin' real nasty, and I guess that mos' usually it would be OK. But I tol' him nah, nuh-uh, 'cause it was him, you know."

"Sure it was him?" Noze whispered.

"Hell to the yeah, Noze. Big Beyoncé don't forget no freaks. That mus' do some good for you and yo' tight-ass cunt. Now Beyoncé want a drink, a big fucker, triple whiskay."

Noze dug out some cash to cover a couple triples. "Thanks, sweetheart. Do me a favor. Tell Chigger about our guy going blond. His rummies will need to know if he sends them out looking."

"OK. And just so you knows, low hanger, I'd do you hard for free."

CHAPTER 24

"Well, now we know something we didn't before coming here," Noze said, pulling away from the curb to go to their next stop. "That crew-cut blond delivery boy who brought us the boxed head was Haynus Geasley. Big Beyoncé told me he cut his hair short and bleached it."

Mary Bliss looked at him quizzically. "How would she know?"

"She serviced him both before and after he made the change."

"Did she give you any description of his behavior or personality or anything else that might help us?"

"Let's put it this way," Noze said. "She won't entertain him again, and her usual standards are pretty low." He plucked a Kool from his shirt pocket and lit it.

"While I tolerate it, I do worry about your smoking," Mary Bliss said. "You know it is very bad for you."

"Don't start with me on that," Noze said. "I'm a man of habits, none of them good for me, but there you go."

"That seems a bit flip and uncaring. I just wanted you to know that I plan on being your partner, and your girl, for a very long time. I hate to think of you abridging that."

"Miss Mary, I get your point. But please put up with it, just like I'm asked to put up with your habits."

"For example?"

"Just the one, really. We never finished talking about your relationships with other men."

"Oh, as I have told you, they are not relationships. They involve no emotion, just playing a role. You should know that you are the only man I have ever felt close to. More than that. No one before you has ever had my heart. I know we have an unorthodox romance, but I do in fact feel there is passion between us."

Noze wanted to ask when that passion might be consummated, but didn't intend to pressure her in any way about it. There was a frailty in her that she had not yet explained, a secret she was keeping that involved a youthful encounter with police. He couldn't imagine what would be so terrible that she couldn't bring herself to describe it, given what she had recently endured. But he too had a memory he'd forced deep down in his consciousness, where that wet evening beside the railroad tracks was lodged in his depression and may even have been its foundation.

He took a deep drag of smoke and menthol then flicked the butt out the window as he luxuriously exhaled.

He glanced at her profile, the look of her as always filling him with wonder and gratitude. His relationships with women before her were vague and ephemeral. They usually had little or no substance. What he wanted from them was physical, atavistic, and when that was done, they were done. He figured that's all he deserved. He never thought about what they deserved.

Mary Bliss was a first, an entirely different story, and one Noze couldn't quite figure out. She says she is his girl, but still calls him Mr. Noze, for God's sake. She speaks of their shared passion, his claim on her heart, but refuses to quit, or even say she'll quit, her transactional enchantment of other men. Did he love her? Inescapably, though he hadn't said so. Nor had she said she loved him, which gave him some reticence in expressing himself on that matter. And he knew she had at least one terrible secret that might well affect their connection, and clearly didn't trust him enough to tell it. Even so, it took one to know one.

Mary Bliss turned toward him and caught the intensity of his gaze.

"A dollar for your thoughts," she said.

"Oh, just admiring the view and still wondering exactly who you are, in your entirety, big secret and all. I'm sure if it was something so horrific, it had to have a strong influence on Mary Bliss, the complete person. Then again, I guess you're not complete if you still rely on 'the kindness of strangers,' showing them your body to buy their support."

Mary Bliss's face registered hurt, then anger.

"You should know I had made a decision about my life that I think would please you. But why did you get mean? I thought I would never hear you like that, not toward me. You shock me. You hurt me. Why did you have to do that? I think I may have made a mistake about you, Mr. Noze."

That shocked and hurt Noze. He didn't know how to react to it.

"I'm confused, is all, Miss Mary. I didn't intend to hurt you. Not ever. It just came out that way. Still, I have the same questions."

She turned away from him and looked forward, silent for a time. Then, "And what am I to make of you? You have shown me nothing but what I thought was love. You have a core of kindness, and I do not think I am mistaken in that. You are rough around the edges, as they say, and that is one of the things about you that charms me. I thought you were incapable of cruelty. Now I wonder."

Noze couldn't back down from his objection to the Miss Ruby school of self-determination. It was wrong by his standards and no doubt those of most other people. Especially so because she presented herself as his girl.

"I will tell you something, Mr. Noze, whether I am right about you or not. I had decided to cease my pursuit of men who can do something for me materially. I was wrong to think that I could show other men my body or any part of it, even without emotion of any kind, and still expect you to regard it as something just for you, as your personal, intimate treasure, if you will. I had decided to give you that, something I have never even thought of offering to any other man. It is a step toward giving myself to you, giving my purity to you. Do you deserve such a gift?"

"Miss Mary, only you can decide that. Whatever I feel about my own worth or what I deserve or don't deserve is a constant struggle, asleep and awake. I'm not using my depression as an excuse. It's a fact."

He was sure he had lost her, and headed toward her house to see her home safely and say goodbye. Whatever needed to be done about Geasley he'd do alone, just as he always had.

When Mary Bliss turned to face him again, she was crying. "I just felt something cleave between us," she said. "I do not know why, but it is raw, a throbbing pain. What are you thinking?"

"I'm taking you home."

"But we have work to do."

"I can handle it."

"Are you saying we are no longer partners?"

"I think that's best."

"How could you? Am I no longer your girl?"

"I'll always think of you that way, Miss Mary. But as it is, we're asking for trouble and will stay that way unless we both share our deepest, most troubling thoughts. They'll always stand in the way of real trust."

Mary Bliss withdrew a tissue from her document bag and dabbed at her eyes and nose. She took a deep breath. "I also would not have thought you capable of emotional coercion. My heart, you are blackmailing me."

"This could have been a very happy day, with your decision about not seeing other men for whatever reason. But it still leaves our secrets."

"We could get to those in time," she replied, almost a whisper.

"I don't see any need for more delay," Noze said. "I'm ready. Why aren't you?"

CHAPTER 25

Haynus Geasley lived for the most part in the mephitic nest he'd created in the abandoned church. He felt comfortable there, breathing in the hellish air and regularly taking an exhilarating peek under the salt to see how LaPierre's mummification was coming along.

Satan's Spawn spent much less time with Tito Flick, showing up only when he wanted something, something like cash or drugs – he'd developed a fondness for cocaine but not crack, which he regarded as a *nigra* drug – or booze or whatever he fancied. In return, he allowed Tito to gaze at him while he stripped, and hungrily play Bury the Boa until both were satisfied. Tito thought the bleached blond buzz cut made him even more irresistible, and lived with fevered daydreams about what could be, if only, and so forth.

Tito's feelings were hurt often enough that he occasionally thought about giving up Geasley to the authorities, and was angered often enough that he even considered handing him over to Jimmy Noze, who might do God knows what to him. Tito had always known that Noze had violence in him.

Still, Tito gave Geasley whatever he asked for, sharing his own stash when necessary. Haynus never stayed with him anymore, and the thought that his wicked protégé might entirely stop coming for their playtime terrified him. Tito Flick had no sex life apart from Geasley except the boys he paid for their lies and ministrations. He prayed the free drugs would be enough to keep him as a special visitor.

So, when Geasley walked through his door this time, Tito promised himself to be happy with whatever he was granted.

"Dear boy, as always it is a delight and a salacious thrill to see you," Tito said. "Please allow me an embrace."

Geasley reluctantly complied, and heard Tito sniff next to his ear.

"Knock it off, Tito," he snarled.

"What?"

"Sniffing on me like I'm somethin' sour."

"Oh, that wasn't intended. But I have to say, darling, the most recent times you have been here, as now, there is about you a sort of woofy aroma – please, please forgive me – that is not pleasant. If I didn't know better, I'd think you work in a mortuary."

Geasley reared back and slapped Tito on one of his chubby cheeks, sending him reeling and almost falling. The little lawyer shrieked.

"Easy does it, you twat. I didn't hit you that hard."

Tito held one mitt to his wounded face and looked like he was about to cry.

"Get a grip, Tito. And make yourself useful. Lay out a couple lines for me and maybe I'll let you give me a bath."

Tito did as he was told, sniffling a little while he shook some coke out of a plastic film canister onto a small mirror. He took the one-sided razor blade also stored in the canister and meticulously chopped the high-grade snow into a fine powder, then scraped it into three even lines. "One is for me, dear boy," he said.

Geasley took a small plastic straw from his shirt pocket and bent to the task, snorting two lines in quick succession. He feigned leaning in to snort the third.

"Please, dear, I need a bump," Tito said.

"I'm just a-shittin' ya, little man," Geasley said, chuckling. "Dive in." When Tito snorked the third line, Geasley blotted up the residue with a fingertip and rubbed it on his mottled gums.

"Damn, Tito, you always manage to find boss shit. Now sit your ass down and I'll get ready for that bath."

As he had done so many times before, Geasley stood

and slowly stripped for his audience of one, dropping his dirty clothes on the floor. He stood naked, arms straight out to his sides, and let Tito enjoy the view, which he did with a squeal while starting to knead his crotch.

"Bath time!" Tito lilted.

"Fuck it," Geasley said. "I changed my mind." He bent to retrieve his clothes and dress.

"Please, Haynus. *Please* let me bathe you as we have always done."

"No, I said."

Tito looked ready to weep. "Would you consider, well, finishing me off here?"

"Fuck, no, ya perv."

Then he was surprised with an entirely new request from his – he didn't know what to call Geasley – protégé, boyfriend, master?

"Looka here, Tito," he said, pulling on his filthy jeans. "Get me some acid."

"Acid? What are you planning to burn with it?"

"LSD, ya pygmy dumbass. Get some windowpane, old-school stuff. Twenty hits should do for starters. I don't want none of that new science-class shit that gives you seizures and shit."

"Dear boy, why do you want to takes chances with that hard-working brain of yours?"

"It's for sorta a religious thing. Just do it, peckerhead. And pack up some of that blow and a ounce of weed and some papers to take with me. And cash. Maybe 500 bucks should do. Now. I'll be back tomorrow to get the acid. And I won't be comin' in so don't beg for your pitiful sex stuff."

"Haynus, I don't think I can get LSD that fast."

"Oh, you'll find a way, or that's it for us. No more fun times."

It didn't occur to Tito that Geasley had far more to lose if that were to happen.

CHAPTER 26

After absorbing the shock of hearing Noze talk of parting, Mary Bliss steeled herself and had something to say about it.

"You are not going to give up on me that easily, Mr. Noze, so get that nonsense out of your head. I have never thought of you as a quitter. Now, I believe we have some business to conduct."

Jimmy Noze had already he realized he couldn't let her go, today, tomorrow, or likely ever. He apologized for trying to force the issue of secrets by emotionally bullying her, and backed off his intimations of a breakup. He felt like a gutter dog, saying what he said, and pledged to himself never to hurt her again. What the fuck was wrong with him?

"I'm truly sorry, Miss Mary. As a reporter, I guess I developed a real aversion to secrets, and it stuck. I still believe we have to share ours. But bullying is wrong, and in my mind bullying you is something like a sacrilege. Please let me off that hook."

"Already done, darling. As I said, we have some business that requires our attention."

In her online research into Haynus Geasley's background, Mary Bliss had turned up the address of his parents' home. It was on Freud Street – the locals pronounced it "Frood" – just north of the quirky canal district abutting the river on Detroit's east side. Noze gave it a lower priority than other stops, reasoning that the turd they had conceived wouldn't be staying with them because of his clandestine activities and the fact that he was an adult. Still, they might know something about where to find him.

After changing course away from her house, Noze picked

up I-75 and took the expressway south toward the city and one of its lesser-known and entirely unique residential areas. After asking Miss Bliss if she had ever been to the canal district, she said she'd never even heard of it.

"That's how it is with a lot of people, even some who think they know their way around," he said. "It's been called 'Little Venice' because of these canals that run roughly north from the Detroit River. I think that name's a little grand, given the variety of homes along these canals. Some are empty wrecks; some have been pretty well maintained and show echoes of what once was. Way back, after a lot of marshlands were turned into buildable ground, the first canals were dredged by a developer who wanted to sell more waterfront housing. Apparently, building on a canal qualified, and the neighborhood grew."

Mary Bliss looked at him, rapt, while he talked, thinking it may have been the single longest speech she had heard from him since they met.

"I'm sure you know about Detroit's history during Prohibition," he continued.

"To be honest," she said, "no. I guess my education in the suburbs left that out. It seems there is a lot about Detroit that I do not know."

"Well, parts of it served bootleggers pretty well for a long time. It was Detroit's second biggest industry after making cars. They'd bring the booze in from Canada on small boats, sometimes on small planes, or even drive it across the river ice in winter. There are old rumors that at least one car loaded to the gills with bonded whiskey still sits in the muck on the river bottom where it settled after breaking through the ice. One version is that it was a hearse belonging to a high-end east side funeral home. Probably my favorite story is about people who completely wrapped themselves in white sheets and walked across the ice carrying hootch by the case while it was snowing.

"There were lots of cops-and-smugglers fights, and big violence from various crime syndicates including the Purple

Gang, an all-Jewish outfit, who had no problem killing competitors. Between them, the smuggling outfits racked up a high body count. Anyway, the neighborhood we're heading for was a real hot spot. I've always thought it's been one of the city's more interesting areas."

Mary Bliss wasn't sure why he was telling her all this, and asked.

"Oh, I don't know. Maybe it's my idea of filling time while we get where we're going."

"I love hearing what you know," she said. "But is it difficult for you to fill the time we have together?"

"That's not what I meant at all. It's just that I'm not one of the great conversationalists, so I go with what I know."

"Well then," she said, "I do not think you know any more than I do about what we may or may not find at the Geasley house. So tell me what you think."

"Hmmm." Noze had to consider that for a minute. "I hope we might find out something about their son we don't expect. I think that unless they're terrible, low-rent people who cared nothing for their spawn, they'll turn out to be meek, embarrassed, maybe even dim-witted 'billies who don't understand why he turned out to be such a freak. Nobody sets out to raise a Satan-worshipping narcissist. Maybe they're Bible-thumpers whose prayers let them down. Maybe Haynus was dropped on his head when it was still soft. Maybe he fried his little brain sniffing glue or huffing paint thinner. Maybe he was a difficult birth whose head was squeezed too hard with the forceps. Maybe they have no idea and he just turned out to be a bad seed. We might not find out anything useful. I hope we do, because our string is running out on him."

They rode for a little while in silence, Mary Bliss resting a hand on his thigh and looking around as they got closer to the city limits at Eight Mile Road, then into it. Noze had noticed before that when they were in territory unfamiliar to her, Miss Mary's eyes were always moving, just like a cop's. Or for that matter, a good reporter's.

She reached into her document bag and pulled out her cell.

"It has been quite a long time since I heard from my cosmetics maker and perfumer, and that is unusual. There is something I want to tell him about our business relationship. I am a little worried that I have not heard from him, so I am going to call his lovely shop."

She punched in the number and listened to the ring. She was about to hang up when a recorded female voice intoned, "The number you are trying to reach is no longer in service. If you have any information about the missing owner, please contact the Oakland County Sheriff's Department at" a phone number that Mary Bliss hurriedly wrote down before disconnecting.

Noze, seeing a look of alarm on her face, asked, "A problem?"

"A recording said dear Mr. LaPierre's number has been disconnected. He is missing. It said to call the authorities with any information. I fear something is terribly wrong. I am calling now."

She punched in the number provided, was silent for a moment, then said, "My name is Mary Bliss. I am a longtime client of Mr. T. Prince LaPierre. I understand he is missing. I have no information about that, but would like to talk to an investigator. I have questions."

She was silent while being connected, then repeated the information about herself.

"I am very concerned to learn that he is missing. How long has this been true?"

She wrote a note about the answer.

"How was this discovered?" Another note, longer that the first.

"Have you been to his home?"

"Is there any indication of foul play?"

"My hair color? It is red, quite bright. Why?"

"Why do you want me to come in?"

Mary Bliss listened in silence for several minutes. Noze saw the color drain from her face.

"Very well," she said. "I have business to attend to first, then I will come in. Is that agreeable? Good. I will be there as soon as I can. Thank you, Detective Gruley." She ended the call and stared out the windshield.

Noze waited several minutes for her to speak, and when she didn't asked, "What is it, Miss Mary? What did they say?"

She turned to face Noze, who saw her eyes brimming.

"Dear Mr. LaPierre has been missing for at least two weeks," she began. "And it seems they think I may have something to do with his disappearance."

"What? Why?"

"As usual, his business datebook was very full, and those who went to his shop and found it locked called and called the sheriff's department asking if it had any information about him. They said he had never, ever missed an appointment, and they missed him. Investigators went to the shop, and other than being closed, they found nothing amiss.

"But they took a missing persons report and followed up by going to his home. The back door was unlocked. They went in and looked around and found that wherever he went, he did not take his cell phone, wallet, or keys. His car was parked in the driveway. They did not find any sign of foul play."

She took a deep breath, and said, "They found printed photos in the desk drawer at his shop. They were all of a woman with bright red hair who was in various stages of undress. Most were taken through a second floor window in which she seemed to be posing for him, nude, from all possible angles."

Noze's stomach lurched.

"It was you?"

"I have to think so, yes. When I first started seeking his brilliant cosmetics and rare fragrances, I didn't know you and was doing as Miss Ruby taught. When I was in his shop, sitting opposite him and discussing my needs, before he could get to the cost, which I knew would be much more than I could pay, I showed him a breast and let him take photos with his Polaroid camera. It meant nothing."

"I guess that depends on your point of view," Noze said, his anger rising.

"Please, dear Mr. Noze, let me continue. He must have followed me home once, and after dark he began window peeping after I had stepped out of the shower and dried myself in front of the bathroom window, as I have always done. I thought no one could see me there, because the tall yews outside block views from anywhere but the thin strip of yard on that side. I never saw anyone in the yard, but did not take into account that the yews make a good hiding place.

"I have no way of knowing how often Mr. LaPierre peeped before I saw someone stir in the yews and was quite sure it was he that I saw there. It was harmless enough, and to keep our commerce on track, I often lingered there after bathing and posed as winningly as I could for him. Apparently he was taking photographs to slake his desire. I think that in his own way, he loved me. And the police told me he had an enlarged photo of me while standing in the window, framed and hanging in his bedroom.

"What I want you to know, darling, is that I was trying to contact Mr. LaPierre to tell him those days were over."

"Why didn't you ever tell me about this?"

"It did not really occur to me because it was so harmless. I am sorry. I should have known it would upset you."

"You told me what you did before we met, and Miss Ruby and all that," Noze said. "But pictures? How often did you allow that?"

"Only for Mr. LaPierre. And never again, but for you if you wish."

Noze swallowed his pique, and breathed quietly for a couple of moments, then said, "Miss Mary, do you have any other surprises for me?"

"No, darling."

"Well, you've said you are done with it. If I don't take you at your word, we shouldn't be together. I do."

As Noze talked, he watched the house numbers on Freud Street and stopped in front of the one they had for Ma and Pa Geasley.

"Let's get our minds in order. You ready?"

"Yes, partner. Should I talk to the man or the woman? I have thought over approaches for either."

"I guess that depends a lot on them. We might not even get in the house."

When the Geasleys answered the knock together and heard that Noze and Bliss were PIs there to talk about Haynus and his whereabouts, they opened the door wide and invited them in.

CHAPTER 27

When his head came off, the fat man, LaPierre, began to speak to Haynus Geasley.

"Well, well," it said, "if it's not Satan's Spawn in the flesh. I said that ironical."

"You're fuckin'-A right, tubby. I'd make you prostate yourself before me, but as we both know, you can't. So you can praise me just talkin'."

"Oh, very well," the head said. "Hail Sperm, Spam, Spawn, whatever."

Geasley had dropped a hit of Tito's windowpane acid before coming home to his nest, amusing himself as he thought, "Melts in your mouth, not in your hand." Soon, he was admiring the pulsing colors that covered everything he looked at on his way to the old church. Now and then an enormous eye stared back at him. "Damnation, that must be the ol' hairy eyeball," he said, laughing. He tried to spit in the eye, managing only to hit the inside of his windshield and watch, spellbound, as the gelatinous glob of phlegm burst into shades of neon purple and slowly slid down the dirty glass.

By the time he parked his beater inside the old church and went down to his lair, Geasley was sweating torrents and tasting metal that he couldn't drink away. When he thought it might be the metallic taste of blood, he wondered first if he wasn't able to remember a bloody good time, then stuck his tongue out as far as it would go and squeegeed it with a grimy finger, studying it closely to see if that's what it was. He squeegeed furiously and inspected minutely until his finger was clean and his tongue was raw and he stopped. At least he didn't have to figure out how blood got in his mouth if he had found some there.

He turned to scanning his habitat to see what kind of fun stuff was happening from the LSD. There were still pulsing colors and several whirlpools of light that wanted to suck him in. In one of them he saw the nude figure of Mary Bliss and squeaked with lust and delight. A pink aura encapsulated her; her hair was electric red and blew about her face as though caught in a cosmic wind. When he reached out a fouled hand to grab her, the face turned to that of his mother, grimacing with a mouth full of brown gums and broken teeth, and leaning toward him with her rheumy eyes closed and her withered lips in a pucker. Haynus reached out to shove away the hag, and she flew apart in rotting wet chunks that he dodged in a spastic dance.

Then his eyes landed on the mummifying body of the fat man.

It appeared to be breathing.

He laid the flat of one hand on the salt-covered chest. Now his hand looked like it rose and fell with each "breath." But he didn't feel it at all. It's the acid, he thought. To be sure, he brushed the salt coating off the head, gripped it between his hands, and raised it slightly for a better look. When he did, it came off with a muted crunch.

The flesh on the face was taut and brown. The eyelids were shrunken, exposing sockets with lumps of dried gunk inside. The lips were drawn back, baring the teeth in what looked like a silent scream. Then it wasn't silent. After the brief exchange about praising Satan's Spawn, it yowled in the voice of a cat in heat and screamed, "Can't stand it! Can't stand the pain!"

The shriveled tongue stuck out and waggled at Geasley. "*Hah*, you little peckerwood! Made you jump!" That was followed with hideous, derisive laughter that sounded like a guitar player using a wah-wah pedal. "You, boy, ain't *nothin'* but a li'l twat!"

That one spooked Geasley. His old man used it a lot when he was just a kid. And then, there he stood, holding a length of coarse rope in one giant fist. "Drop them pants, Haynus. Bend over and grab ankles. I'm gonna whup your ass raw!"

Geasley opened his pants and started to obey, but stopped when LaPierre's head squealed with laughter.

"You're such a baby, even when he's not there!"

Just like that, Geasley saw his old man disappear with a poof, like a cartoon, in a dissolving cloud and the word "Poof" appearing in its place. The head roared with laughter.

"You didn't sound like such a smartass when I was carvin' on you," Geasley shouted at it. "I can still do anythin' I want to you, fatty." He reminded himself that this all had to be an acid dream.

Another hideous laugh. "Look here, nancy boy. I've got nothing left to feel with. All my nerves are dried up and black. You could use my noggin for a bowling ball, far as I care, oh, right after you go fuck yourself. You do all your tough guy stuff by sneaking up on people. Scaredy-cat! Punk! Pussy! Double pussy! You couldn't even go face to face with a dead mouse. If your baby-mama wasn't dumb as a box of Fruit Loops, she woulda laughed at that little thing you call a dick, kneed you in your teeny little nuts, and walked out on you before you could breed. *Ooh, Satan's Spawn*! You fucking joke. You couldn't even face me without getting the jump on me, asshole! That reminds me. I know the icky things you do with your clammy lawyer boyfriend. So, *gimme a kiss*!"

Its tongue was no longer withered, and stuck a full foot out of the mouth. It cracked like a whip. It waggled and flung thick, neon-blue spittle onto Geasley's face. "Glig, glig, gliggle-a lig! *Kiss me, baby*!"

Geasley jammed the head face down where it had come from.

"Now what you got to say?" he screamed.

The dank room filled with thunderclaps, then a voice at the same volume.

"Flip me over and give me some of that good loving you give Tito, needle dick!"

For a moment, with the acid still at work and his perversions in full gear, Geasley thought about it, then dismissed the idea as possibly uncomfortable.

He dragged a couple of bags of rock salt over to the tub, and in turn heaved them to the rim, slit them open, and poured a fresh layer over the head and chest. He didn't remember buying rainbow hued crystals.

"Colors," he said. "Pretty."

CHAPTER 28

"Name's Cable, and this here's my woman Coral." Cable Geasley stuck out a paw that engulfed Noze's when they shook hands. Coral was at least two heads shorter than her husband, and just nodded to their visitors when she was introduced. She kept her gaze on the floor.

Cable towered over Noze. He had the hardened physique of a man who spent his life doing brutal work. He was beetle-browed, his eyes almost touched over a nose that looked like it had been broken more than once, had blue-black stubble on his cheeks and chin and thick black hair on his arms and head, though the mop on his head was going white.

Coral wore a faded, shapeless cotton housedress that fell just below her knees. Her calves and ankles were nearly solid blue with varicose veins, phlebitic pellets scattered over all. Opaque pressure stockings were rolled down to her ankles atop furry pink house slippers. She wore her dull ashen hair pulled into a sloppy topknot. Her eyes were a startling emerald green. They were surrounded by lines and creases that spoke of constant worry, or unrelenting fear. She held an unfiltered cigarette in one hand, smoked down almost to her nicotine-stained fingers. She looked up from the floor when Mary Bliss spoke.

"Miss Coral, because of your husband's accent I think you must be from the South. My dear grandmother Miss Ruby was from the South, her beloved Tennessee. And you, dear?"

Before she could speak, Cable said, "Kentucky. We's from bluegrass. Bell County. I worked the mines over to Harlan, but the boss didn't like me much so I switched closer to home at a surface mine. The money was bad, and Coral was takin' in warsh daytimes. We met when I saw her dancin' in a county-line titty bar. 'Scuse me, Miss Mary, but it's the truth." Coral flushed deep red. "If she wasn't the purtiest thing I ever did see. You wouldn't know to look at her now. Sorry, swee' pea, but you let yourself go, didn't ya? Anyways, other ol' boys kept throwing cash money at her, sometimes jus' change. I busted one up purty good for somethin' he yelled at her. I grabbed her and pulled her right offa the stage. That's how we met up, and she made me marry her." He threw a side eye to his wife and grinned. She returned a tight, thin-lipped almost-smile.

"'ventually we hauled up here for me to work in the car plants. Told 'em I could lift a engine block if I needed, and proved it to 'em. Case you don't know, I'm a strong fucker."

"Language, please, Mr. Geasley," Mary Bliss said. "May I call you Cable?"

"Cable's good," he said. "Sorry, miss. Shoulda knowed you was delicate, way you look." He winked at her, and her stomach flipped. "Say," he added, "what happened to your leg?"

Noze almost spoke up, but Mary Bliss replied, "I was born without it. The replacement I am wearing serves almost as well. Let us stay on track, Cable."

"OK, miss. Hey, Coral, go mix 'em up one of your specials. You know the one."

Coral shuffled off into the kitchen. "Set down," he told his guests. "Spose it's time to talk about that kid, our devil-worshippin' rock 'n' roll dumbass." Noze took a seat on the stained threadbare davenport. Mary Bliss stayed on her feet and looked around the living room while waiting for Coral to return. The couch and a wicker rocker. Old TV with a coat hanger and foil antenna. Cardboard fireplace, fake logs. Jesus on the wall. No books. No magazines. Nicotine streaks on the walls.

She heard clinking and saw Coral slowly shuffle into the room carrying a metal tray with four water glasses holding cloudy ice cubes and brown liquid. Her hands were trembling. She approached her husband first, and he took a glass, then served Noze, then Mary, and picked up the final glass herself, setting the empty tray on the floor.

"Up yours," Cable said with a grin, raising his glass in a toast. He took a big slug from his drink as his guests took tentative sips.

"Never tasted anything like this before," Noze said. Mary mumbled, "Nor I."

"I like drinking good, clear corn whiskey when I can get me some," Cable said. "But the little woman is some kinda wizard with cocktails. She thought it up herself. Tell 'em what's in it, darlin'."

Coral was startled by the request to speak. In a voice almost too low to hear, she said, "Dr. Pepper's and gin. People seems to like it."

"Yum," Noze said. "Inventive." Then, "So have a seat, Cable. Let's talk."

Mary Bliss caught Coral's eye. "Miss Coral," she said sweetly. "I'd love to see your kitchen. Will you show me? Maybe you and I could sit at your table and chat." She looked at Noze and he nodded very slightly.

"All right, then," Coral said, and walked into the kitchen, Mary following.

Cable settled his bulk onto the sofa, leaned to one side, and farted – "Had to hold that'n while the women were here" – and said, "So what's this all about, then?"

Noze sat as far from Cable as he could, and set his drink on the worn wood floor. "Don't tump that glass over, you," Cable said. "Ol' Coral'd have a conniption."

"I'll be extra careful," Noze said. "So, we've had a couple of run-ins with your boy, threatening ones, and want to talk to him about it. He's slippery. Seems he doesn't want to be found."

"Well, that one never likes to stick around to take his medicine. No matter how often I whupped his ass or striped his back with my rope when he was comin' up, he stayed a coward. Whu'd he do?"

"It started when he called me after getting out of prison

and blamed me for all his troubles, including losing his son. Said I owed him a debt. Said he'd find something I cared about and threatened harm. My truck was pipe-bombed not long after and I know he did it. Maybe worst, he sent me a box with a fake woman's head that had bright red hair and was splashed with stage blood. Along with it, he included a handwritten note that said he was coming for Miss Bliss, my partner. The delivery boy had a bleached blond crew cut. We later found out that your son has cut his long black hair and bleached what was left. Sure wish I'd known that when he delivered the package."

Cable drank the rest of his cocktail and sighed. "Well, butter my butt and call me a biscuit," he said, his face serious. "We ain't seen that little shit in a month-a Sundays. His mama's birthday is comin' up and he ain't even sent a card nor nothin'."

"Oh?" Noze said. "When's her birthday?"

"Eighth day of September. Why?"

"No reason. I'm just a curious guy. We want to talk to your son, see if we can straighten out some things. Any idea where he hangs out or lives or what he does for a living?"

"That lazy little twat ain't never had a job. Maybe he does stuff on the street to make money. Prolly steals. Cops brought him home one day when he was a whelp and tol' us they caught him stealing lady underpants at a Kmart. Tol' me he was fixin' to give them to his mama for her birthday, like that was a good reason. Bullshit. I gave him a pile of licks with my rope and left some fresh marks on his back for that. 'Nother time I caught him gulpin' from my whiskey jar, and he got another taste of the rope. It's rougher than a cob and I don't know why he never learnt his lesson from it. Say," he added, "what kind a name is Noze anyways?"

"My dad told me it was Belgian or French, but he didn't know for sure. Had a lot of fights about it with other kids, called me 'Noze-hair' and 'Noze job' other things."

"Did ya whup 'em?"

"Usually."

"They learn their lessons?"

"Mostly not."

"That's the way it is with some," Cable said.

"Tell me something then, Cable. Was Haynus one of those? Did you have to beat him often?"

"I reckon. But no more than he had comin', and he had it comin' a lot. Sometimes I roped the skin right off his back, and it still didn't change the little twat."

"I guess that's the way it is with some," Noze said.

Mary Bliss took another sip of weak coffee from Coral Geasley's beat-up aluminum percolator. "Mmm," she said. "You have a way with coffee."

"Well, Cable likes it anyways," Coral said, looking down at her own cup. "He gets mad if I don't have it waitin' for him when he gets up mornings. When I make it for him, it has to have some corn, some corn whiskey in it."

"Excuse me if I am prying, but does he ever hit you?"

Coral's face reddened and her eyes grew wide. "I shouldn't say. He's my husband and my provider, just like he says."

"Please tell me," Mary Bliss said. "He will never hear anything about it from me. I am just doing my job and trying to understand the person I am talking to."

"You sure talk proper," Coral said.

"Please tell me, Coral."

"Oh, only when I got it comin'. Sometimes I can't stop from giving him sass, and he slaps it out of my mouth. Sometimes, no, I can't say. Oh, well, sometimes I'm too tuckered to give him what he wants in our bedroom. He's so big, ever' way, and he acts like a animal when he wants it. Always leaves me bruised and, 'scuse me, burnin'. God blesses me, though. He only needs it four or three times a week. When I was younger and prettier, he wanted it ever' day, sometime more than oncet."

Mary Bliss let her hand rest on one of Coral's tiny, work-weathered hands. "No man should ever do that to a woman, any woman, Coral."

"Maybe it's different for you," she replied. "You're so young and fetchin' and all, Miss Mary. But I married him, and when we did our weddin', I promised to honor. I pledged my troth and I keep it." She paused, then said in a nearly inaudible voice, "Even if he doesn't."

"Why does he treat you so badly?"

"To be whole honest, Miss Mary, I don't believe he ever forgive me for not bein' a vestal, like in the Bible. Cable's big on the Good Book. Sometimes he calls me a Jezebel, like in the Bible. I know what he means. I know the Bible too."

Mary Bliss thought it best to quit pressing Coral on her private life before she shut down.

"As Mr. Noze said, we came here hoping to learn about your son. He has done some bad things to us, threatening us, and last time he chose me for his threat and said he was coming for me. So we hope to find him before he carries through on that."

"I'm so sorry he done that," Coral said. "You're such a sweet lady and all, and it's just wrong to do that. But I don't think I have anything to help you with."

"Was he a troublesome child?"

"Well, yes, and him and Cable tangled a lot and a course Haynus always got the worse of it. Sometimes Cable left bloody marks all over his little back and later, when Cable had some corn and drifted off on the davenport, I cleaned his marks best I could and put a balm on 'em. He always tol' me he loved me after I done that. And he kissed me on my mouth. One time when he was a teenage boy he put his tongue inside a little bit. I tol' him don't never do that again, and I never let him kiss me on my mouth no more."

"We do not have to speak about that any more," Mary Bliss said. "Tell me this. Was he ever violent to people or animals."

"Maybe there's some I don't know about, but oncet he was at a boy friend's house and the boy let Haynus hold his little pet. It was a hamster, I think. Anyways, as soon as he got the hamster in his hands, he threw it hard down on the floor and clomped on it with his foot."

Mary Bliss kept her composure. "How did you learn about this?"

"Cable was tol' it by the boy's daddy. He come home with the devil's fire in his eyes and beat Haynus for a real long time. Most ever, I think. When I found him, my son's face was bloody, he was nekkid, and he had rope cuts all down his back, his little bottom, and his legs. I tried not, but I cried hard when I warshed him that time."

"I am so sorry. I will stop bothering you, but can you tell me anything about where he might be found?"

"I don't have no idea, miss. I wished I could help you."

"Do not worry. Just one more thing. Does your son have any health problems that might take him to a doctor regularly?"

"No, but there's one thing. One time he fell out with his conscious and the doctors who tested him said there was some kind of trouble with his heart. They said it was dead at the bottom. Maybe you unnerstand that. I don't."

CHAPTER 29

Jimmy Noze and Mary Bliss traded notes as they drove north, headed for the Oakland County Sheriff's Department in Pontiac. Cable's brutish treatment of his son may explain Haynus's obvious mental illness and hateful acts. But that didn't offer a way to find him. Coral's tenderness and her son's sexual response no doubt added their own kinks to his derangement. Still, it was more useless knowledge.

"I feel terrible about Coral's circumstances, about her life with Cable, her neglect and abuse by him, and her neglect of herself," Mary Bliss said. "The entire time we spent together was filled with sorrow, and I had very strong inclinations to help her, even if it was just making suggestions about hair and skin care, cosmetics, and other means of possibly cheering herself. I am aware that sounds silly and ineffectual, and it was not my place anyway. I was there to do our job, and it also occurred to me that Cable would punish her for it. That poor, piteous woman."

After describing their conversation as thoroughly as she could remember, she told Noze about Geasley's heart condition and wondered if staking out a hospital might be a way to find him.

"Miss Mary, I'm sure you know the answer to that."

"Yes, I do. We have no idea which hospital he might visit, or when he might need care. I am just struggling to find something in Coral's statements that could help us."

Noze said he too almost struck out with Cable. There was one thing though.

"He was sour about his son's disregard for his mother. Said her birthday is coming up and the scumbag hasn't bothered even to send her a card. He told me her birthday is September 8."

"Why is that significant?"

"It's only a couple of weeks away, so there's still time for Haynus to send birthday greetings to his mama."

"Or maybe, yes, I see, *maybe* he will decide to deliver them in person!"

"Exactly," Noze said. "It's not much, but it's the only thing we've got. I've thought a couple of times that staking out Tito Flick's place might be worth it because maybe he lied to me about his lack of contact with Geasley. No, not maybe. Most likely he did lie, but I can't think of a reason why Geasley would visit that slimy troll. Tito didn't keep him out of prison, and we know Geasley nurses grudges."

Noze explained to Mary Bliss who Flick was – a greasy bottom dweller and ambulance chaser who scoured the streets for clients – and his ties with Geasley.

Mary Bliss gasped, and her eyes went wide.

"What is it," Noze asked, alarmed.

"I cannot believe I have forgotten this until now," she said. "There was one time when I saw a heavyset man step out of the yews and trot off, and I am still quite sure it was Mr. LaPierre. But there was someone else in the trees that time. He was much thinner than Mr. LaPierre and had a distinguishing characteristic." She paused. "Mr. Noze, he had very short, very blond hair."

Noze gaped at her. "Geasley? I don't believe much in coincidences, and this is definitely not a coincidence." He paused for several minutes, staring at traffic. "Now, if Geasley was watching you in the window at the same time as LaPierre, maybe he felt a similar attachment to you." Paused again. "Maybe he had an overwhelming lust for you, like the Viking." He stopped.

"Mr. Noze? Darling. What is it?"

"I'm thinking. Hold on." He continued to drive without speaking for several more minutes, then, "Wait! Maybe he was jealous of LaPierre. We know he has a temper. And he has a lot of screws loose. Maybe he was *very* jealous of LaPierre and wanted to know who this was, this guy eyeballing you. Maybe he followed LaPierre to find out what he could. That's it. He followed him home. At some point, out of his own obsession with you, he went back to LaPierre's house and grabbed him and did God knows what with him."

"My God!" she said. "That makes perfect sense. Do you think that's it? Do you ... Oh, my God. What if he followed Dick Sloane when he kidnapped me? Do you think he is capable of such brutality?"

"We don't know what he's capable of. We know that when he was a kid, he stomped on his friend's hamster. That's a great leap to savage murder, but it's how a lot of serial killers got their start. And I'm sorry about your special friend, but something like the Viking's slaughter might have already happened to him too."

Mary Bliss's hands began to tremble and her eyes welled. *No*, she quietly said to herself. And she calmed.

"Do I tell the sheriff's detective?"

"No. Except for Ma and Pa Geasley, we haven't told anyone. Telling the cops now will get us tangled up in all kinds of ways. You were witness to a murder and could be charged with obstructing justice. We both could be suspects in the Viking's death. They might blow off Geasley as a suspect. As far as we know, the only thing on his sheet is what sent him to the joint. If you looked at him now, would you think he was up to destroying Sloane the way he did?"

"Actually, no. But I am not a cop, so I probably do not have the same instincts."

"I think your instincts are very good after years of sizing up potential gentleman friends, if that's the term."

"Mr. Noze, do you still believe they were something more?"

"No, not really. I guess it will take me a while to get rid of the reflexive snark."

"Work on it," Mary Bliss said, and added, "Are we making a mistake not letting the cops take over?"

"Probably. But you don't trust them, and I still don't know

why. I trust or don't trust individual cops once I get to know them. If they don't know me, they tend to be suspicious. I want to play this out to the end, whatever that might be."

"Very well," she said. "I trust you implicitly. And I am with you to the end."

CHAPTER 30

"My name is Mary Bliss. I am here to speak with Detective Gruley. He is expecting me."

The deputy at the reception desk punched a few numbers into his phone and said a Mary Bliss was there with a man to see Gruley. There was a short pause, and he said, "Got it," and hung up the phone.

"Gruley said he'll see you now, but your companion will have to wait out here." He explained how to find Gruley's office. "Sir, have a seat over there."

Noze turned to Mary and said, "Are you going to be alright?"

"Of course I am, Mr. Noze. You know that."

He smiled weakly and gently squeezed her shoulder, then went to sit down as the deputy at the reception desk buzzed her into the building. She entered the hallway, and disappeared at the first right.

After several more turns, she found Gruley's door open and knocked on the wall to get his attention. He waved her in without looking up from the file on his desk. "Sit there," he said, pointing to a chair directly across from him. She complied, crossing her left leg over the right to see if Gruley would comment on her cosmesis.

The detective was old school. He wore a white shirt and a drab tie with the knot loosened. A crumpled navy blue sport jacket crookedly hung on a hat tree in one corner. His brown hair was cut in a flattop and part of his scalp showed pink where the hair was thinning in the center. Whitewalls were cut around his ears. A burn-scarred black Melamine ashtray sat on one side of his desk, overflowing with Marlboro butts. His wastebasket held wads of paper and maybe a dozen cardboard coffee containers.

When he finally looked up at his visitor, he said, "Well, Miss Mary Bliss herself. I've only seen you in pictures until now. It's special to meet you, Red." He grinned.

Mary Bliss straightened in her chair and replied, "Well, it is not good to meet you. Is that a proper way for a sheriff's detective to begin an interview?"

"Just trying to set a casual mood."

"First, my name is not Red; it is Miss Bliss to you. With a remark like that, detective, you show that you have no respect for me. I should tell you the feeling is mutual."

"Do you know me?"

"Only insofar as you are an officer. Long ago, I had a bad experience with cops."

"Don't you mean 'law enforcement officers?'"

"I mean cops. You are all cops."

"Rough you up a little when they arrested you?"

"I have never been arrested. I am a law-abiding citizen. Let us just say that when I needed them, they were not there for me. In fact, they blamed me for my plight at that time when I was clearly the victim."

"What was the problem?"

"That is none of your business."

"Want to try me on that?"

"Surely. I will leave and come back with an attorney and she will tell you the same."

"You're here because I have questions about your relationship with a missing person, Mr. Tug Prince LaPierre, nothing else."

"Tug?"

"That's his given name."

"He never shared that with me, if that tells you anything about our so-called relationship. Am I a suspect in whatever this is?"

"Let's see how it goes."

"I hoped to get more information from you about Mr. LaPierre's disappearance. He is important to me."

"Apparently so," Gruley said, reaching under the documents he was reading and withdrawing a stack of photos. "So tell me about your relationship." He looked for Mary Bliss to blush at the sight of the photos. She had no visible reaction.

"As I already said, I do not regard what we have as a relationship. That seems to imply, at least the way you say it, as something other than a platonic affinity. I like to think that we are friends. And our camaraderie was based on commerce."

"*Commerce*?" Gruley said. "Like the exchange of one thing of value for another thing of value? For example, like a prostitute and her john?" His revolting grin returned.

"You truly are a vile man, detective. Everything you say is with a leer. It is not easy for me to sit here and allow you to sneer at me and assault me with innuendo. Let me ask and answer the questions for you. Do I have anything to do with the disappearance of dear Mr. LaPierre? No. Did he pay me to let him take these photographs? No. Do we have a physical, sexual relationship? No. Did I know he was taking all of these photographs? No, not all. Not most of them. I suspected he might be peeping in the trees outside my bathroom window, but I did not know he was photographing me. I believe it was harmless. Mr. LaPierre is needy. For that, I feel pity. Did I ever pose specifically for him to take photos? Only once. I was in his shop and bared a breast to show him the color of my nipple. I said I wanted him to create cosmetics for the eyelids, lips, and nails of a color precisely matching that of the tip of my breast. I suggested he take a photo so he would have it for reference. That is the Polaroid you have there.

"Our commerce was in barter. He would create whatever cosmetics, lotions, emollients, bath oils, custom perfumes, hair-care items, and anything else I desired for prettification. As one of southeast Michigan's most sought-after creators of such things, his prices were far more than I could afford. So when I placed orders, I sent him photos that I took of myself in varying poses of undress. It was all he wanted. We agreed our arrangement was in service of the exquisite. It was no more licentious than a model requiring a fee from an artist. Now, have I answered all questions to your satisfaction?"

Gruley leaned back in his chair and locked eyes with Mary Bliss. He said nothing for several minutes as she glared at him.

"Tell me, Pussy Galore, do you ever turn tricks?"

Mary Bliss stood, her face flushed, her right hand in a fist. "If you were not a cop investigating the disappearance of my well-mannered friend, I would strike you! I should anyway. I came here willingly to help with your investigation in any way I could, and all I get from you are suggestive, lascivious imputations about my own character. My heart aches with the fear that my friend is in danger. You have abused me with your leers and implications. You might consider seeing a therapist to deal with your attitude about women."

"Oh, I'd say my attitude about certain women is right on the money."

"You are a filthy pig," she said. "Go do your job. Find Mr. LaPierre. I am done here."

"I'll decide when you're done here," Gruley said.

Mary Bliss turned and walked out of the office.

Gruley stared out the door long after she was gone, then shook his head and smiled.

"Lot of sass for a gimp," he said.

CHAPTER 31

Mary Bliss moved as close as she could to Noze on her plush davenport, rested her head on his shoulder, and stuck her hand inside his robe, combing his furred chest with her fingertips. She sighed as he reached inside her robe and caressed her thigh.

"Glad to wash this day from us," he mused, still damp from the luxurious hot shower they shared. After they patted one another dry, she had misted herself with the plumeria scent that always powerfully beguiled him, and he thought he could sit and enjoy just that for a very long time. "I'm satisfied that all the effort has shown us a few ways to find that scum bucket. It also seems pretty likely that we've been chasing a budding serial killer." He felt Mary Bliss shudder. "We'll get him, don't worry."

"I am not worried, darling. It turns out we make a good team. We will get him; I have no doubt. It is just the idea such people exist that shakes my body and soul. I hope dear Mr. LaPierre is missing for a simple, benign reason. I have to admit my worst fear, however, that Geasley has him and is doing unspeakable things to the gentle man, or he has already finished with that, and Mr. LaPierre is dead. If indeed Geasley was the goggled maniac who butchered Sloane, then it is rational to believe he did the same to my friend out of the same jealousy. It grieves me to think that I inspired such gruesome acts."

"Wait a minute," Noze said. "I hate to even think about it, but there's one way we didn't talk about that might be just the thing to allow us to nail him."

"What do you mean, my heart?"

"Think about it. We don't know all that much about Geasley, about his personal likes and dislikes, about his obsessions, other than seeing himself as some kind of dark lord of evil and blah, blah, blah. He has delusions of grandeur, it seems. Big, bad Haynus Geasley. Maybe that's an obsession. And we know of at least one other."

"Do we?"

"You inspire obsession, Miss Mary. I have felt it myself, after the first time I saw you. I simply had to see you again, to look at you. I'm sure it was obsession of one degree or another that kept you in goods and services from the men you attracted. Pretty clear that the Viking was so obsessed that he kidnapped you to have for his own."

"When you put it that way, I suppose you are right."

"Of course I'm right. And you have another obsessive that we know too well. Geasley has murdered for you. And you saw the blond version of him pop out of your trees."

"Yes, we already talked about that."

"But we didn't talk about setting him up, luring him back there, and nabbing him while he peeps your window. For all we know, he's already been back."

She took her hand out of his robe and shifted so she could look him in the eye. "Are you seriously talking about using me as bait for a murderer?"

"Think about it, Miss Mary. Of the few ways we have to possibly find him and put an end to this, using his obsession with you seems to be the best chance. I wouldn't even think about it if it wasn't true."

Mary Bliss looked into his eyes and saw nothing but sincerity and a touch of fear, for her, presumably.

"Yes, of course you are right. I hate the idea of displaying myself for his pleasure, but it does make sense. How do you propose that we manage this?"

Noze knew it was going to have to be foolproof, with no risk at all for Mary Bliss. Her house will be locked up tight before she ever appears at the bathroom window. The only question is where and how he could lay low while watching for Geasley and getting the jump on him. Once he sees Satan's Spawn take to the yews, with no way out but the way he went in, it should be a fairly straightforward matter of stepping out of his own hiding place and pointing his Glock at the prick's face. Then put him on the ground face down, lock his wrists up tight with a couple of heavy duty zip ties, and haul him inside the house to interrogate him and lay a little discomfort on his punk-ass.

While he thought, eyes closed, Mary Bliss leaned in and tenderly kissed each of his eyelids.

"Are you lost in there?" she asked. "Any light bulbs go off?"

"Yeah, a couple. The hook is that we don't know if or when he peeps you. Can't think of any way to deal with that than trying it out for a few nights to see if he shows." Noze went on to describe his plan to her, then, "So what do you think?"

"It sounds doable and as safe as we could hope to manage it. How soon do you want to try?"

"I don't see any reason to delay. As long as that loon is lurking somewhere, you aren't safe, I'm not safe, and who knows what other people might be in danger. Are you absolutely sure that you don't want to bring the law into this?"

"Yes. I do not know what your plans are for him after we capture him, and I do not care. I may have to leave those choices entirely to you. I have never meted out justice, or violence, and whatever you decide, I do not want to falter at any point. And especially after my experience with that gawping, foul detective today, I am even more set in my disdain for cops. They are just as liable to fail us as to help us. I hate them."

Noze silently looked at her face, shockingly beautiful even without her carefully applied makeup. Her silver-gray eyes glittered with their own light; her lips were the color of moist, ripe peaches; her cheeks roseate even without benefit of blush; her brow and chin both masterpieces.

"I have a question I have asked before, and think maybe a little cold Jack will calm you enough to give me an answer."

"Whatever can you mean?"

"Would you like me to fetch our drinks?"

"Very well," Mary Bliss said, as a shadow of discomfiture

passed over her face.

Noze stood and went to the sidebar to prepare two double Jacks on the rocks. He returned to Mary Bliss and handed her one, then took his seat and held his glass to tink hers just because. They each took a serious sip and set their glasses on the table.

"What is it, darling?"

"It's this: Why do you hate cops the way you do? I'm guessing it has something to do with your dark secret. I think it's time we share the things we have held back from each other. Will you do it? Can you do it? I believe it's absolutely necessary that we have no secrets between us. And I think we both need to unburden ourselves with the person we trust more than anyone else."

Mary Bliss quickly gulped more Jack and asked for a refill. "Yes," she said. "I will do what you ask but I think I will need to be a little sedated for it. I have never told this to another person, not one. Telling you will be an act of my devotion to you, my devotion to us."

Noze refreshed both of their drinks and settled in beside her.

"I suppose it is fitting that we drink whiskey with this story. My nightmare began because of it."

CHAPTER 32

By age 16, like many of her schoolmates, Mary Bliss had tasted liquor and liked it. Just a slug or two made her tingle all over, especially in the parts that were particularly sensitive and pleasurable when piqued. She was not aware that thinking about boys had the same effect, just that it made her feel good. She had never dated, because she was more an outré curiosity than an object of desire, despite being surrounded every school day by hormonally thunderstruck boys.

She was a curiosity to girls too, but it was a crueler interest in a potential rival. When they spoke to her, if they acknowledged her at all, it was with a malice she could not then fathom.

Mary Bliss was always lonely, and even Miss Ruby's constant reassurance and love couldn't change that. So it came as a disorienting surprise when six of her schoolmates, a tight clique of three boys and three girls, approached her at her locker one afternoon and invited her to a clandestine party.

"Mary," said a girl named Jeri, the unattainable blonde who lived in the lizard brains of boys throughout the school. "We feel bad if it seems like we're ignoring you. We just didn't know how to talk to you. You're so pretty and have such a cute shape that we thought you might, I don't know, shun *us*. I mean, can you even *imagine*?" Jeri laughed at this outlandish idea, and the other kids joined her.

"Listen," Jeri went on. "Al knows how to pick the lock on the concessions stand at the stadium. And he managed to get some whiskey, plenty for all of us. Miles' dad is a jazz musician and he copped some of daddy-o's reefer for us too. We're going to party hearty. Who knows *what* we might do?" The girls giggled, a naughty sound. A girl called Juliet leaned in close to Mary Bliss's ear and whispered, "Wanna *come*?"

The who-knows-what part intrigued Mary as much as the prospect of some whiskey. She looked around at each of the kids, wide eyed, and said, "I guess so. Yes. I would like that very much."

"Wow, Mary, your eyes are so sexy," the one called Miles said. "I been watching you, even with the fake leg and all." It made Mary feel like she was something less than the rest of them, friendly as they seemed. "C'mon you guys," Miles said. "Let's get to it."

It was fall and cold and they all wore winter coats. Al's was roomy enough that it was easy for him to conceal the quart of Old Overholt. They all carried their books. Ambling along like just any group of kids leaving school, they made their way to the concessions stand, unseen, and Al jimmied the lock. They rushed into the small block building's darkness and closed the door behind them before turning on a light. There was no game tonight, and no practice. They wouldn't be disturbed.

So far, it was going just as Mary's new friends had planned.

Miles had an ancient transistor radio and fiddled with the tuner until WHYT came in clear. He kept the volume low, but loud enough for dancing, which they did after passing around the bottle of rye. When it was Mary's turn, she thought she tasted apples. Soon, the whiskey and their body heat warmed the room enough to take off their coats.

Miles pulled a joint out of his shirt pocket, fired it up, and passed it to Jeri. She took a heavy hit, held it in, and exhaled as she passed it to Mary, who said, "I've never..."

"Oh, go ahead, chicken. You'll love it. Mellows you out."

Mary toked gently, and coughed it back up. "C'mon," Jeri prodded. "Hit it good. Hit it, girl!" Mary took a bigger toke, and coughed that up too. But her head felt – she couldn't think what – maybe lighter? "Oh, I see," she said.

As others took their turns, the boys and girls started pairing off for a slow tune – Wham's "Careless Whisper." Mary stood alone to one side. She noticed that each boy's style was to clutch his partner's butt with both hands, pull her flush against his body, and hump. It seemed like it was agreed upon. The girls didn't object. A couple of them, including Jeri, kept their crotches hard against their partners' and leaned back at the waist, languorously waving their arms. Neither did they object when one hand strayed to a breast, kneading it. The girls giggled. One pretended to be faint, then snapped to, grabbed her partner's crotch, and rammed her tongue into his mouth. She let him slide a hand under her sweater. There was some slobbering. She was raven-haired and her name was Delilah. She swore it was the one her parents gave her. "I know how to take a man's strength, just like Delilah in the Bible," she told Mary. "My way has nothing to do with a haircut. It makes his legs wobbly." The others laughed.

Next up was "I Want To Know What Love Is" by Foreigner. The couples continued to make out during the segue. Delilah peeled off her sweater, raising the temperature in the other dancers. Mary watched as she recoupled with the boy, whose name Mary didn't know, and whispered something in his ear. He glanced at Mary, and then held her eyes with his as he slowly smiled. The booze and pot had emboldened her, and she returned it. She thought him especially good looking when he smiled – dark, with chocolate-brown hair, bright blue eyes, perfect white teeth, and a certain archness that hinted at danger. He broke from Delilah, who boldly stood wearing a lace bra, her hands in the back pockets of her jeans, and a defiant look on her pretty face.

The boy kept his eyes locked on Mary's and poured on the sensuality as he slowly danced toward her. She blushed and looked at the floor. When she looked up again, he stood in front of her with his arms open.

"May I have this dance?"

"I am sorry. I do not know how to dance. I have never

danced. And I do not even know your name."

"I'm Gil," he said. "It's short for Gilbert, but I hate Gilbert. So I'm Gil."

"Well," Mary Bliss replied with a nervous tremolo in her voice. "I am pleased to meet you, Gil. But I worry that Delilah may not be as pleased."

Gil laughed, and Mary thought his voice was even more pleasant when he did.

"Look at her," he said. "Does she look like she's pissed?"

Delilah danced alone, shaking her hips, jiggling, swaying, hugging herself, and otherwise drawing the boys' attention. Their girls were not to be outdone, and they shimmied out of their pants and began gyrating in front of the boys wearing only thongs, shirts, and nasty smiles.

Mary felt confused. If not for the intoxicants, she would be appalled. She looked at Delilah – clearly the catalyst for this nascent teen orgy – who caught her inquisitive eyes, raised one hand and waggled her fingers, a friendly gesture. "Let's see yours," she said to Mary, shaking her breasts to show what she meant.

"See?" Gil said. "This was actually her idea."

"OK," Mary said. "But I could never do that. I am not so bold. And as I said, I do not even know how to dance."

Delilah fetched the bottle of whiskey and took it to Mary, who declined to drink. "C'mon, Mary," Gil said. "Loosen up a little and have fun. Delilah will show you how." Mary again waved away the bottle.

Gil put his hands on Mary's hips and shook them. Then he slid his hand up her waist to her breasts and squeezed. "Oh, uh, no, please Gil. I have never ..." He gripped her shoulders and shook them. "See," he said, eyes settled on her breasts. "That's how you shake them. Delilah will show you more. You're going to be sexy as hell."

The others started to gather around her. Jeri began to chant, "Mary! Mary! Mary!" and the others joined in. Delilah handed the bottle to Gil, who took a deep swallow, then grabbed

Mary's hair and yanked her head back while he poured liquor into her open, gasping, upturned mouth. Mary coughed it out. He poured in more and clapped a hand over her mouth and nose. She swallowed.

Mary again coughed and reeled a little from the effects of the whiskey. She turned and came face to face with Delilah, who no longer smiled. "I said, let's see yours!" Delilah grabbed the neck of Mary's demure white blouse and yanked, tearing it open and sending several buttons flying. Mary, her brain swimming in sauce and unsure on her feet, yelped and tried to cover herself. Behind her, Gil pulled off her blouse. "Now we're getting to it," he said to the others.

"You know what to do," Delilah ordered. "You all said you were in. So do it!"

It took them only a minute of struggling with Mary to pull off her jeans, and rip away her bra and panties. She swooned and Gil caught her as Al said with a laugh, "Whatta ya know! Her hair really *is* red."

"What a mutant," Jeri said. "Look at her leg. I mean her almost-leg. *You think you can be one of us with that leg, crip*? You're ugly, broken, disgusting."

Gil let Mary drop to the concrete floor and slipped one foot under her head before it could hit hard. She fell on one side, moaning, and Gil again used his foot, turning her onto her back.

They all stood around her and Mary looked up, too woozy to understand what she saw, as Al grinned and said something like "circle work." The boys unzipped. Mary heard the zizz but couldn't clearly see what made it. Then she saw that each of them was fishing around in his pants and pulling something out. Their girls hugged them from behind, reached around and got their action started. Mary wondered briefly about how those things got so much bigger. The boys brushed their girlfriends' hands away, took hold of themselves, and began rhythmically jerking. This turned to frenzy until release, and Mary saw and felt ropy streams of something that landed on her chest and belly like hot honey. Her mind cleared enough to scream.

"No! Oh! Oh! No! Please! What are you ..."?

All six of her new "friends" laughed and pointed. "Geek!" Miles said. "You don't belong with us. You oughta be in a sideshow." The three girls were now without pants or underwear and straddled their breathless, trembling prey. Jeri took a position over her belly, Juliet over her chest, and Delilah chose her face. Mary tried to cover her face as she felt the hot splash of their urine. It seemed to go on forever.

The horror of this putrid insult, of this utter mortification, of such hatred, followed Mary Bliss into unconsciousness. One by one, each of her teenage assailants stood over her body and spit on it. Then they high-fived around and left her corrupted, desecrated young body on the cold concrete floor, her bright red hair pooled around her head like a neon bloodstain.

CHAPTER 33

She was sobbing when she finished. By halfway through the horror story, she was shivering so hard that she could barely get the words out. She managed, then looked at his face and asked, "Can you forgive me?"

"What?" Noze couldn't imagine he'd heard her correctly. "What did you say?"

"Can you forgive me, my darling?"

"Forgive you for what? For being demeaned? For being disgustingly abused? For being a victim? How do any of those things require forgiveness?"

"I feel as though I have deceived you about being pure."

"My God, Miss Mary. You remain pure, as you call it. And even if you weren't, it wouldn't mean anything to me. You are true to me and spend so much time and effort honoring me and making me happy in our relationship. There is nothing to forgive about this or anything else you might tell me."

"This is everything, Mr. Noze. I have no more secrets from you. I have been terrified about telling you this one."

"I can understand being hesitant, but terrified? Do you really think the actions of rotten kids when you were just a girl would turn me away from you or change my opinion of you? Or my feelings for you?"

"If this just relied on my intellectual examination of what happened, no, I know you better than that. But everything about it was, is, emotional, about disgust for letting myself be flattered by their sudden attention to me, about disregarding any suspicions or instincts about their motives, about drinking whiskey and smoking a marijuana cigarette with them, about becoming so vulnerable in the company of my antagonists that I ended up alone, unconscious, naked, and covered in filth, all for their entertainment. I was so dreadfully stupid."

"But dear Miss Mary, you were just a kid yourself, and I'd guess you were awfully lonely. How could you be blamed for any of it?"

She was calming, slowly, and Noze handed Mary Bliss her drink, which she sipped at. "Can I ask you one question?" he said.

"I have now completely opened myself to you, Jimmy Noze. That has never been true for anyone else. You can ask me anything now, or in our future."

"What does this have to do with your feelings about cops?"

"That is actually the end of the story," she said. "When I awoke in the concession stand, I cleaned the filth out of my hair, off my face and body as best I could at the sink, then spent a long time regaining my composure as I dressed and waited for my hair to dry. My plan was to go to the police alone and never tell Miss Ruby, who I feared might succumb to her anger and go after my assailants in a deadly serious way. They would have deserved anything they got, but would have been very bad for her. I also feared for the effect all this might have on her failing health.

"So I did go to the police, who had a station within walking distance of the school. I did not worry that Miss Ruby would be concerned that I was not home yet. I often went to the library after school and she was used to my habits. I told my story to the man, a sergeant, at the front desk, who seemed to be fighting the urge to smile the entire time I spoke.

"I grew angrier as each second passed, and finally said, 'What do you find so amusing, Sergeant? I have been defiled, assaulted.'"

He said, "You sure it was an assault? You look like a hard partier who has to find an excuse about your appearance for the folks at home. You smell like liquor, your eyes are red as a monkey's ass, and I see inside your coat there that your blouse is open an indecent amount."

"My blouse is like this because they tore it from me, ripping off buttons."

"Let's be honest here, young lady. You pulled off those buttons to make a believable picture, didn't you? Huh? Isn't that it? You girls all seem to put on makeup like whores, but *your* face isn't painted. Another ploy to prop up the lie? Are you wearing underpants, or did they make them disappear? Here's what I think. I think you went to a party, got lit up, and tried to act like a woman instead of your age. And now you want to involve the police in your lies?"

Mary Bliss looked at Noze as said, "That is where it ended. That is what was imprinted on me about our so-called friends, the cops. I think he made assumptions about me based on his own prejudices – and fantasies, for all I knew – and refused to believe the truth. I turned and left without saying another word, and he did not try to stop me."

"You've kept a very hard grudge for a long time," Noze said. "Do you think talking about it has relieved you at all?"

"That remains to be seen, I suppose. But I know this. I will never willingly subject myself to being minimized, marginalized, or disregarded by a cop ever again. I spoke to that repulsive detective today only because of the threat that I might become a suspect. It reinforced my feelings about cops. When I could not take another word, I left, against his wishes. I hate cops, and now you know why."

Noze knew what was coming next, and tried to think of a way around it. There was no hope.

"And now, finally, my darling," Mary Bliss softly said. "It is your time to speak freely of your own most terrible memory, of the unlit place you have never taken anyone. You have to do it. It will join us completely."

Besides betraying her trust by refusing to tell his secret, Noze could think of only one way to get around it.

"Miss Mary, I've seen a lot of bad things that most people can't even visualize, and have already shared some of them with you. This world is filled with everyday horrors, any one of which could ruin a person's faith forever. I've read that depression sleeps in the depressive until a triggering event wakes it, and it can stay awake forever. I've always thought this was my trigger, the most vile, revolting, and mind-bending thing I've ever seen, and it wasn't just the aftermath. I watched helpless as it happened.

"You were upset when I told you some of the ugly things I saw as a reporter. I'm afraid this one will steal your essential softness, your belief that some things couldn't possibly happen in a sane world. I'm pretty sturdy, and it nearly ruined me. I don't know what it might do ..."

"I am sturdy too! Far more than you seem to know. Now keep faith with me and do what you must."

Noze picked up his empty glass and started to rise to go refill it.

"No," Mary Bliss said. "You will tell it without any help from that."

He set down his glass and said, "There was a child."

CHAPTER 34

In the library for his first visit in a long time, Haynus Geasley – had an epiphany, though he didn't know it was called that.

He stopped in to revisit images of the Grand Guignol for that special tingle in his jeans. Blood had an ever more personal meaning for Geasley now that he had spilled plenty in his campaign to evolve into ... *something*. He didn't know what it would be until he switched his attention to references about demons and the things they were known for. Then he found it.

Asmodeus. He read it aloud: "ASS-mo-doos." The filthy hebes called him Ashmedai. He didn't try to pronounce it.

This was the boss demon, he read, king of the demons who did their nasty work on earth, not waiting for human chumps to go to Hell. Better, he was the demon of lust, which Geasley knew something about. Even though it didn't say so anywhere he could find, Geasley knew this meant Asmodeus had a big dick, just as he imagined his own Boa to be.

He would no longer be Satan's Spawn. Satan must have a gazillion spawns. No, this is who he was meant to become after doing some dirty work, slicing, stabbing, skinning, baptisms in blood. Asmodeus was a bad motherfucker, just like himself. He was now the boss demon on earth. In accepting his role and reading further, Haynus Geasley – no longer just a spawn of Satan, no simple slimy drop of the Black Lord's jizz – knew he was the obvious fit for this evolution.

Some said Asmodeus was a real looker, slick and desirable, and had perfect manners, all the better to weasel his way into humans' lives. He could shift his shape into just about any appearance he needed, which was handy because his real look was monstrous and repulsive. Even transformed into the most attractive and sensual of all men, he always had one leg like a rooster's, which gave him a permanent limp. The other foot had claws instead of toes. In his real form, he had three heads. One was a bull. One was a sheep. And one was a man with jagged teeth, pointy ears, and a hooked beak above a fire-breathing, foul mouth. And – it makes sense – he had a scaly tail.

He loved human women as objects of lust, torment, and cruelty. In Bible times, he got men liquored up while he used their ladies for perverse entertainment. Geasley pictured him swinging his huge cock around like a fire hose, splashing his conquests with 'jaculate, and putting spells on their minds and bodies so they couldn't resist.

As Geasley read further, he found that Asmodeus also loved revenge, making use of a wide variety of cruelties to kings and commoners alike. He tricked Solomon into exile, then took over his harem of more than a thousand wives, desecrating them all. But it was Sarah, the daughter of archangel Reguel, who claimed his heart and his loins. Other men wanted Sarah, but in a fit of demonic pique, Asmodeus killed all seven of her husbands, one after another, on their wedding nights with her.

This last convinced Geasley that he was the heir to Asmodeus – that he was Asmodeus incarnate. Didn't he have his own Boa? Wasn't he consumed with lust? Didn't he live for revenge? And wasn't he on his way to repeating the murders of Sarah's husbands with the horrific murders of Mary Bliss's own men, first the Viking, then the tubby cosmetics wizard.

And next, next, next. The worst of all. The cockroach Jimmy Noze.

"I will claim him!" Geasley shouted in the carrel. "I will make him pay.

"I am the boss demon! I. Am. ASS-mo-doos!"

A voice from a neighboring carrel said, "Why don't you Ass-mo-douche your ass out of here?

CHAPTER 35

As Noze said, there was a child.

The first time Jimmy Noze heard of Goodluck Garcia, he figured Ma and Pa Garcia had to have a sense of humor. Their son didn't. The guy was a low-rent creep of the first water who shaved off his eyebrows and replaced them with thin arched lines using red eyebrow pencil. His eyes nearly touched over a narrow, crooked nose that looked like it had been broken more than once. He covered his blue-black beard shadow with cheap makeup foundation a shade or two lighter than his neck, forehead, and scalp. He kept his dome shaved bald. Whatever look he was going for came out as grotesque, deviant, and indelible.

He had a sheet with just a couple of misdemeanors – weenie-wagging at kids – and got a few months in Wayne County Jail for each of them. While it wasn't uncommon for a repeat flasher to be charged with a felony and get prison time for the second offense, his given name seemed to fit when the judge either decided that prison was too harsh, or he just couldn't worry too much about indecent exposure compared to all the other stuff on the court's docket.

When Goodluck Garcia came to Noze's attention, he seemed to have become a bigger fish to fry. He was picked up in Hamtramck and charged in the disappearance of a six-year-old boy after several witnesses saw him eyeballing kids getting off a school bus. With his makeup and mustard-yellow harem pants, he cut a memorable figure.

By the force of witness statements and his record alone, he was picked up at the flophouse room he called home, one of a dozen located above a used CD and comic book shop on 12th near Clairmount, where Detroit's 1967 riots jumped off. The desk clerk sat in a cage at the bottom of the stairs leading to the flop.

On the advice of his counsel, Tito Flick, Goodluck entered a not-guilty plea and was released to await preliminary hearing. The night clerk and other witnesses were called to testify. Noze and a few other reporters were allowed to sit in the unused jury box because the notoriety of the case drew a full house of angry citizens. Noze had a special hatred for any crime against a child, and had to guard against bias in his reporting leading to and including the prelim.

The night clerk was an addled old geez with his back up for being bothered to come to court. When sworn in, he answered "Yaz!" to telling the truth. When asked if he saw Goodluck Garcia in the courtroom, the old man pointed to him and said, "Yaz, that the muhfuckah right there." The judge upbraided him for the language, which made the night clerk even more resentful.

He answered "yaz" when asked if he had made a note of Goodluck leaving the building on the night in question, but seemed confused when asked to describe what he was wearing. "Clothes, man," he said, "what you think?" The prosecutor followed by asking if there was anything unusual about his attire, for example, his trousers. The old man half rose from the witness chair and shouted, "Man, I don' look at no mens below dey wais'!"

Everyone in the courtroom, including the judge, burst into laughter while the old man glared at them all. The judge called a brief recess to allow them to compose themselves.

By the time the hearing was over, it was clear the case shouldn't have been brought. No witness could place the missing boy with Goodluck. And other than witness testimony, there was no other evidence to make Goodluck Garcia the bad guy. A peeved judge dismissed the charge against him and reamed the prosecution for overreach.

Noze didn't buy it. His instinct was waving red flags that told him Goodluck Garcia was the guy, whether or not the cops and prosecutors could prove it. The child had not been found, alive or dead. There was no ransom demand. Ransom wasn't what the abductor wanted.

However Goodluck got the kid, he got him, and that was what he wanted. That and whatever he planned to do with him, or to him. Noze despised this guy and wasn't going to let him get away with it. Not with a kid.

He began to stalk Goodluck Garcia at night and whenever he could grab time during the day. If Goodluck went to Farmer Jack, Noze went to Farmer Jack. If Goodluck went to buy a copy of *Playgirl*, Noze followed him. Noze shadowed the aberration everywhere he could and made sure Goodluck saw him each time. Once, waiting outside the flop for Goodluck to emerge, the deviant walked directly to Noze, eyes blazing.

"The fuck you harassing me for, newsboy?"

"I'm not harassing you, Goodluck. I'm your biggest admirer. I want to see you and follow you and learn everything about Goodluck Garcia, fashion plate, master of the eyebrow pencil. I don't know why you aren't happy about that, having your own one-member fan club."

"You're cramping my social life, asshole."

"Yeah, your social life," Noze said. "Who exactly do you socialize with? Is there a one-digit age limit for your social circle?"

Goodluck started to take a step toward his nemesis, and Noze put up a hand.

"Wouldn't do that if I were you."

"What you supposed to be, some kind of badass or something?"

"Oh, it's just a friendly warning, Goodluck. You can try me if you want."

"I'll have my lawyer deal with you," Goodluck said.

"Who, Flick?" Noze said. "I've known Tito for years. It'll be good to hear from him."

"Fuck you, Noze."

"That's all you can come up with?"

"You'll see," Goodluck said, backing away. "I'll show you. That's a promise."

"Okey doke, man. I'll see you around."

Noze continued to shadow him for nearly two more weeks. At the time, he was working on the newspaper's investigative team, and talked his editor into giving him the time to find what he could about Goodluck Garcia. He and his target never spoke during that time until Noze got a phone call and immediately recognized the voice on the other end.

"You remember the railroad tracks between the greenbelt and the old Kelvinator plant on Plymouth Road?" Goodluck said. "You should. You grew up near there, yeah?"

"I remember," Noze said. "What's with the trip down memory lane?"

"Meet me on the tracks about where Castleton would hit them if it cut through the greenbelt. Eight p.m. sharp. I have a little surprise for you."

"It's raining like hell and is supposed to keep it up tonight and tomorrow," Noze said.

"What, sugar, you afraid you'll melt in a little water?"

"See you then," Noze said, and hung up.

If he hurried, Noze could make it there by eight. He tucked his Glock into the back waistband of his black jeans, put on an old Carhartt duster that did a pretty good job of keeping out rain, pulled on a stocking cap, and headed out.

The rain was falling in sheets as he turned onto Shirley Street along the greenbelt, pulled up onto the grass, got out, and locked his car. It was hard to see in the cascade, so he walked up to the fence beside the railroad tracks and followed it until he saw a cut he could fit through. Squeezing through the hole in the chain link, he snagged his coat a couple of times then got in. There was ambient light from the neighborhood and infrequent lightning; it didn't help much. He looked up and down the tracks but didn't see Goodluck. Then he heard him.

"Hey, scoop, over here! You're a punctual motherfucker."

Noze squinted through the dim light and rain toward the sound and spotted a dark figure. He began to walk toward it until he had a better view.

"Close enough, shithead," Goodluck said. "I've got something to show you."

Goodluck reached behind him and pulled out a young boy, maybe five or six, who was shivering. He started to shout something to Noze in a quavering, reedy voice, and Goodluck slapped him hard. "Shut your fucking mouth!" The boy obeyed.

"This is the brat all of you are looking for. It has to feel great to know you were right all along. We've been having a lot of fun together. Sometimes when I do something to him he bitches, but then I do something else to shut him up. Can't talk with your mouth full."

"You piece of shit!" Noze shouted. "Let him go."

"Oh, I told you I've got something to show you, and it's not just the kid."

Noze gaped as Goodluck grabbed the boy by his hair and lifted him off his feet. The child squealed. "For all you do," Goodluck yelled at Noze with a rictus grin, "this one's for you!" He lifted his other arm high and Noze saw something in his hand, about two feet long and glinting faintly. He swung it at the boy's neck where it made a sickening sound, swung again and the little body dropped into the mud with a splash.

The fiend still had a grip on the boy's hair as he raised the small head high, turned his face up, and let the streaming blood cover it. His tongue was out.

Noze wasn't sure he was seeing what he thought as he began to tremble uncontrollably. He continued to gape as Goodluck dropped his abominable handful in the mud, raised his machete and charged at Noze, who snapped to, reached behind his back, drew the Glock, and fired twice at his chest and once at his head, dropping him cold.

Jimmy Noze, who thought he had seen it all, clutched his spasming stomach and violently dry heaved, and then vomited into the mud and the blood of an innocent boy.

CHAPTER 36

"I have to go see Tito Flick," Noze said after recounting his soul-scarring experience, and stood to go to the bar and see to drinks. Before he could take a step, Mary Bliss gripped his hand and pulled him back down on the davenport.

"Be still." She kissed his forehead and rose to fetch their Jacks. Returning with two stiff ones on the rocks, she handed one glass to Jimmy Noze and settled back down beside him. She saw his hand was trembling.

"Darling," she said, "that is the most heartrending, unspeakable thing I have ever heard. And yet you saw it and spoke it to me out of love, I think. I cannot even imagine what it must be to live with such a memory.

"But if you spoke of that fellow Mr. Flick to divert your mind, I believe it is a bad idea. Deal with the lawyer later. I want you to drink your drink and face down the appalling memory that has hectored you for so long. Face it down! Dare it to hurt you again! Tell it *Mary Bliss orders it so*. Then close it up and tell it to leave. Be *fierce*. If you mean what you tell it, it will comply. I truly believe this because I succeeded in doing that to my own dark secret, my own worst memory. It is still there, somewhere, but commands almost none of my attention.

"Do it, dear man. I believe with all my heart that you can."

Noze tossed down his drink and went to replenish it. Mary Bliss sipped at hers.

"And there is this," she said, lightly licking her lips. "In sharing the worst moments of our lives, we are bonded ever more tightly. We are a living, breathing Gordian knot; it cannot be untied. It is a forever bond. You are an integral part of me as

I am to you. With this bond we are strong enough to confront anything that may come our way, and put the past where it belongs."

Noze sat, eyes down. "I listened to what you said. I promise I'll give it a shot. I can't promise how it will come out, but I'll give it a real shot. Try to shove it deep in the back of my skull where depression hides. When it starts to creep out, I've learned to concentrate on all my memories of Mary Bliss. Head to toes. Every gorgeous inch of you. And mostly, it seems to work."

Mary Bliss stood and straddled Noze's legs. It allowed her to fully press her body against him, feel his warmth, kiss him when she wished, rest her head on his shoulder.

She pressed her lips hard against his, then lightly on his forehead, and leaned back to take his face in her hands.

"Darling," she said, "do you feel up to telling why you mentioned this Mr. Flick as soon as you finished describing that hideous event?"

"I thought of Tito because he has a connection to Geasley as a client. I think it's more than that, and I don't think he squared with me way back when he said he hadn't seen or heard from Geasley since the punk got out of prison. We're not having much luck catching up with the scumbag. I think it's time to ask the question again."

"When are we going?"

"I'm going alone, Miss Mary. It will work best."

"But we are partners, are we not?"

"Now and always. But Tito Flick has a strong theatrical streak that he loves to show off when there's an audience to play to. I'm not such an audience; you definitely would be. He's never met you, doesn't know anything about you, at least as far as I know. I intend to go straight at him, up in his face, and get the whole truth out of him. I might have to squeeze him a little. I don't see a need for you to watch anything like that. So please, understand why it's best I go at this one alone.

"I'm going to call him to be sure he's home when I arrive."

Noze punched some numbers into his phone and put it to

his ear.

"Tito? *Jimmy Noze*. I have some questions for you and I'm on my way over. Be sure to be there or I'll track you down like an overfed dog. Oh, I hurt your feelings? I'll hurt more than that if you stiff me." He hung up.

Noze couldn't remember ever seeing Mary Bliss pout, but now she did, and it was so winsome that he almost softened. Almost.

"I am disappointed," she said. "But I suppose I understand as you explained your reasons. Still, I am concerned for your safety. Will you be in any danger?"

"From Tito? He's as soft and skittish as they come. If you saw him, you'd know. Don't worry, partner. I'll be as safe as I could be."

She walked to him, took his face in both hands, and kissed him as though she'd never see him again. Then he was gone.

CHAPTER 37

Jimmy Noze nursed a mad-on since hearing the little slug's irritating whine on the phone. He'd have had nothing to do with the loathsome lawyer back in his newspaper days if it weren't for the fact that Tito was a fount of street tips, some good, some not. It was what reporters referred to as "every other round a tracer."

He'd been to Tito's apartment only once and had to refer to his phone listing for the address. It was in a stately old building on Whitmore in the Palmer Park area, which had long been known as much for its gay community as for the sometimes safe, sometimes not, city park that it bordered. Small bands of predators occasionally amused themselves by harassing, or beating, or even killing trannies and gay hustlers they cornered in the park.

Another sort of hustlers worked over newbies who thought they'd try the adjacent golf course, which was flat as the streets that surrounded it but had a good number of tricky holes. These were the purview of a resident pack of gamblers who set up unsuspecting duffers and took them down for all the cash in their pockets, and sometimes watches and jewelry.

Besides the gay-bashing, Noze knew the neighborhood was never as safe as its cheerleaders insisted. A short walk to a raggedy store on Six Mile for some beers or smokes or a green glass keg of Mickey's Malt Liquor could end in an armed mugging or an assault just for the hell of it. Noze knew a cop who was relieved of his gun and badge in the vestibule of his apartment building by a large mugger with a large pistol, which he used to knock his victim to the ground.

Noze found plenty of street parking, which hadn't always

been the case. In the alcove outside the main door, he pushed the doorbell labeled "Tito Flick – Legal Superstar!" in tiny letters written by the shyster himself.

A little speaker in the panel crackled with something that sounded like, "Yes, dear?"

"Open it, Tito," Noze said. A loud buzzer made an electric burp and Noze yanked on the heavy door to enter. He trotted three flights up the stairs, found the apartment, and pounded on it the slab with his fist.

"My heavens, James," Tito almost shouted when he opened the door. "You could wake the dead. Do come in, my valiant comrade."

"Save the grease, Tito. I'm here for a reason, and it's not because of your charisma. Sit down."

Tito plodded over to his magenta, button-tufted, throne-like easy chair, made himself comfy, and took a dish of dates from his side table, plopping one in his incongruous Cupid's bow of a mouth. He widened his porcine eyes and raised his plucked eyebrows, saying, "Well?"

"I don't think you were square with me when I asked about your punk-ass client, Geasley, after he was kicked loose. The more I think about your claim that you hadn't seen him after his release, the more I think you were exactly who he'd go to see first.

"Maybe he thought you owed him after failing to keep him out of the joint. Maybe he thought he could trade on that to milk you for this, that, and the other. I'm here now because he is a threat to me, which doesn't concern me, and to Mary Bliss, my business partner. That does concern me, a lot."

"Hmmm," Tito said. "Could it be this Mary Bliss is something more than a business partner?"

"A business partner. Anything more is none of your fucking business."

"So now I know the urgency of your visit. Prince Charming, are we? Sir Galahad, perhaps? Her hero. Yes. I have no doubt about it." Tito stuffed another date in his face. "Is she as sweet as these dates I enjoy so much? I can almost picture her."

"There's no way that steaming pile of shit you call a brain could possibly create an accurate image of her. Your boy Geasley knows what she looks like. That's one major reason for my concern."

"James, dear boy. I've never known you to be so taken with any of your many *affaires d'amour.*"

"How would you know?"

"Oh, I see things. I hear things. They are the basis for much of my usefulness on and off the streets we both know so well."

"Enough jaw flapping, Tito. Where can I find Geasley?"

A voice behind him said, "Right here."

Noze turned just in time to see Geasley swing the heavy receiver from Tito's Victorian princess phone and connect with the hinge of his jaw.

The world went black.

CHAPTER 38

"You're number three."

Noze heard the voice through loud crunching and a frantic timpani solo in his skull. He felt his throat spasm as he fought the urge to puke. There was a cloying, rotten stink that combined with the booming in his brain to make his stomach violently roil. His jaw hurt like a bitch. He couldn't see or move his arms and legs.

"*Hello. You in there?*" Crunch. Crunch.

He couldn't see. Geasley had bound his head with a black cloth over his eyes. He knew it was Geasley because he'd seen him for a split second before he was knocked cold. The vile punk got the drop on him and brought him here, whatever here is.

"*Yoo hoo, Schnoz!*" Ridiculous giggling. Crunch. "See what I done there? Noze means Schnoz, right? You gotta give me that one."

Noze tasted sour funk and cloying sweet in his dry mouth. "Give me some water."

"Oh, don't think I'll be doing that."

"Sweet. I smell sweet. I taste it too."

"Could be that ether you been sucking down since we left Tito's. You'll like this. I'm real clever. See, I got some a that spray for starting cars and it's got lots of ether in it. I laid a rag over your face and kept it soaked with the stuff. Smelled kindly sweet to me too."

"It's a different sweet, a stink."

"Hmmm. Lemme see here. Ah, I know. You spent a lot of time around rotten bodies? I'm gonna guess yeah 'cause you was some hot shit crime reporter. Could be that. I got one right over there, but I can't keep enough salt on him to keep him from smellin' high."

Geasley yanked the blindfold off Noze's tortured head and squealed, "Ta-dah!"

Noze squinted at the light before his eyes adjusted and he could scan the room. Symbols of some kind were daubed on the walls in garish hues. A crude network of extension cords fed cheap incandescent clamp-on shop lights that gave the chamber a yellowish tinge. The ceiling, walls, and floor looked like concrete. Mold bloomed in every corner and down the walls. Besides the cloying sweet smell, he now detected a thick, musty odor. He strained his neck trying to see his own situation and saw that his wrists and ankles were bound to a heavy wooden frame that seemed to have once had a fine varnish finish. A cross? Was he crucified with rough rope instead of nails? That was a benevolence Geasley wouldn't seem to have.

Noze's throat felt like it was lined with crepe paper.

"Where is this?" he rasped.

"Oh, you're honored to be a guest in the lair of Ass-mo-doos, the boss demon, the heavy-hung fuckmaster with a million brides. I bet your Mary Bliss still has her sweet cherry. She wouldn't give it to you. She'll pretty soon lose it to Ass-mo-doos, which if you don't know is me. My great big dick will make her squeal. With you out of the way, she should be easy pickins. Every since I saw her showin' off in that bathroom window, I had to get me some. That red hair, up and below, has got me half crazy."

"Only half?"

Geasley snarled at Noze and was out of his sight for a minute before returning with a hammer and a two long, heavy nails.

"Yeah, OK, say something smart ass again." He jabbed a nail hard into the palm of Noze's right hand and drove it halfway home with the hammer.

Noze nearly shrieked but clamped his aching jaw shut and concentrated on keeping that pleasure from Geasley.

"Uh, oh, a tough guy. Lemme see how tough." He pounded the other nail through the left hand. Noze felt every muscle in his torso tighten, arched his back, and saw lights inside his eyelids as if glinting off shards of glass. Still, *fuck you, Geasley.*

"I'm going to play with you for a while just 'cause I like it," Geasley said, holding his face close enough to his victim's to nearly touch noses. Noze almost gagged at the fetid breath, like rotting chicken in a toilet bowl. "But we're here for a serious reason why, a big honor for you. See, you're number three."

"Three?"

"Yeah. See, I read somewheres that to be a real-deal serial killer you have to make at least three kills. You're my third."

I'm not dead yet, Noze thought.

"You don't have to worry about getting spikes through your feet, like your punk-ass lord and savior. I got other ideas." Geasley skipped out of Noze's vision like a depraved grade school kid. When Noze could see him again, Geasley stood at his feet, facing him, munching on a pretzel rod.

"You know that Chin-ee thousand-cut thing? I'm thinking to see how far I can git."

Geasley's hand moved and Noze felt a small sting on the sole of his foot. He didn't make a sound.

"That's the first cut. Little bitty thing. When there's a thousand of 'em, I betcha it's gonna be worse."

He surprised Noze with a deep stab in his sole while turning the blade a bit. Noze gasped and held it. "I know you think that's not a cut, but I'm gonna count it anyways. Now here, little cut number three." It wasn't enough to hurt much. Only smarted. Not even a bee sting.

"Just 'cause I don't want your other tootsie to feel left out here."

With a grand sweep of his arm that grossly exaggerated the size of the cut he left on the other sole, Geasley said, "Don't wanna move too fast. Got to stretch it out some. So how 'bout I give you a tour of my cozy torture room? Don't know if I can officially call it that, since you're my first visitor." He took another bite of the pretzel rod, then paused to stare at it.

"How about some water, what's your name, *Ass*-mo-*douche*?"

Geasley winced. "Uh, sure."

He went out of Noze's sight and quickly return with a discarded chili can. "Drink up, visitor."

He held the can to Noze's lips, then poured in the contents when he opened his mouth. This time, Noze couldn't contain himself.

He spit out the mouthful and nearly vomited. "The fuck is that?" he croaked. "Jesus."

"Hmmm, there's that guy again. Anyways, I was going to tell you that over there is a big ol' bathtub holding the body of that fat man, the one who served your whore with face paint and what not. Couldn't believe I was so jealous of the slob, but I was. So, I brung his big ass here and skinned him. He was whining a lot, then he wasn't. I flopped him into the tub. I keep a lot of salt on him to make him a mummy, but he still smells. I kinda like it. Prolly the sweet smell you said. The mix of the salt and his melting soft parts makes some liquid. Proud to serve some to you. Kindly like fat man broth."

Noze gagged. "Clean water."

"OK, if it'll shut you up."

Geasley fetched a bottle of water and dumped it in Noze's mouth. Nearly breathing it in, Noze gagged again.

Geasley picked another pretzel rod from the bag and turned to face Noze. He stepped close to his face. "Ya know, I found somethin' innerestin' about these sticks." He took a bite. "Most ever' time you bite off some," crunch, crunch, "it makes a sharp point on the rest. See?"

He held it close to Noze's face.

"Great," Noze said. "You're a real big brain."

"Look," Geasley commanded, and he used a thumb and finger to hold Noze's left eyelids apart. "I said *look*." He held the point close to the eye, then plunged it in." Noze shuddered, and clamped his mouth shut. Geasley left the pretzel stub in his eye.

"Oh, man, it's funny when you move your eye and the stick waves around. Ain't that crazy?"

CHAPTER 39

Jimmy Noze was a bit old school and didn't easily let go of things. So a black desktop Rolodex with a patina of dust sat beside his rotary phone. Flipping through the index, Mary Bliss was relieved to find a card with Tito Flick's address, cell, and landline numbers.

After he left for Flick's apartment the day before, she assumed he wouldn't return until late afternoon at the earliest. Mary Bliss gave room for Jimmy Noze to attend to another matter if he had one, but by 8 o'clock she began to fret. Repeated calls to Noze's own cell went unanswered for the entire night. She struggled to swallow her panic, and dialed Flick's landline number.

"Tito Flick Esquire here, fully at your service."

"Mr. Flick, my name is Mary Bliss, and we have a mutual friend, Jimmy Noze."

"Indeed, my dear. Forgive me, but what did you say your name is?"

"Mary Bliss, B-L-I-S-S."

"And is this your birth name or an enchanting *nom de guerre*?"

"It is the name I was born with."

"My, I must certainly say it makes my own sobriquet more grievous still. How do you know our mutual friend?"

"I am his partner, a fellow investigator who adds a unique skill set to Mr. Noze's own expansive one. We complement one another quite well."

"And," he said with a lilt in his voice, "are you also *romantic* partners?"

"Whether or not is none of your concern, Mr. Flick. I am investigating Mr. Noze's disappearance overnight and have questions for you. He left to meet you at your home. Did he arrive?"

"Yes, indeed he did. And it was pleasant indeed to commune with my old brother in arms. We have long plied the streets of the city and beyond in our mutual pursuit of justice and truth. He asked me if I know the whereabouts of one Haynus Geasley, once a client of mine. I assured him I do not. Certainly I will alert him if I do. Did you try his cell phone?"

"Of course I did. You must think me a fool."

"Oh, my dear, no. Of course you did."

"He has not answered my repeated calls. You know Haynus Geasley, and you know he is a bad person. He has threatened both Mr. Noze and me. I am going to come to your home, and I want you to tell me, to show me, everything you have about him. I may see a clue to his whereabouts that you do not."

"I don't know what that might be, dear. Perhaps I have an old file here. I'll have to look. Although now that I think about it, I do have some things that relate to him. To help him when he got out of prison, I gave him an old car gifted me by another client. It is still in my name. I am chagrined that he ignores parking rules that govern the rest of us, and I have quite a sizeable collection of tickets he has amassed. Please feel welcome to come and look at them, though I cannot imagine what help they may be in your investigation. Certainly, I will help Jimmy in any way I can, but I have nothing else."

She said goodbye. "I will be there shortly."

***

When she pulled the Miata into a curbside parking place opposite Flick's apartment building, she saw he was standing in the main entrance waiting to greet her. As she got out of the car, locked it, and walked toward the stubby lawyer, he said, "Oh, my, as one who appreciates beauty in all forms, I must say Jimmy is a very lucky fellow."

"Thank you. Now please take me inside. As you can imagine, I have a need for urgency."

"Very well," Flick said, offering his hand. "It is a great pleasure to meet you."

Mary Bliss accepted his hand and thought it felt like nothing so much as a small bag of oatmeal.

She followed him inside and up two flights of stairs and he let her enter his living quarters first.

"May I offer you some refreshment, perhaps a glass of fine wine?"

"As I just said, I am in a hurry."

Flick had a thick stack of parking tickets waiting for her, bound in a neat package with red ribbon tied in an ornate bow. "As you asked, my dear."

"Thank you for this," she said, turned and left the heavily scented room, ignoring the little man's urging to bide just a while.

CHAPTER 40

Mary Bliss parked herself in a non-Starbucks coffee house, examined the tickets one by one, and listed the time and place of each on a yellow legal pad. It took two coffees and somewhat more than an hour to get through the stack. Then she punched each address into her cell's search engine, ignoring those for stores – there were several for an army-navy surplus outlet – and keeping only those that didn't have a commercial connection. Eleven were left.

All but three were for parking in handicapped or other "no parking" zones in residential areas. The three were all for the same place: an aged church that, according to Google, had been vacated and abandoned about a decade before. It was one of the countless ruins the City of Detroit never seemed able to demolish. The three tickets were for the apron outside a loading dock at the rear of the stone structure. They were issued three days in a row.

This had to mean something. It was plain that Geasley had some reason to go to the old church; certainly, religion had nothing to do with it. Mary Bliss packed up her things and headed out to visit the building and try to discern what that was.

Following the route on her cell, she arrived at the old church and parked in back, the heck with a ticket. She locked the Miata and looked for an entry. The only thing that suggested itself was a large, well-worn piece of plywood near the middle of the wall. She pulled on one side of the board, expecting it to be attached. It was not. The weeds along its bottom were crushed, probably by the large "door." She tried sliding it to one side and it gave, roughly dragging along the macadam as she pushed. When it cleared a space about the size of a garage door, it revealed a ratty Geo Metro parked inside a large open space. She knew from Geasley's parking tickets that it was the sort of car he drove.

Leaving the entry unblocked behind her, she pulled a penlight from one pocket and began scanning the space for doors of any kind. A set of double doors that may have led to the interior of the church proved to be locked and squealed in protest when she tugged on it.

An open doorway to the left had curved stairs leading down. Mary Bliss stood at the top for several long minutes before she heard faint voices down below. One maniacally cackled and she knew she had found what she was looking for. It hadn't occurred to her to bring a weapon, nor did she own one. Though she was dressed down in a white cotton blouse knotted at the bottom and loose black jeans, she decided to trust her ability to distract men and hope for the best.

She put the penlight in one pocket and carefully picked her way down, following the curve of the staircase until the voices became louder and she could see faint light. Then she walked back up several steps until behind a curve that would hide her.

Mary Bliss screamed in her highest register and kept shrieking until she heard footsteps just below her. Planting her left leg as steadily as she could and leaning against the curved wall, she kicked hard with the other as Geasley's face appeared from around the bend. Her block heel hit him squarely on the nose and he fell backwards, noisily rolling down the stairs. She followed close behind and when he settled face down, she kicked hard at the end of his spine, pounding his tailbone and making him freeze for several seconds.

She stepped around him and at the bottom of the steps looked across the chamber and saw Jimmy Noze, his hands nailed to a cross on sawhorses. Hurrying over to him, she wept quietly when she saw the nails piercing his hands and something ugly protruding from one eye.

"Behind you," Noze shouted at her. As Mary Bliss was half

turned, she saw Geasley on his feet with a fearsome look on his gaunt, bloodied face and he backhanded her, nearly spinning her around when she lost her balance and fell to the floor on her butt. She lost her breath and grunted.

"Bitch!" Geasley screeched. "Cunt! I'll make you sorry for what you done to me." He kicked her belly as she tried to get to her knees. It nearly lifted her off the floor, and she fell on her side. He grabbed her cosmesis and ran in a circle around her, pulling, until it came off with a pop. She shrieked with fury, "You are no man. No real man would treat a woman like this. You are a sick, sick child, a demon changeling, a worthless waste of skin and bones." He kicked her again, flipping her onto her back.

Geasley saw that she was crying, and it stirred him. "Worthless, huh? Waste of bones?" He straddled her on his knees. "I'll give you a bone like you ain't seen before." He pulled open his filthy pants and withdrew a small erection. Hefting it in one hand as if it had weight, he undid the waistband of her jeans with the other. "Lemme see that red kitty a' yours and I'll give you somethin' to remember." He leaned over her, poking his stinking tongue in her mouth.

Mary Bliss bit hard on his tongue, chewing as Geasley squealed, until it came off in gouts of blood. She spat the tongue and the blood in his stunned face and bucked him off to one side.

"Cuh'! Bish! Muhfucker!" he babbled. "I guh ki' you!"

Blood pouring over his chin and down his chest, Geasley grabbed at her right leg and missed. She raised it and kicked him on the side of his gory face. He fell flat and rolled, hurrying to his feet and trotting to a satchel sitting against one wall. He rooted inside and withdrew a pistol. Mary Bliss recognized it as Noze's.

He stood and pointed it down at her and she froze.

"No need for that," she said, breathless and raspy.

"Bish! You come 'ater whe' I have my way wi' you."

They both heard a loud, pained growl and turned to see Jimmy Noze wrench his hands free of the nails. He began to sit up when Geasley pointed the gun at his chest and pulled the trigger.

Nothing. Not even a click.

Geasley gaped as Mary Bliss kicked his legs out from under him, grabbed the pistol from his hand, and tossed it to Noze.

Noze sneered. “It works like this.” He racked a round into the chamber of the Glock and shot at Geasley. Because Noze had only one working eye, the shot went wide. He adjusted and shot again, hitting Geasley square in the face, and the already bloody freak dropped like a sack of cornmeal.

Mary Bliss scooted around his body and steadied herself on the cross as she stood on her right leg. She threw herself at Noze, sobbing.

“Oh, Mr. Noze, I thought I had lost you.”

Noze fell back on the cross, exhausted.

CHAPTER 41

Mary Bliss called 911 as soon as Noze fell back on the cross. She said an ambulance was needed for a conscious man who had been terribly tortured, and that police were needed to attend to the hideously abused body of another, a dead man in an advanced state of decomposition. Oh, she said almost as an afterthought, the body of the man who had abused them both was also there, dead of a bullet to the head.

She stood and stroked Jimmy Noze's damp and greasy brow until help arrived a short time later, and she could hear them shouting in the church above. She answered, and the cops hurried down the curved steps as the EMTs toted a stretcher behind them. They all nearly collided when the first of them stopped cold at the bottom, gaping in mixed wonder and horror at the foul *mise-en-scène* there.

The cop first thought he saw a severed leg lying to one side of the chamber, but there was no blood from it, while gore was otherwise splashed and spilled in many places near it. A one-legged woman stood next to a cross with a bleeding man laying on it, blood coming from his hands like the crucified Christ.

The cop moved aside to let the others in, and they quickly got to work helping the couple. One cop stood by an old bathtub, examining the remains of an obese, partially mummified man. Another squatted beside a corpse with much of his head blown apart.

EMTs attended the mutilated man and were stunned when they asked about the sodden brown mess protruding from one eye. "Pretzel nub," he said. He held a pistol in one hand and surrendered it when asked. The woman at his side told them she was beaten by the man now dead and could use their help. The leg lying on the floor was hers, she told them, though they figured as much.

By the time they collectively pieced together an astonishing story that ended with the tableau in this basement, the cops and EMTs had the man and woman ready for transport, carried them up the curved staircase, and out to an awaiting ambulance. As they headed to the hospital, one cop stayed behind to meet the crew from the meat wagon that would take both corpses to the Wayne County Medical Examiner's Office. After they had gone, he strung crime-scene tape around the olid room.

Mary Bliss was released from the hospital after a thorough examination, the dressing of several scrapes, and learning how to ice and otherwise treat her bruised ribs and belly at home. When she asked, they explained to her that bruised or broken ribs were no longer taped as they once were because the compression prevented deep breathing.

Noze was kept for several days, as much to monitor his condition as to dress his wounds and remove every trace of the blinding pretzel from his eye. Of course, the eye itself was ruined, and he was counseled about getting a prosthetic replacement. For the interim, if he chose to get one, he was fitted with a black eye patch. Mary Bliss told him he made an irresistible pirate.

"Well," he said to her just before he was released to recover at home, "I guess the story is over. We got our man, at a price."

"Yes, we did, partner," she replied. "I welcome the end."

"Time for a new story."

CHAPTER 42

If the night indeed has a thousand eyes, as the poet wrote, Jimmy Noze thought they must all be on Mary Bliss right now.

As always, her makeup was meticulous, somewhat more extravagant than usual in what she said was a tribute to her lamented intimate friend and personal care wizard T. Prince LaPierre. Besides, she said, an intimate night calls for smoky eyes.

Her bright coppery hair that often flowed like liquid about her face and neck was fashioned into an elegant chignon, with a red silk plumeria blossom tucked above one delicate ear. She wore ruby studs in each lobe, and a sizeable matching ruby pendant – pear-cut with the point down – hung from an ornate silver chain. Mary Bliss said she inherited the necklace from her grandmother. A banker who adored Miss Ruby had the namesake stone cut for her own luminous bosom, which the banker had been allowed only to see, never touch.

Mary Bliss was altogether elegant in a sleeveless black sheath dress cut to the knee, nearly backless, and with a décolletage that framed the centerpiece gemstone. As was her habit, Miss Bliss wore no stockings and tonight hazarded red open-toe pumps with heels as high and slender as she dared.

She smelled of gardenias and ylang-ylang.

While he had waited for her to appear at the side door, Noze reflected on his fake eye. He was becoming accustomed to it. The pretzel stub did far more damage than piercing the cornea. It destroyed both the iris and the retina and scarred the eye socket. With little recognizable eye left, he had to undergo enucleation, the removal of all eyeball matter from the socket.

He had to wait about seven weeks for the socket to heal, then got an ocular implant to fill his gaping eye socket. Waiting for the artificial eye itself and all the instruction that comes with it forced Noze to wear the eyepatch he hated.

Being a details man, he was fascinated when told that as his artificial eye is made, tiny blood vessels will be simulated by red silk fibers. And he got a strange kick from knowing that once the fake eye is in place, he can treat itching around it by placing a few eye drops on his fingertip, and wiping it over the imitation.

When Jimmy Noze stepped from his beater outside her home shortly after four in the afternoon as she'd asked, he gave himself one last inspection to assure that he looked as good as he could. Miss Mary always took such trouble with her appearance that he wanted to do the same, hoping it might charm her. He'd shopped at Lord & Taylor, putting himself entirely in the hands of a personal shopper who assured him that such service was offered free to any patron, and pirates were favored.

"As you can see," he said to her with an unaccustomed twinge of discomfiture over his usual rig of Hawaiian shirt and black jeans, "I don't know much of anything about style. Got a big date tonight. Very special, I'm told. Please help me."

The young lady turned on some heavy flirt and, for no practical reason, squeezed his broad shoulders, reached around his chest as if to take its measure, and slid her hands down to his narrow waist. "Mmmm," she said, raising her eyes to his, "I know just what you need." She took her time showing him suits, many shirts, belts, socks and, "If you'll allow me an indiscretion, boxers or briefs?" He said, "Boxers." She picked through a selection of custom-label examples, chose one, and held it against his waist, letting it fall in place. "Black form-fitting silk," she concluded. "It's the only possible choice. And if I may say, please forgive me, should it get that far, your special date will find them very provocative." Noze hoped she was right.

By the time they were done, he had a slim-cut single-breasted navy blue suit that fit like it was custom tailored, a slate gray silk dress shirt with a point collar, a carmine tie with thin gray diagonals, and a black leather belt with a simple gold-toned buckle.

"I'm very sad to have to let you go," she said. "You've been a wonderful customer, so rakishly handsome that you turned my head, as they used to say, and I would give anything to see how you look for your special date."

Noze blushed, and the color deepened when he said, "Could I ask you one more favor?"

"Oh, yes. What can I do to, um, excuse me, *for* you?"

"Would you please tie the tie around my neck so I can loosen it and just slip it on later?"

She gave him a painstakingly elegant half-Windsor knot, trying not to betray how she felt about having her face so close to his.

Mary Bliss heard his car and came to the door to greet him.

"Mr. Noze! I have always been charmed, no, more than that, *stimulated* by your rugged good looks. But this, this new refined presentation has me close to melting into a pool at your feet. I know I told you about the restaurant's dress code, but this! You might well be a model for a sophisticated men's fashion glossy. I have always loved your voice, your manner, your intelligence, and knowledge. Your new look alone, however, inspires a *frisson* of desire that I can barely contain. I know other women will see you the same way, so I must be ever watchful lest one or another of them attempts to impinge on my territory, my partner, my very own boyfriend. Kiss me, now! Do it!"

He enveloped her in his sturdy arms, and lowered his mouth to hers, lingering there, besotted by the taste of her, the sweet warmth that captivated him every time they kissed. Then he held her by the shoulders and stepped back to look at her. This was when he thought of the night and its thousand eyes. She was lovely, as always, and her attire was hardly provocative. Mary Bliss herself was.

After they entered her house to wait for a cab – a ride

that would show better than the beater when arriving at their destination – Miss Mary told him that this night would be unique among those they had spent together, more than special, with a celebratory dinner that she insisted on buying to mark the hard-won success of their first case together as Noze & Bliss, Private Investigators.

"There is a singular restaurant not so very far from here where I have been privileged to dine several times on the generosity of men in my past, a past I will never, ever revive."

Noze reddened and smiled.

"This time I want to treat you, and have been so bold as to phone the owner and ask for a sumptuous meal comprising only amatory, even prurient, ingredients. He is an extraordinarily charming fellow who has few rivals on the subject of food and wine, and always directs patrons' attention to a large painting of a nude woman, languidly laid out to seduce. He never tires, after observers have sufficiently oohed, of revealing that the enticing model was none other than his own sister. It has the power to shock some of his customers. I think it is delightful.

"He phoned me this morning and said he has set a special table for us directly below the painting. His chef, he continued, will prepare an eight-course feast. I had to write it down." She plucked a small piece of peach notepaper from her décolleté and read: "Ice-cold oysters on the half-shell with yuzu mignonette, a dozen for us each; seared foie gras that I remember being so smooth and delicate as to be blatantly erotic; sautéed sweetbreads with Meyer lemon and caper sauce; an amuse-bouche to cleanse our palates with tangy Mexican hibiscus sorbet and a whisper of habanero chili; seared duck breast so red inside as to be suggestive, with Amarena cherry coulis; another palate cleanser, this time Italian *sorbetto* of honey, lavender blossoms, and bits of the somewhat rare, very phallic long pepper; braised beef cheeks bourguignon scented with fennel pollen and more specks of the roguish long pepper; and finally, passion fruit mousse with *mignardise* of Pure Nacional, said to be the world's rarest chocolate, and garnished with flakes of 24 karat gold – gilding the aphrodisiac in a real sense. Before and throughout the meal, at my request, we will be served various styles of French Champagne. And accompanying dessert will be the old and very special Kopke Harvest 1957 port, which the owner selected just for us from his personal cellar, for its hints of citrus and, perhaps the most enticing flavor in all of nature, honey."

"Miss Mary," Noze said, "how in the world are we supposed to eat all that?"

"Slowly, one bite at a time. Dare I say, lubriciously, thoroughly tasting what we put into our mouths and onto our tongues. Our feast begins at five o'clock sharp, and three full hours are being allowed us."

Although Noze was unaware that these ornate plans had been put into play the evening before, it was no accident that, seeing the early evening light was especially warm and lovely, Mary Bliss asked him to take her to his home. There, as he watched, she slowly disrobed in his makeshift atelier and posed in the western light just had she had for his sketch, now insisting that he at least begin the oil painting it was meant to become. It had taken only a glance for her to see that it was having the desired effect on him, as he blended colors to mimic the tones of her illuminated skin.

———

Their feast ended as it began, with the tuxedoed proprietor approaching Mary Bliss, smiling broadly, placing a hand on each of her perfect shoulders, and kissing her lightly on both roseate cheeks. "I see more blush in your charming face than when you arrived," he said. "I hope everything was to your satisfaction, Miss Bliss, and that the selections and preparations have had the desired effect, which if I interpreted correctly, is desire."

She and Noze assured him that the meal, the service, and the mood set by the nude painting were more than could ever reasonably be expected. They thanked him profusely, and in addition to a very generous tip, Mary Bliss kissed him on each cheek. He thanked her, saying, "Now that is priceless," and saw them to the door.

The cab ride home was gravid with expectation. Noze couldn't take his eyes off Mary Bliss, especially her own eyes that even in the dimly lit cab still glinted more than usual with silver in the unexpectedly fetching circle of gray. As he looked deeply into them, his dinner date slowly and gently raked his face with her brazen ruby nails. They spoke only a little as she occasionally let her hand fall to his lap and stroke one thigh.

"You do want me, do you not, Mr. Noze?"

"Is there some misgiving about that, Miss Mary? I thought by now you would have absolute certainty. I would have to be dead inside not to."

She smiled the perfectly tantalizing smile he had come to adore, one that prompted him to hope that there might be a different ending to this evening than every other evening before. He tried to resist the longing as a matter of self-preservation. She reached behind his head and cradled it as she leaned in and kissed him, gently at first, then wantonly, running the tip of her tongue across his top lip, then using it to gently explore within.

When she stopped, she looked at his face and giggled, rubbing his mouth with one thumb. "My lipstick looks lovely on you," she said, her giggling like birdsong. She held up the thumb to show him. "Do you know the song where the singer sings, 'lipstick was *everywhere*'? When we get home I think I will refresh it."

The ride was blessedly short. Noze insisted on paying for the taxi as he had on the trip over, and included a generous tip to thank the cabbie for his discretion. If he even glanced at them in the rearview, Noze didn't catch it.

Once inside, Noze embraced his date, holding her body as tightly as he could against his own, and kissed her mouth, her cheeks, the tip of her nose, her forehead, and lastly her chest just above the ruby, then released her.

"Oh, Mr. Noze," she said. "You seem almost rabid."

Noze stood and reached to remove his tie.

"Please pause and sit back down. In my mind, since seeing you so magnificently attired, I have thought in great detail about disrobing you myself." His own mind conjured a scene where he was slowly bared, and ended in her bed. He forced himself to avoid reading too much into what she said. He should expect only what he had come to expect from their sensual evenings together, respecting Mary Bliss's "purity."

"Before settling on the davenport in the parlor," she said, "prepare a glass of Jack for each of us." With that, she turned and slowly walked off to her sanctum, Noze entranced as always by the little hitch in her step that created the provocative sway of her hips. When she was gone, he prepared their drinks and settled onto the plush davenport, its color as deep red as Shiraz. The smell of jasmine was heady once he lit the incense, and Noze took a deep swig of Jack, savoring its sweet burn.

By the time Mary Bliss appeared, Noze had started a fire in the grate and poured himself another Jack at the bar, which he nursed. For the first time, he heard music quietly playing from a corner of the parlor.

Then there she was.

Mary Bliss stood in the doorway, one hand up on the jamb, knowingly backlit from the hall outside. Her hair was down, parted in the middle and pulled forward over her collarbones. A real jasmine blossom was tucked above one ear. The smoky eye treatment was gone, and replaced with subtle peach shadow and deep pink liner. Her lips and nails were still bright red. She wore a short crimson kimono that fell to the tops of her thighs, and slowly turned to show Noze that the collar drooped low in the back, baring her graceful neck in the way of the geisha.

"Tell me, Mr. Noze, did you think the sweets after our feast were the only dessert?"

She dropped her arms to her sides as she turned and padded barefoot toward him, moving sinuously to the music. "Are you familiar with the opera *Salome* and its voluptuous 'Dance of the Seven Veils'?" she murmured. "I do not have seven veils, but will this serve?" She raised her arms shoulder high and turned slightly at the waist, back and forth, letting the kimono's voluminous sleeves flutter at her sides while briefly exposing herself as the crimson hem rose.

Noze nodded. He couldn't prevent his gaze from dropping to her bared legs, thighs just touching as she positioned them next to his.

She idly ran one finger through Jimmy Noze's hair, up and down his cheek, over the rim of his ear, and continued her affections, stopping to lean over and tenderly leave some lipstick on his mouth. She stood, turned around and sidled to him, carefully raising her left leg over his knees to straddle them.

"I have a favorite line of poetry," she murmured. *Graze on my lips, and if those hills be dry, stray lower, where the pleasant fountains lie."*

She stood, intending him to catch the scent of her dew, then took him by the hand and led him toward her bedchamber. He stopped after a few steps and picked her up, enjoying her warmth as he cradled her in his arms. Mary Bliss wrapped her arms around his neck and kissed his face the rest of the way.

"I have never said this before, although I have felt it almost since we met," she said, taking his face in both hands. "I love you, Jimmy Noze. I love you more than can be measured. I am yours, entirely yours, and always will be. I love you." And she kissed him as deeply as Noze could remember.

He set her on the edge of the downy bed. As he squatted to remove her cosmesis, she parted her legs to release more of her fragrance.

"Do you know the French word *cassolette?"* she asked, her voice almost husky, in a way Noze had never heard.

"I think it's a kind of cooking pot," replied Noze, the now confused, autodidactic chef.

"There is another meaning, much less known. It is French slang for 'scent box.' I do hope you enjoy my *cassolette*, darling."

Noze, speechless, stood and stepped around the boudoir, lighting unscented candles as he went. Their glow enveloped

Mary Bliss in fluttering gilt as she rose on one leg, loosed her belt, and let the little kimono drop free. She sat as he returned to stand facing her. He felt his face and grinned. "I suppose now your lipstick is everywhere," he said.

"Oh, no, Mr. Noze, not as yet."

She stopped him as he unbuttoned his dress shirt. "Please let me," she said. When she finished there, she unbuckled his belt, then the button at the waist, and slowly worked the zipper down. It made a throaty zizz as she returned his grin.

"No, my love, lipstick is not yet everywhere."

The trousers dropped to his feet, which Noze raised in turn to pull off his socks. He caught her staring, her pretty lips just parted, at the thick *bas-relief* in his fitted black boxers. She slowly caressed its length, once, twice, three times, and once more, then peeled the briefs off him and giggled when the perfect sculpture sprang free and insolently targeted her face. She started to reach for it.

"Miss Mary," Noze said, almost breathless, "are you sure about this?"

"Please, my love," she said, as she gripped him, "do call me Mary."

Moving her hand in slow, torturous strokes, she looked in his eyes and said, "Do you remember when I told you that many men think red hair, especially fiery red hair, means we are wanton, lustful, lascivious, sexually available, that we are X-rated? And when I told you that if a deserving man comes along, that is true. You, Mr. Noze, are more than deserving, as I will now demonstrate."

Her skills were extraordinary, artistic, as she used every part of her mouth – lips, tongue, teeth – to please him. Her silver-gray eyes never left his. When Noze started moaning, she stopped abruptly, looked at what still stared arrogantly from her little fist, and said, "Ah, yes. *Now* lipstick is everywhere." She laughed, music.

Mary Bliss lay back on her comforter, her knee still over the edge of the bed, and opened her thighs a bit more as Noze knelt before her to test if her dew was as sweet as its fragrance. Her reactions were nearly feral throughout his long, careful attentions. She raised herself on her elbows so she could watch his ministrations.

He raised his face to look at hers, the silver eyes nearly closed, her lips parted to make way for throaty moans. "I love you," he said. "I will always love you."

He had never said it aloud.

"My darling man," she cooed. "My love! I want to do everything. Do you understand? There is much to explore, to experience, to become besotted by, humid burrows holding timeless pleasures, and we must follow our passions everywhere and do *everything*."

She trembled as Noze stood, then bent to kiss her little belly, to taste her navel, to kiss her breasts, and on to her throat. He gently turned her onto her belly and kissed with small kisses from her neck, down the irresistible valley in the small of her back, to her buttocks, where he stopped short and again began kissing, starting with her feet and continuing up to return to her bottom, which he slowly and greedily kissed all over. He returned her to lie on her back.

"At last, it is you," she said, her eyes half-lidded. "So relinquish any doubt about accepting my gift." She clutched his waist and pulled him toward her, nearly onto her and, with a tiny mewl, opened herself fully to him.

"Is it time, you ask? Yes, yes, yes – *aah!* – yes!" she said. "I am saying it as plainly as I can. Yes," she whispered. Her voice caught.

"Jimmy!"

ABOUT THE AUTHOR

Ric Bohy

The author spent his adult life as a journalist, first in newspapers, then magazines, and online. While he has written several non-fiction books for commercial clients, this is his first novel. Born, raised, and initially educated in Detroit, he holds a degree from The University of Michigan, and has been honored with more than 50 writing and reporting awards. He is included in Who's Who in America.

Made in United States
Orlando, FL
24 April 2023

32410530R00134